SUCCUBUS HEART
SUCCUBUS SIRENS BOOK TWO

LINA JUBILEE

Crimson Fox
PUBLISHING

CHAPTER ONE

PUSHING ASIDE THE FLAP OF MY TENT, I RELISHED IN THE WARM touch of the fading sunlight on my skin, at odds with the chill of the hard metal *tumba-ler* that kept my tea cold.

Metal was a part of this planet, but these humans... they'd mined too much of it, shaped more than their fair share. Used it for frivolities such as this strange, perspiring cup that protected my herbal tea.

I took another sip. It was refreshing, actually, how cold it was—how long the beverage stayed cold. How beautiful the sunset looked across this wide-open prairie, the tree line entirely out of sight.

Roots and sediment, I just might be letting myself be charmed by this planet—as it is. Not as it could be. Not as my brother, Alarik, had struggled for many orbits of the moon, many months, to make it. Not as Xerxes, Alarik's former best friend and my one-time fiancé, had insisted *he* could make it when he'd detained my brother, the king, and tried to lead our people in his own way.

Xerxes hadn't minded if the humans on this planet suffered. Alarik had directed us to try to avoid bloodshed as we'd torn through the concrete and steel to uproot the soil

1

beneath and let it breathe—though the humans here had viewed our efforts differently regardless.

I knew that now. I knew, too, that we had caused harm, though there had been no loss of life. Xerxes wouldn't have cared if there had been.

Shuddering, I tried to push all thoughts of Xerxes away. I was here—he was on Nelia. I'd remained on Earth so I could get away from everything that reminded me of home. Of Nelia. Of my fellow elves.

Of Xerxes.

My heart cinched at the echo of his name through my thoughts. My first love. The man I'd once promised to marry. Dark of eyes and dark of skin, his long, flowing hair as green as the moss soaked in rain, often gathered behind his head in a bun. He was broader of shoulder than my brother, though the two had had a sort of brotherly bond as children and perhaps looked more like siblings than Alarik and I did. Alarik and I were both lean and tall, but Alarik's darker complexion took after our mother's, whereas my fairer skin took after our father's. Only the deep green of our hair, the pointed tips of our ears was the same.

The three of us had had a special relationship once. The two of them had been the only ones who'd accepted me, who could laugh and smile and spend time beside me without their joy curdling to bitterness.

I took another sip and let my mind empty. The sun sunk lower and lower and then there was this incessant buzzing, like a swarm of insects, at my hip. The unyielding vibration sunk through to my bones.

Ah. The fo-na. The phone, I corrected myself, remembering Kouta's explanation. Kouta and his teammate Torynt, both of the Renegades, had been especially kind to me in the months since my self-imposed exile to Earth. Their leader worked with my brother in changing the Earth for the better, and they'd taken it upon themselves to see to my wellbeing after that last assault on Earth, during which Xerxes had recklessly attacked a human settlement in his eagerness to see the planet conquered.

If I could have found the humor in it, I would have laughed at that idea now. There was *so much* more of this planet than we'd imagined—so many more humans, Natches and Typicals—powered and non-powered—alike. The Natches were common in this world, though perhaps only one in four people was born with powers. Compared to home, it seemed odd, as all Nelians were born with something this planet would consider a superpower.

Except for me. My "superpower" was more like a poison.

Setting my metal cup down amidst the dry grass that grew to my knees, I pulled the phone from the pocket of the *geen-za*—*jeans*, surely, I could remember that one—my new Earth allies had procured for me and touched the silky-smooth flat screen. That wasn't enough for it to stop shaking in my hand, the too-bright screen causing my eyes to squint as I tried to remember. The words "Aurora Haddix" hovered over the green and red circles, along with an image of her, her long, brown hair framing a rosy, oval face and a bright smile. I wouldn't have needed the image to know, though. Our Nelian language was close enough to this part of this world's tongue that my brother and I had had little trouble with it.

The *tik*—*tech*?—on the other hand, was still often beyond me.

"Green for go," I said aloud, jamming my finger over that circle. Clearing my throat, I spoke loudly. "I am speaking to you."

Faint laughter rung out from the device in my hand. "Alanna! I was wondering if you remembered how to answer." Aurora's voice was so quiet, it could have been produced by a mouse.

I craned my neck closer to the now-black screen emblazoned with numbers that reflected this planet's form of time-keeping. "Can you speak louder? I CAN BARELY HEAR

YOU!" I made sure to shout as loudly as I could in case she was having the same issue.

Aurora screamed a faint little scream and then chuckled again. It was like tiny little children were laughing somewhere nearby. "Alanna, hit the 'speaker' button. No need to shout."

Turning the phone this way and that, I searched for this button she spoke of on every side of the device.

"On the screen," added Aurora's soft voice.

Ah. I hit the button. "Can you hear me?" I asked more quietly.

"Yes! You found it," said Aurora. Her voice was stronger now, almost as if she were standing here in front of me.

But no, I was alone, as I ought to have been. Alone but for the fluttering birds and the other little critters rustling through these fields.

"How are you doing?" asked Aurora. There was something giddy in her words, something I couldn't quite make sense of—unless my inexperience with the phone had proven that amusing for her.

"As ever," I replied, betraying no emotion in my voice. The sun was almost entirely set now and the rustling through the field was growing closer. Nothing scared me here, though. Their larger creatures were not so wild as our Nelian boars, though Torynt had told me there were other giant animals in other places that were just as frightening.

Not so here, in this quiet little place where no one roamed.

"Your brother really wishes you would talk to him more often," said Aurora. Bent down to extend my palm out to the fuzzy little gray creature that approached, I'd almost forgotten I was talking to her.

"I answer when he calls," I said. The *quir-elle* stepped forward cautiously, its little nose twitching in the air.

"Come now, sister," said a deep, sonorous voice—Alarik. Over the phone. "You know I'm even more inept at this thing than you are."

"Says the elf who won't let his generic MP3 player out of his grip," said another voice—a male one. The name Flayme —Nash?—jumped to mind. One of Aurora's consorts, as was my brother.

"The year 2002 called," said another man's raspier voice. That one was more familiar. Zander, another of Aurora's consorts, and the leader of the Natch Renegades. The Renegades had once been opposed to Veras, Aurora's group, despite the fact that Aurora included the Renegades' leader among her group of lovers. They made it work somehow. My brother had been even more of an enemy to Aurora and her Veras friends—and I'd known from the moment I'd seen them together that they were destined to be as one. Nelians could sense that between pairings, like a fine perfume that these humans and Natches seemed unable to pick up on.

"He doesn't understand that reference," said another man, this one's voice somehow both quieter but more severe. Then he let out an airy chuckle. "Look at his face. I'm sorry." He kept laughing. "No, honestly…" This one had to be Jayden, the final member of Aurora's consorts. Though, truth be told, I'd pictured him as more reticent than that the few times I'd met him.

Expressing their love for Aurora as a group—being there for her, together, despite their differences—had made my brother so blissful. Aurora had visited me—Zander, too—to check on me, though it was usually Kouta and Torynt. But it'd been months, and I hadn't seen my brother face to face. There was still Xerxes hanging between us.

I'd asked him to stay away. I had no reason to be around any of them, really. I'd grown weary of my nullification. Weary of the harm it had on those around me.

For my "gift" was seemingly invisible, but it was there. Unmistakably. Around me, those with super abilities lost their powers, became as useless as an average Typical human on this planet. Even leaving my side, there were lingering effects, leaving them unable to access their gifts for around the length of one Earth hour.

The *quir-elle* was in my palm now and I brought it closer to my chest, rubbing its soft back with my thumb. It chewed on something it had between its front legs—a dried piece of corn.

"*Anyway,*" said Aurora, the laughter echoing out behind her now practically a chorus. "Your face looks fine, hun," she said, probably to my brother. "Beautiful as ever. You just looked sort of... lost." There was a smacking noise, most likely lips on lips, a sound that was like a dagger to my heart as I remembered the feel of Xerxes' lips on mine.

"Perhaps I can take you aside for a moment and find my way again," purred Alarik between smacking noises.

"All right, all right, all right," said Zander. "Can we save that for later, please? Darlin', are you going to tell the aunt-to-be or not?"

The *quir-elle* jumped up my arm, bouncing right up to my shoulder as I stood back up, dumbfounded. "Aunt?"

"Way to ruin the surprise," teased Flayme.

"We're having a baby!" squealed Aurora. She tittered. "No, two, I mean! We're having two babies!"

"You... are?" I asked. My furry friend was jittery on my shoulder, holding his little snack tightly and taking quick and successive bites.

"We didn't think it was possible for Aurora to conceive," said Jayden. "But she has."

I could almost see the five of them in that moment, even without their images on the screen. The way those men looked at her...

My heart thundered. The image of Xerxes on the ground, bleeding out, lifeless... That same man had looked at me like that once, had held me as if he'd never wanted to let me go. He lived, thanks to Roulette, another member of Veras, but I hadn't seen him since he'd lain there, his life ebbing from my grasp as I'd rushed to examine him.

"She's carrying the future heir to the heart of Nelia," said my brother. "The future guardian to protect our planet, to take up my cause to better this Earth as well."

"Let's not get ahead of ourselves," said Flayme. "We've barely had time to discuss names, let alone whether we're going to let *our* babies move to elf fantasy land. I want my babies to know about pizza and reality TV, okay? Not just giant boars and shooting vines or whatever you've got there."

"We really need to let you take a tour of Nelia," added Aurora.

"*Really*?" said Zander. "Reality TV? *That's* what you care about sharing with my children?"

"We have more than just boars and vines," said Alarik, clearly affronted. They were having a strange, jumbled conversation at this point. "And of course I wouldn't take my sons or daughters there for all time. I want them to know their Earth heritage, too."

"Okay, guys," said Jayden. "Let's save these discussions about our kids for later. We still have Alarik's sister on the phone."

"Blessings to you and your fellow parents," I said, giving Aurora the customary congratulation one gave on Nelia for such an occasion. Multiple consorts were fairly commonplace on Nelia, and everyone involved identified as the parents of their lovers' offspring.

It was commonplace, but I'd only ever had one lover. I'd only ever felt the call to Xerxes.

Not that Alarik had let his lack of the call—until he'd met Aurora—stop him from making occasional pairings. But it wasn't the same, finding your lover—or lovers. I'd known since childhood I'd been in love with Xerxes. I hadn't wanted anyone else. Now, I couldn't imagine going back to him. Which meant I was doomed to never feel that kind of utter joy again.

"Thank you," said Aurora, bringing me back to the moment. "We can't wait for you to meet them in seven

7

months. But please let it not take *that* long for us to see you again."

"I wish you well," I said, instead of commenting on her remark. I hit the screen twice, bringing light back to it and then hitting the red button.

The world went quiet around me once more.

My little *quir-elle* friend rubbed his fuzzy cheek against mine and then went back to working on his morsel.

I slid the phone back into my pocket, staring up at the stars as they came into view, the bright blue of the sky more visible here than it was back home. Our sun shone wildly through trees, the few fields we'd cleared away used only for growing food and cotton, and even they were surrounded on every side by the never-ending trees of Nelia.

It was so… open here. So wide and vast.

I didn't know how long I stood there, but my little fuzzy friend eventually tittered, jostling down my arm and leaping to the ground, disappearing back into the tall grasses.

Whipping around, I brushed aside my long, green hair, exposing a pointed ear I knew marked me as a Nelian, to listen.

A crunching noise grew louder, the sound I'd come to recognize as a metal people-transport *car*, or *beeacal* as humans call them, approaching. I crawled into my tent, peeking out between the flaps, knowing that my little shelter was well-hidden amidst the tall grass.

I exhaled quietly as the two lights on the front of the car blinked once, twice, three times in a pattern.

The Renegades have come to check on me.

One of the car's windows rolled down and Torynt stuck his head full of yellow, coiled hair out, laying his hand on the wheel in front of him and causing his metal carriage to let out a loud, shrill cry. "Hey, princess!" he shouted. "Welfare check!"

Sighing, I pushed aside the tent flap once more and stood. "I just spoke with my brother," I said as the car slowly moved closer. "I am fine." *Why do they come so often? Don't they care that around me, they'll lose their abilities?*

But despite what my aura would do, they would approach me with pity. It was almost crueler than the stares, the whispers, the rejection back on Nelia.

Can I not just have peace? Away from others, I can do no harm.

"We have groceries," said Kouta, leaning out of his own window as the car rolled to a stop and went quiet. His black hair was cropped closely to his scalp, his beige skin and dark, expressive eyes differentiating him from his somewhat reddish companion. "We won't bother you more than a sec." The lump at his throat twitched.

Despite his kindness, he hates being around me. How could he not?

"You don't miss it until you actually can't use it, do you?" said Torynt as he opened his door. "I mean, it's not like I shoot wind out of my hands for kicks, but—"

"You totally do," said Kouta, shutting his own door behind him and shifting a big, brown paper sack in his arm. "Who was it who was trying to use a miniature cyclone to get the TV remote closer to him last night but who wound up slamming it against the wall and busting it?"

"And who was it who was so startled, he knocked his girlfriend off his lap onto her cute little ass on the floor?" said Torynt with a grin.

"Eyes off my girlfriend's ass," Kouta snapped. His brows narrowed, but he shook his head and rolled his eyes. "I liked it better when I could kick *your* ass."

"I don't recall you doing much ass kicking until you joined my side."

"I joined Zander, not *you.*"

"As I recall, the man recruited *me* for the team," said Torynt. "Turned me from a petty anarchist to a man with a mission." Winking at me, he slid one hand into the pockets of his pants, then snapped the fingers of the other in front of him. "Nope." He wrinkled his face. "No powers."

Kouta shoved the paper sack at his chest, forcing Torynt to catch it before it dropped. "Thanks for the update, Captain Obvious." They were both so... amiable. I didn't deserve their kindness. Kouta turned to me. "Is there anything in particular you need next time—"

Before he could finish speaking, a massive lightning bolt shot out to strike the car—and not from the clear sky above, but from somewhere far down the path whence the car had come.

CHAPTER TWO

I crouched into the tall grasses on instinct just as Torynt whirled around, dropping the sack. Kouta backed toward me, but it was over as soon as it had begun. The bolt collapsed into nothing, fading instantly as it neared the car—or more accurately, neared me.

I'd negated a Natch's powers. I knew it could not be a Nelian's. I was the only one who'd immigrated here permanently, and I'd never heard of one who could wield the very flashing, scorching light of the skies. Torynt opened his palms in the assailant's direction, aiming them like a weapon—like he'd tried to use his powers. "Did some asswipe just *attack* us?" he asked, emitting a little growl I could easily identify as frustration.

"We can't fight without our powers," said Kouta, standing beside Torynt, fists up, ready to strike our unseen assailant.

"No duh, genius," Torynt snapped. "So now what?"

"Zander told us to be ready for this," said Kouta. "Ever since we learned about this elven princess and her negation powers—"

"I'd leave, but you'll still be without powers for some time after," I said, stepping forward. I drew my daggers from the dual sheaths on either side of my hips—the two Nelian things

I still wore amidst these Earthling jeans and cotton T-shirt. Or B-shirt? I'd forgotten.

"Smooth. I forgot you learned to kick some *ass* Typical-style," he said, the "Typical" referring to the non-powered humans of this planet. He gestured for me to step in front of him. "Ladies first, then."

"Torynt, we're supposed to keep an eye her—" started Kouta.

I let out a battle roar, running through the tall grasses, feeling them whip and sting my arms as I moved between them. I didn't worry about stealth—they'd attacked first.

"Alanna, maybe hold up a second?" Torynt's voice grew fainter by the word as I put him behind me.

"Wait!" shouted Kouta, trying to catch up. "We can—"

I didn't hear what else he had to say. I had distance to cover and an attacker to investigate.

"It's not—it's not working!" A new voice a short distance in front of me shouted, the smooth, deep cadence of his words sending a shiver down my spine that arrested my steps.

"Neither are mine. Damn it!" Another man. Husky and baritone. I slipped forward silently, crouching so my head wouldn't appear above the stalks, willing my heart to stop pounding so loudly. Cautiously, I peeked out.

There were four men, each more striking than the last— and I didn't know how I felt about even thinking that at that moment. They were four attackers, I reminded myself, my eyes narrowing to adjust to the dying light. We were outnumbered. The two nearest me were having the conversation, another was bouncing nearby on the balls of his feet, his fists at his side. The fourth was a few steps back, clutching the door of a car bigger than the one Kouta and Torynt used—a truck. Or a *pickdown*. No, pickup. It had a long, flat area in the back behind a carriage part that had two benches, enough seats for all four.

"We've got to get out of here," said the one bouncing on his feet. He had short, thick, wavy black hair through which he ran one of his shaking hands. His profile looked carved out of wood, his features sharp and his skin tawny.

"Those fuckers move around," said another of the men. He was so much paler than his friend, with short hair the color of amber, a clipped layer of the same dotting his chin. "We can't lose this chance."

"What chance?" said the man by the pickup. He had ochre skin and silky black hair that came down past his shoulders, framing the bulging muscles his too-tight shirt could just barely contain. The shape of his eyes reminded me of Kouta's. "None of us can use our powers," the man continued. "Why can't we use our powers? It's hopeless, Bo."

So Bo was the amber-haired pale one.

"Goddammit," said the fourth man. He flung his hands out in front of him as Torynt had earlier. As I expected, nothing happened. He stroked his sleek, rosy chin. His dark hair was so closely cropped to his scalp, it was more like little bumps than hair. I had to fight the urge to reach out to feel it. It looked so soft. He cocked his head toward the pickup. "Something weird is going on around here. Maybe it's a trap. Let's go."

Footfalls broke through the grass behind me, my Renegade companions, no doubt. They kept moving, not noticing me, breaking through the grass headed straight for the intruders.

"You go, Monroe," said bearded Bo. "I'll cover you."

"How?" asked Monroe, the one with the close-cropped hair. "You couldn't lift the truck when you tried. That means your super strength is gone, too."

"Just go!" said Bo, taking a few steps in front of the others. "Rhett, start up the truck."

Rhett—the man with the eyes like Kouta's—jumped back inside the truck and it roared to life.

"Well, what have we here?" spat Torynt as he broke into the clearing and approached the man called Bo. "A gathering of douchebags?"

"They look familiar," added Kouta more quietly. He remained tense.

The fourth man walked up beside his friends, standing so close to me, I could reach out and grab him by the thick, sculpted arm I could perceive even through the black leather jacket he wore. He smelled of leather, of hide, earthy and slightly sweet.

"Caspian," hissed Bo through clenched teeth. "Get in the truck!"

"Not until you do," Caspian answered.

Something hit me then, something that took the breath from my throat.

No. No, it can't be…

Caspian put a hand on Bo's shoulder. "Wait a minute," he said. "They can't use their powers, either."

Kouta and Torynt did their best to seem menacing, both in a fighting stance, but they had no weapons. They were clearly too used to relying on their powers.

"What's going on?" asked Caspian. He turned just slightly to check over his shoulder. The other two were already in the truck.

"It's about time I kick your ass, that's what's going on." With a great roar, Torynt charged toward Bo, locking hands with him as Bo went to reflect. Torynt laughed. "Ha! Not so impressive without your powers, are you, bud?" He pushed forward, slamming Bo against the front of the truck.

My heart sped up. "No!" I said, standing upright and revealing myself.

Everyone's eyes turned toward me, even the two in the truck, who froze as they'd started climbing out of the open doors.

"It's a Nelian." Monroe spoke those words half in surprise, half in awe.

"A stunning one," added Caspian, his jaw agape. His head dipped as he took in as much of me as he could see behind the grasses.

The tips of my pointed ears felt incredibly hot.

Clearing my head, I raised my daggers and shifted my legs into a fighting stance. "Stop it. All of you."

Torynt backed up, a stony expression on his face as he shook his head. "These assholes had it coming."

I didn't know what was going on—this world was still new to me, and besides, I'd purposely abstained from company as much as possible.

Rhett and Monroe jumped down and stood on either side of Bo.

Kouta shuffled by my side, but Caspian didn't flinch, his lips parting as a slow smile built on his face.

"I remember now. They call themselves the 'R.I.A.'," said Kouta.

"Stands for 'Risk It All,' *hermosa*," said Caspian.

Torynt snorted. "Yeah, but do you know what you're risking it all *for*?"

"Justice," said Bo, standing straight and wiping his mouth with his forearm. A red stain smeared on his pale skin.

"Freedom," added Rhett beside him. His eyes narrowed as they trained on me, his fingers lightly caressing his throat.

"Love," said Caspian, thrusting out his chest toward me.

"We don't expect our enemies to understand," Monroe said.

Torynt chuckled and kicked up a storm of dirt with the toe of his shoe.

"Are you my enemy, *hermosa*?" asked Caspian. Kouta moved to step between us, but I lowered my daggers.

"I don't even know who you are," I said.

Caspian let out a deep sigh. "We're not fans of Nelians and Renegades acting like they fucking own the government."

I flinched. It was my brother who was doing that, telling the people what to do, how to change the way they ran things. All in the name of saving the planet. Humans couldn't be trusted to save the world on their own. Couldn't these men see that? No. They'd attacked Torynt and Kouta.

"I guess by default that makes you our enemy." Caspian actually looked sad, the lump at his throat bouncing noticeably.

He was right. But I couldn't bring myself to lift my daggers again. It was *that feeling*. I sensed it. I couldn't believe it, but I sensed an attraction, one I'd never felt since Xerxes. But I couldn't tell with which of these men.

It crashed hard over me with the force of a gale, so overwhelming, my knees were beginning to buckle under its weight. My palms were clammy on the hilts of my daggers and I blinked hard, trying to follow what was going on in front of me as Caspian threw another punch at Kouta and the fighting began again.

Both sides were taking hits—fist blocked by forearm, leg against shin—but the Renegades, who'd found me this place, who brought me food—they were outnumbered. I needed to step in.

But I was frozen in place, my legs trembling like jam. I *felt* it. With someone here. One of these men I didn't know.

And they, being humans, had no idea that a fire was roaring at my core. A Nelian would have sensed it instantly.

"Well, maybe if we could *rely* on the government to protect all its citizens..." Torynt grunted as he narrowly dodged a punch Caspian had launched his way.

"This isn't up for debate." Monroe spat on the ground. "Dictatorship is never the answer."

"We're *dictators* now?" Torynt *tsked*. "Then who do we talk to about getting some better digs?"

"So what was the plan?" asked Kouta, jumping out of the way of Rhett's kick. "You wanted to take us out?"

"That wouldn't get your tyrants to back down," said Monroe, grinding his teeth. "We need a hostage. A live one." His gaze flickered toward me.

I should have felt something other than a racing, fiery inferno shooting up from below my abdomen.

Focus, I told myself. But I couldn't move. The feeling I hadn't asked for—the *need* for someone who stood nearby—was overwhelming. It hadn't even been this strong with Xerxes.

Torynt threw another punch, which grazed Bo's cheek, and the other man fumbled somewhat, his eyes wide, as if shocked to discover that a blow could hurt.

Who are these men? I still didn't fully understand.

"Yeah, we're not gonna just sit back and let you take us," Torynt said, blowing on his bleeding, scuffed knuckles. He took a sharp breath in between his teeth. "Goddamit, I wish I could use my—"

Kouta slapped him across the chest, his eyes narrowing on the four assailants.

"Forget this!" shouted someone—Monroe, I thought. It snapped me out of my state. "There's too much we don't know about what's going on here. Get in the truck!"

Torynt turned his head and spit out a small amount of blood. "Aren't worth a damn without your powers, are you?"

Kouta let out a grunt as Caspian dodged his punch, but the R.I.A. member kicked the Renegade's calf before joining his friends in the truck.

"And what were *you* doing?" asked Torynt, facing me. "I thought you were leading the way. You just froze. Oh, forget it."

The pickup backed up at top speed, its weird, flimsy car wheels kicking up dust and catching in my throat. Lifting my arm up to my mouth, I coughed as the truck sped down the hard surface I'd learned was here called a "road." We had roads similar to them for our carriages back on Nelia, but they didn't mar the nature around them in quite the same way.

I lowered my daggers, sliding them into their sheaths. It

was hard getting used to not thinking of Earth innovations with disgust. My brother worked to correct the technologies that went too far—that threatened the health of the only homeland the humans had. But these men, they'd decided to "risk it all"… for what? To stop my brother from saving them?

What was… a "dictator"?

"Let's pack up," said Torynt, sliding an arm around Kouta, who moved forward with a limp.

"Pack?" I asked.

"We can't leave you here," said Kouta with a grimace. "They'll know where to find you again. And they're clearly looking for trouble."

So that was the end of life in my peaceful pasture.

I didn't know if I could face the world yet. Face the looks on my allies' faces as they felt the effect of my aura wherever I went.

But if I waited here, those men would return. And I couldn't say for certain I'd be strong enough to resist the scorching, demanding *urge* to give in to them.

CHAPTER THREE

"I'm pulling in here," said Torynt after an hour in the car. "I'm hungry and your vegan whole-grain crap isn't going to fly."

I stared at the brown paper sack of food they'd brought me, now headed off with me to wherever I landed next. My people ate boar sometimes, though it was true we didn't consume the flesh of animals as often as many of those on Earth seemed to. When asked for foods I'd eat, I hadn't bothered to request roast pig.

"Really?" Kouta grunted as we turned off the road and pulled into a food place that styled itself as "Sideshow Diner." "We're like twenty minutes from base. Can't we just eat there? Zander isn't too worried about those assholes despite their threats, but—"

"I'm not leading them right to the others," said Torynt. "Got to make sure the coast is clear, even if the boss isn't too concerned. Is that what you want? The R.I.A. showing up where we're crashing to attack your girlfriend?"

"She could handle them better than me right now." Wincing, he massaged a bruise forming on the side of his face. "Even without powers. She's better about training without them than I am."

"Comes with your powers being more defense than offense," said Torynt. "And I think we all should do better with that training, now that we've got Miss Nullifying Princess under our care."

I tried not to flinch at the thought that I would be causing them such trouble. They were so *kind*, so reasonable. Their kindness hurt more than the icy stares of the Nelians I'd left behind. They'd ached to have access to their own powers in my vicinity. Only Xerxes had always been kind about it, and even he had had periods where he'd asked me to stay behind, to stay away, so he could access his gift as Nelia's only known truth-puller.

Not that we'd had much cause to rely on that. Nelians didn't lie. It wasn't that we couldn't, it was just that we *wouldn't*. His gift had seemed nothing more than a useless trick until we'd encountered humans and their deceit.

But these humans... I trusted them. They were kind to me.

"They called my brother a 'dictator,'" I said, speaking for the first time since we'd left my pasture behind.

"Don't worry about them. They're nobodies." Torynt scratched the side of his nose.

"They wanted a *hostage*." I wasn't sure what that word meant, either.

The car rolled to a stop and Torynt shifted the lever at his side. He adjusted the mirror over his head until the reflection of his eyes met mine. "A hostage is like... a person they take with them—against the person's will. Your people have done that before, remember?"

Aurora and her Veras friends. My brother *had* taken some of them, had tried to learn from them. Then he'd given in to the call of the bond and fallen irrevocably in love with Aurora.

"Only this person is used as a tool for negotiation," Torynt continued. "'Give us what we want and get this person back unharmed' type of thing. They wanted to use one of us to convince Zander and your brother to stop, um, *intimidating*

20

our nation's government, I guess." He shrugged, as if it wasn't something he was concerned with. "But they're wrong if they think Zander or the king of the freaking elves will stop what they're doing to save the likes of him or me." He gestured to Kouta beside him. "We don't have much to do with all the planning and laws and whatever they do up on Capitol Hill."

"We're the muscle," Kouta said. He was typing on his phone. "Well, the wind and water, when we can use our powers." *When* they could use their powers. Of course. The car went quiet, the only sound a quiet snapping from the front of the *beeacal* before even that ceased.

"What's a dictator?" I asked.

Torynt and Kouta exchanged a look. "Well," said Torynt, "your brother and Zander view themselves as more like *consultants*."

"Lobbyists existed around the government before all this," added Kouta. "You didn't see little rogue Natch groups caring much about it then. *And* the pro-Natch groups didn't really have the kind of capital necessary to influence anyone."

"Capital." Torynt snorted. "Only now instead of money, we're making those lawmakers snap to attention via the threat of giant vines replacing the nation's roadways. And maybe mentioning how Typical armed interference might just end up as fertilizer."

Kouta cleared his throat. "Right, well… Now with King Alarik and Zander's *unique* form of lobbying, we're finally getting things done—it's all aboveboard. Technically. They find sponsors for bills, take them to committees— "

"Dude, you're losing her." Torynt jingled the keys to the car in his hand. "You're losing *me*."

"You are *determined* to know as little as possible, aren't you?" Kouta asked him.

"I just want a fair shake for Natches and some food in my belly. Is that so bad?"

Kouta shook his head. "You make it all seem so simple."

It felt like anything but. I still didn't understand what a "dictator" was, but I could see that those R.I.A. men were confused. My brother was only doing what was best for this world.

Shoving his phone into his pocket, Kouta opened his car door. "Lila texted to bring her something back." He looked down at his clothes. "We're filthy," he added. I looked at mine. There were bits of dried grass stuck here and there, but my clothes didn't exhibit the same level of dirt and grime—a testament to my inability to act when called to it.

Torynt had a visible bruise beneath his eye, his jacket torn in several places. "We're fine. Places like these are used to all types."

"Yeah, well, maybe not *her* type." Kouta limped over to the back of the car, knocking on the rear of it until Torynt pressed a button on the keys and the back portion popped up.

"Here," said Kouta, handing me a hat. It was deep blue and round and had a little portion that stuck out on one side.

"What's this?" I asked, tapping my finger on that extra bit.

"A baseball cap," said Kouta, shutting the back of the car.

"*Baseball*," I said, grabbing my hair into a tail and shoving it up beneath the hat as I slipped it on my head. "What about this part?" I tapped the extra bit again.

Kouta stared at me. "A visor."

I made a mental note of the lesson.

"She's like a kindergartner and a wise old woman all at once," said Torynt as we headed for the door. I got the bulk of his meaning, not wanting to ask what a "kindergartner" was and prove his point further.

"Whoa, rough night, huh, boys?" A woman in a peculiar yellow dress with a flap of white cloth over the front of her legs brightened as we walked inside. The place was lit with this world's electric lights, so bright, I had to squint to take in the view. Nearly every surface was white and dingy. There were many tables and a long, long table with strange high chairs beneath them. The woman carried a clear pot filled with a dark liquid in one hand. Steam rose up from the top of it as she went to grab a stack full of thick, shiny papers from beneath a tall box near the doorway.

"You could say that," said Torynt. "But my friends and I just seem to attract trouble." He grinned from ear to ear as he draped an arm around Kouta and another around me. Kouta winced and I almost fell over at the weight of his touch. He was the first to even brush against me since my exile. But though he was attractive—odd-looking but pleasing—he did nothing to stir my insides.

Nothing like the searing, tantalizing urge I'd felt back there.

The woman led us past a few other humans seated at tables, some with food between them, some with just drinks. Their eyes fell on the three of us as we went by. Not a single one ignored us, and I instinctively went to tug on the *visor* of my hat.

"Well, I hope you won't bring any of that trouble here," said the woman as she led us to our table with two bench-like seats on either side of it. "We run a clean establishment." She winked as Torynt let us go and both he and Kouta slid together on one side as I sat on the other.

"Oh, come on… Dana," said Torynt. He'd leaned forward to read her name off the little plain, rectangular broach above her breast. "Surely, a *little* trouble might spice up a dull night?"

"Oh, stop," she said. "I don't care how cute you two are. I won't allow any shenanigans."

I sat down across from the men and made a mental note to ask someone what *shenani… shenani…* whatever was.

Kouta picked up one of the shiny papers, so I did the same. The paper was stiff to the touch, hard to bend. I ran my finger over it and it came back a little sticky. I shuddered. It had pictures of food and a lot of words, as well as numbers. I didn't know where to start. Only some of the words looked familiar.

"Coffee?" asked the Dana woman.

"Yes, please," said Kouta. He flipped over a glass cup. "Caffeinated."

Dana poured the liquid from the pot she was holding into the cup.

"None for me," said Torynt, picking up his own sticky, stiff paper.

"Hun?" said Dana once she'd finished pouring.

I stared up at her.

She jiggled the pot beside her head. "Coffee?"

I tipped over my cup like Kouta had and nodded.

Dana chuckled. "Caffeinated all right?"

I nodded again.

"Doesn't talk much, does she?" Dana asked Torynt.

"Shy," he said, offering her another smile.

"Be back in a minute." Dana left to approach a man nearby who'd lifted his cup in the air. I wondered what he was celebrating, to whom he offered a toast. But it seemed to be some kind of signal instead. I stared as Dana poured more of her pot's liquid into his raised cup. She was going to run out soon enough.

"You drink coffee?" asked Kouta, cradling his cup. He'd grabbed some very small white containers from near the window and tore them open, dumping the white liquid into his cup.

"I don't know," I admitted. I picked up the cup by the little handle grafted to the side of it. A warm, earthy aroma wafted through my nose and down through every inch of me. Such an inviting scent. I raised the cup to my lips, and as soon as the dark liquid hit my tongue, I let out a small cry and spit it back out.

Hot. Bitter. *Terrible.*

Kouta and Torynt laughed, the fair-haired one only looking up from his paper for a second.

"Here," said Kouta, sliding his glass cup toward me and taking mine from my grip. "Try it with cream."

Cream? The Earth people kept cream on their tables? The liquid in Kouta's cup was paler than mine had been. I sniffed it. It still *smelled* nice, but I didn't know whether or not to trust it.

"Just give it a sip," Kouta said, repeating his cream-dumping into the other cup.

I did, and my muscles instantly relaxed. It tasted much better, this coffee and cream. I cradled the cup as I sipped it slowly, rejoicing as the sweet liquid moved down my throat.

"What are you going to eat?" asked Kouta, turning his attention back to his shiny paper.

"*Coffee* is fine," I said, trying to remember the new word. Did my brother have as much trouble adjusting to this world? Maybe I would have known if I'd spoken to him more often. But he was going to be even busier now that he was going to be a father.

And what did *he* think about those men, the R.I.A.? Kouta had spoken to Zander over the phone and had told us that Zander hadn't been concerned. Zander and my brother worked together. He had to be speaking for both of them.

But I couldn't shake the feeling that this wasn't the end. I stared outside, my heart quickening at the thought of them out there, somewhere.

"You have to get *something*," said Torynt. He shook his hard paper. "Look at your menu."

Menu. I was learning too many words today, meeting with too many people. I kept sipping the warm drink, feeling the calming sensation in my fingertips as I held it tightly in my hands.

"Never mind." Torynt stacked all of our menus into a pile as he got the coffee woman's attention. "Dana? Two All-American combos and one shortstack."

"He got you pancakes," Kouta explained, but that didn't really help me understand, either. Cakes. Pans. We had those in Nelia, but I didn't know that on Earth people had to specify the tool with which their cakes had been baked.

Dana gave both men a wide smile as she came to collect our menus. "It'll be just a few minutes," she said. "More coffee, honey?"

My cup was nearly empty. I nodded.

Dana laughed as she stepped away. "I'll get you talking yet."

Placing the cup down, I stared out the window as Dana came back to give me more, as Kouta checked his phone. He practically shouted after it buzzed. "Lila says Zander's going to be a dad?" he blurted out. "I just talked to him. Why didn't he tell me?"

"Hush," said Torynt, and I looked around to see a few other heads had turned our way. "That name isn't exactly common, and our Zander is sort of infamous these days."

Dana came back with three plates—one stacked precariously up her arm—and beyond the window, a *beeacal* neared. I had to squint to keep its front lights from blinding me until they finally cut off.

Dana placed three rolled napkins besides each of our plates. "Anything else I can get you? Want some syrup for your pancakes, hun?"

Turning away from the window, I gazed at my stack of cakes. They were flat and brown—like they'd been over-cooked. There was a glob of what I presumed to be this planet's butter oozing out from the very top. I shook my head *no*, picking up my fork, its cool metal still strange in my hand when I was used to the wooden ones back home.

"Let me know if you change your mind," she said, tapping my shoulder.

I stiffened. People seemed very apt to touch you here. I wasn't used to being touched by anyone besides Xerxes.

Torynt and Kouta talked some more in quieter tones between bites of their food—laughing about the idea of their leader being a father, of *sharing* the title with three other men. I opened my mouth to say something about how that wasn't so strange on Nelia, but I got caught up in the bites of my

26

pancakes. They were fluffy—better than I'd expected them to be.

I cleaned my plate of every morsel and then felt a strange rumbling in my stomach.

"I have to relieve my bowels," I said.

Kouta spit out some of his coffee as a bit of egg tumbled down from Torynt's lips. Then he laughed. "You could just say you need to take a shit, princess."

Kouta was cracking up so hard, his face was turning red. "Don't teach her *that*." But he couldn't say anymore—his laughter just wouldn't stop. Perhaps Earth people found the natural process funny.

I nodded and stood, looking toward the right door. Kouta's girlfriend, Lila, had told me once that some bathrooms didn't have baths in them. "*Look for the little stick person in a dress,*" she'd said. I headed toward the back of the *diner*.

Once finished, I lathered my hands with soap, rinsing and then drying them, tucking a few stray strands of my green hair under my cap after looking in the mirror. Reflections were so clear here in these mirrors—we used natural crystal growths or bowls of water back home. We had no glass to speak of, though I'd found it a more soothing material than many of the minerals these humans had mined from their planet's core.

My finger went still on the mirror's surface as murmurs echoed out in the hallway beyond the bathroom door.

"...there are bystanders here."

"Well, then, we'll wait to jump them when they come out."

"What if they spot us first?"

"That's why we're covering the back door."

"My powers still aren't back."

"None of ours are. Let's hope it's the same thing for them."

The voices were all familiar—each sending a shudder down my spine.

The R.I.A. They'd found us somehow, were here to attack my friends.

I had to warn them.

My hand rested on the handle. The voices didn't let up. I wouldn't be able to pass them by without them seeing me. And there was that tingling *feeling* again, starting small and growing, building to something unyielding. If it were from a Nelian man, I knew I'd be destined to be with him—though that feeling had led me to Xerxes, and he had led me to heartbreak. But a human? Could I do what my brother had done?

Focus. It didn't matter. I couldn't be with someone who thought my brother was a *dictator*—though I still needed to research what that word meant. But first, I'd need to run for the table and get the Renegades out of there quickly.

Setting my jaw, I pulled open the door and stepped out.

Three of the four members of the R.I.A. stood to my right, gathered in front of a cracked-open door that led out to the darkness of night. Crickets chirped loudly as the men fell silent.

Caspian, Bo, and Monroe. All staring at me.

My heart palpitated, the burning of my cheeks at war with the clamminess that invaded my limbs. There was that feeling again. Like my body knew—a man I was destined to love was among them.

Only it was so, so much *stronger* than it had been with Xerxes.

Impossible. And so wrong. *How can my body react this way to these men? Men who attacked my allies, who spoke of my brother with contempt?*

"She'll do. Grab her," said Monroe, and he pushed past Caspian to snatch my arm. I flinched, swung my leg out on instinct, and flipped over his back, clenching my teeth through the pain in my limb until he let out a yelp and let go. The moment where my front had pressed against his back had been exhilarating—dizzying. My breasts still ached from the sensation, my nipples erect. I panted as I crouched on the other side of him, ready to attack while at the same time fighting the urge to latch on to him again—to just keep myself there, my breasts and groin pressing hard into that muscular back.

My mouth opened to scream, to alert my friends, but my mind was overwhelmed by the scent—the ravishing musk radiating off of a man I was supposed to think of as an enemy. "Torynt!" I finally said, but my voice was hoarse, too quiet, like it was at war with my desire to melt into a nearby embrace. "Kouta!" I fared no better my second try.

"Shit," said Caspian. "They probably heard that." He sidled up beside Monroe. I was trapped. Caspian and Bo on one side. Monroe on the other. "Hello again, *hermosa*." Not a single bit of Caspian's face seemed to be disingenuous as he grinned down at me.

Monroe seethed through his teeth as he rolled his arm around. A thickness in my throat made me hesitate as I stared him down, my chin quivering even as I tried to look tough.

"Grab her," said Monroe bluntly. He would not be subdued. A foolish part of me liked that. Cradling his shoulder, he squinted his eyes as he stared me down.

"What about the Renegades?" Bo asked. His gaze darted hesitatingly toward me, quickly averting, only for him to stare unabashedly me again. He swallowed visibly.

The Renegades. If they hadn't heard me before, I'd have to scream louder. I'd call and they'd come running and then we'd take them together, powers or no powers…

Powers or no powers…

I had an idea then. An idea I had to see through—regardless of what my brother or these Natch allies of mine thought of it. "Leave them be," I said, standing straighter, my palms out before me. "I'll come with you quietly."

Caspian let out a low whistle. "Let's go with that." Thrusting his chest forward, he slipped a hand around my upper arm. I let out a little moan. It didn't hurt, but I was taken aback by how much I *liked* the feel of his skin on mine.

Which man was I feeling this foolish attraction toward?

Bo cleared his throat and grabbed my other arm. I could have fought them off—despite my poison powers, I was skilled in combat—but I wouldn't yet. Not if they agreed to take me and leave my allies alone.

Monroe muttered something about him being the only one who got his butt kicked for trying that and brushed past Bo, squeezing behind him toward the propped-open back door. "Well?" he said, standing in the doorway. "Let's go."

Caspian and Bo both grinned, a fire flickering in their eyes. "Yes, sir," they said in unison.

Monroe rolled his steely eyes but said nothing.

Stumbling, I let the two men guide me, my heart thundering and my skin warming at the feel of their touch. This was maddening. I couldn't tell where the attraction was coming from—it seemed to be everywhere all at once.

And even though I'd known Alarik had felt it for the Earth Natch Aurora, I never—*never*—would have imagined I'd find the same on this planet. That wasn't why I'd banished myself here.

"Wait," said Monroe, stopping my escorts as we rounded the corner. "I'm going to text Rhett to meet us around back." He pulled his phone out of his pocket.

I stared through the window to the inside of the diner. It was much easier to see inside than it had been to see outside when I'd been sitting there. Torynt and Kouta were still at the table, Kouta sipping his drink and Torynt looking over his shoulder back toward the hallway where the bathrooms were.

A short while later, the pickup truck from the prairie rolled quietly toward us, its two front lights blinding me for a moment.

"You have a phone with you?" Bo asked me.

I blinked. Then I nodded, pointing down at my pocket, though I was careful not to move my arm too much, lest he think it a threat.

"Lucky bastard," Caspian mumbled as Bo dug into my

pocket. Then Caspian chuckled. "Though we can't really have you armed to the teeth now, can we?" He grabbed for the hilt of the dagger on the side nearest him, then reached across my abdomen to grab the other, his forearm lingering against my belly as he moved. My groin began to tingle and I let a small gasp escape past my lips. His eyes met mine as he yanked his limb back. "Sorry," he said, rubbing the nape of his neck. It was the first time since I'd met him that I'd seen the fire drop out of his eyes.

"All right, all right, Mr. Hotshot," said Monroe, taking the daggers from him. He turned to Bo. "Is it locked?"

I didn't know how a phone could be locked.

Bo shook his head as he stared at my bright screen. "The contacts could prove useful," he said.

"And the phone could prove useful for tracking her, too," said Monroe. I didn't know what he meant. He sighed. "Toss it."

"Shouldn't we get the info down first?" asked Bo, his head tilted slightly.

"Guys," called Rhett from the open window of the truck, "we've got a problem."

Inside the diner, Torynt and Kouta were both on their feet, Torynt running toward Kouta from the direction of the bathrooms and Kouta's expression growing tense.

"Get her in the truck now," said Monroe, knocking my phone from Bo's hand. "*Now!*"

Caspian and Bo tugged quickly and I stumbled, Bo opening the back door of the car and climbing in, pulling me as Caspian shoved me inside and climbed in after me.

"Step on it!" said Monroe as he slid into the seat up front beside Rhett.

"Don't have to tell me twice," Rhett said, and he pushed his foot down hard, which caused the truck to squeal as it surged forward.

Pressed flat against the seat, it took extra effort to turn around and glance out the back of the truck as it hit the road and started to speed off. Torynt and Kouta were where I'd just been standing, Kouta bending over to pick up my phone and show it to Torynt, who tossed his hands in the air and shouted so loudly, I could hear something of the sound.

Caspian let out a hearty laugh, shaking his fist in the air, punching the roof above us. "Take that, motherfuckers!"

The others joined in the celebration, proud of taking me of my own free will—though they likely thought they'd subdued me into agreement.

But I had other ideas, other reasons for being here.

To find out which of these men roused that feeling deep within my loins—and to keep them all from using their powers against my brother and his allies as long as I could.

CHAPTER FOUR

After the laughter and glee died down, an air of solemnity hung over the interior of the car as everyone went quiet once more.

These men were an odd collection of Natch species—so much heat and cold, energy and sobriety all at once.

I wondered what they could do—not that I'd ever see it firsthand. They'd mentioned Bo had super strength, and I assumed one of them had been responsible for that lightning strike that had vanished as it had come up against my aura. But I didn't know which.

Monroe sat with my daggers on his lap, examining them even as he rotated one of his hands in the air.

"Nothing?" Rhett asked after a while.

"Nope," said Monroe. "You?"

Rhett squeezed the wheel in front of him tightly. "No," he said after a while.

It was hard not to notice the way Bo stared pointedly at me at that. "We lost our powers when we followed the Renegades."

I didn't so much as flinch, though I hoped he didn't notice the way I clenched the edge of the seat.

"Ease up, *hermano*," said Caspian. "She's frightened

enough as is." He gently touched my shoulder and my face grew hotter.

"Forgive me if I don't really care how scared the *Nelian* is," Monroe muttered. He shifted in his seat to face me. "Don't think I've forgotten how you pointy-eared freaks attacked our city for months on end."

"No one was killed," I said quietly. "We made sure of that."

Caspian's hand slipped from my shoulder.

"So you *did* participate firsthand," Rhett said from behind the wheel.

My shoulders slouched as I slunk back into the seat.

"What were you doing out there in a field?" asked Bo. "What were you doing with the Renegades?"

"That should be obvious enough," spat Monroe. "The Renegade leader is just as much a dictator as his buddy the Nelian king—but at least he's from Earth and I can get behind his desire for better Natch treatment." He went quiet on that last part, his finger tracing the tip of one of my daggers' blades.

"I don't know what you mean by *dictator*," I said.

Monroe sneered. "Passing laws by threat of harm? That's as good as taking the government hostage."

Hostage. Like what they wanted me to be.

"The government is banning the production of new plastics," said Bo, shaking his head. "Do you know how difficult it's going to be to rely on recycling plants to reproduce enough for what we need?"

"They've given automakers a deadline for producing only electric vehicles," added Caspian. "And there's supposed to be some bullshit program for all of us to swap the engines in our cars for battery packs."

"Don't forget that electricity can only be produced through solar and wind going forward," said Rhett. "There's a tight deadline on converting old power plants and building new ones, too."

"I don't understand. Do you not wish for the Earth to be healthier?" I asked. "For it to flourish and provide your people with sustainable resources for generations to come?"

"Of course we do," Caspian said beside me. His voice had lost some of its usual swagger, which he seemed to notice, as he quickly sniffed and rested an elbow against the window. "But this stuff costs money. Who's going to pay?"

Humans and their *money*. "It will be done," I said.

"How?" Monroe snapped. "People need money to live. You can't just force them—"

"An army," said Rhett quietly. "A Nelian army—poised to invade through portals all across the nation if corporations refuse to comply."

I opened my mouth and then shut it. "We don't want it to come to that," I said. I didn't know whether or not to explain that our "army" was hardly as large as they seemed to think. Granted, we could do a lot of damage with a small force. Besides, until they could be made to see reason, they were my enemies. "We *invaded* before. We're trying a different way now."

"Yeah, dictatorship," spat Monroe. "We're a democracy. At least, we're supposed to be."

I didn't understand. They believed in the Renegades' mission—in the Nelians'. My brother and Zander worked together to direct more environmentally responsible practices while at the same time guaranteeing better protection and more respect for Natches—still not always looked upon positively by the Typicals on this planet, according to the Renegades.

So what was the problem? These R.I.A. men—they didn't like *how* my people or the Renegades did things. The laws had been passed, the *corpornations* forced to change their ways, and sustainable practices were becoming a reality across this country, with plans for the rest of the world to follow suit.

The Renegades had had to turn away new recruits, so

beloved was their work by some—Zander had said it was too much to operate, too much to oversee when he had other things he'd rather focus on.

"What about Veras?" I asked, knowing that despite their differences, their leader had come to an agreement to cooperate with my brother and the Renegades, to offer his views.

"What about them?" asked Monroe, snorting. "Those weak-willed kowtowing traitors give Natches a bad name."

"Rumor has it it's because the guy who runs Veras is in love with Mr. Renegade himself, Zander," said Caspian, wriggling his eyebrows.

I didn't know about that. But I didn't want to let these men know more than they had to, didn't want to explain about my brother's beloved and put her at risk—or her babies.

"They're good people," is all I said instead. "All of them, Veras and Renegades alike."

"They used to be your enemies," said Rhett.

It was dark on this road and there wasn't much around us. If I remembered right, we were headed in the opposite direction from the city where Aurora and her team were headquartered, the city where the Renegades took up their temporary headquarters as they moved from one place to the next to avoid detection. Not because the police would do anything to them now, Zander had explained, though I didn't quite understand what he meant, but because of their "adoring fans" and them just wanting a "little privacy." Privacy I did understand.

"I don't believe we should be enemies," I said, my heart tightening at the memory of Xerxes going up against my brother, of his brief time claiming the throne through betrothal to me, the heir—until my brother had children at least. "Nothing good comes of working out differences through violence."

"We're not *trying* to be violent," Bo said softly, clenching a fist in his lap.

"They leave us no choice," said Monroe.

A moment passed in silence.

"We've definitely lost them by now," Monroe continued. "Take us home, Rhett."

Rhett turned the wheel and the truck moved sharply down an empty road. A car passed by us on the other side— the first we'd encountered in ages. We passed houses and other small buildings spaced great distances apart. Everything looked old and dusty, dull beneath the occasional flickering yellow overhead light.

At last Rhett pulled off the road, to a building that seemed bustling in comparison. Six cars were parked under a harsh, brightly-colored sign in the shape of a woman wearing a big hat with a wide, wide *visor* and swinging what looked like a yellow vine above her, the loop flickering in and out of existence. "Drake's" read the brightly-colored lights beside the woman. I wondered if she was "Drake."

Rhett drove behind the building, bringing the truck to a rest in the dark and turning off its twin lights. Blinking, I let my eyes adjust until I could make out the shapes of everything around me. The silhouette of that woman lingered behind in my closed eyes for a bit, even after we'd left her behind.

"You okay?" asked Caspian.

Monroe climbed out of the door he'd opened. "Can we not focus so much on the welfare of our *hostage*?"

Bo swallowed visibly at the word as Rhett got out and joined Monroe. "We've never done this before. How are we… What do we…?"

"Toughen up," Monroe said, opening his door.

"We'll treat her right." Caspian jumped out and reached up both arms toward me, the corner of his mouth twitching upward. "We're not bad guys," he whispered as I slid forward and he helped me out of the truck. I stumbled. My muscles quivered as he caught me by the waist to steady me. "Hey there," he whispered, lingering for just a moment before letting me go. A shiver wracked my body and a light pain seared across my chest.

Bo walked up beside me and adjusted my cap, holding out a lock of my long, green hair that had fallen out until I snatched it from him and tucked it back under the top. "Natches and Typicals do play around with hair color," he said, "but I don't know any who would choose green after you elves started ripping up cement with your giant vines."

Rhett went tense in front of me, like he expected me to whip him with a giant vine right then and there. "Your powers gone, too?" he asked.

My mouth went dry. How much did I lie to protect the people who'd been kind to me—to protect my own people? Especially considering the rapid beat of my heart, the scorching flush to my cheeks that wouldn't abate around these men. It was almost like I felt the calling to be with them *all*. But that couldn't be. I'd never taken more than one lover. The thought, as natural as it was for many other Nelians, caused me to open my mouth in an effort to inhale enough air. My breaths grew more and more shallow, the air never enough.

"All right," said Monroe, reaching past Caspian to grab my arm. "I assume if you could shoot vines, you'd have shot them by now. Let's get going."

His hand on my elbow, he led me to the back door of the building, producing a key from his pocket that he slipped into the lock. A repetitive thunderous boom echoed as he turned the key, escalating in volume as he opened the door—some of the Earthlings' music, though not like any I'd heard before. I pressed my free hand over my cap to put pressure on that ear.

"I guess elves don't like country," said Caspian from behind me. Bo elbowed him in the gut and he let out an *oof*.

"Hey, sugar," said a woman rummaging through a stack of boxes. There were shelves and boxes everywhere back here, all lit up with a single faint yellow bulb. The woman had curly, dark red hair, and she wore one of those strange hats I'd seen on the lighted silhouette outside, a checkered red shirt tied beneath her breasts exposing her abdomen and a pair of jeans cut too short, exposing about three-quarters of her legs. "I see you have company?" She raised an eyebrow and leaned an arm against the box.

Monroe put a finger to his mouth, his other hand still gripping my elbow. His muscles were tense as his gaze explored the hallway leading out there to where the music thundered loudest, the light only slightly brighter.

"Oh, don't you worry about them, sugar," said the woman. There was something different about the way she spoke, something I hadn't heard from Natches and Typicals before—not that I'd spoken to many. Her words had an almost melodious quality to them. She turned back to her box and started pulling stacks of white papers out of it. "Next thing you know, those assholes are going to demand we use reusable napkins," she muttered. "Like I've got the time to wash the stains off cloth napkins made by these clowns." She hitched a thumb toward the open hallway.

It took me a moment to process what she might have meant—Alarik had been concerned with the way humans used disposable items without properly letting them decay to the Earth. But paper napkins had the opportunity to decay if disposed of properly. They weren't on the top of my brother's list of behaviors to correct.

Bo, Caspian, and Rhett stepped beside us, heading up a dark, narrow staircase I hadn't even noticed before. Monroe directed me toward them and indicated for Rhett to take my other elbow. I let Rhett lead me up the stairs as I watched Monroe down below, whispering something into the beautiful woman's ear. My ribs squeezed tightly as my mind raced to recover what was *mine*.

But Monroe wasn't mine. None of them were—and they couldn't be. They stood against my loved ones, my allies.

Besides, as Alarik explained, his human consort didn't *feel* the attraction in quite the same way we Nelians did. Whoever was my destined among them wouldn't necessarily feel the same way.

I could walk away from them eventually, refuse to give in to nature's inclinations.

The squeak that the door at the top of the stairs let out made me tense. As I squeezed past Rhett in the narrow space, I swore he hesitated, his mouth a bud's length from mine in the hot, cramped space, my breath growing shallow once more.

"Come on, *hermosa*," said Caspian, and he reached down to take my free hand. Rhett dropped his grip on my elbow.

With a click, a dim source of light turned on in the corner of the room where Bo stood, pulling the chain for an electric lamp. The room was large—it must have been the size of the entire building below. There was a large chair big enough to seat five people with one of those large, flat rectangles the humans used to watch moving images, like a large phone, only you couldn't speak through it. There was a small kitchen in the opposite corner—the humans' equivalent of a cooking fire, what was the word? A *stoven*. A shelf with books, a plush chair beside it. And in the other two corners of the room, there were four plush mattresses covered in an array of blankets, three on one side and one on the other.

"Sorry about the mess," said Bo, rushing to one of the mattresses and fixing up the blankets to make it look neater.

"She's not a guest," Rhett said glumly from behind me. "No need to straighten up."

"*Au contraire, hermano*," said Caspian, running his free hand through his sleek, black hair. "She's the best guest we could ever invite here to our little bachelor pad." He squeezed my hand and led me to the messy mattress by its lonesome in the corner across from Bo. "You can have my bed." He leaned in and spoke in a hushed tone. "If you want me to fluff your pillows, just ask." His smooth, hot breath sent bumps to my skin.

Caspian frowned, staring at his hand in mine. "You

feel…" His thumb traced a feather-light circle over my palm. "Your skin feels different." He raised his voice, jutting his chin out toward the others behind me. "Did you notice that? It's almost like there's a rubber quality to it."

"To what?" Rhett grunted.

"Her *skin*," purred Caspian. His voice was steamy, inviting.

Bo shuffled around his now-tidy bed. "May I?" He gestured toward my other hand, but then pulled back. "That's a weird thing to ask of you, isn't it? Never mind." In answer, I took his hand in mine. My shoulders relaxed as both men's fingertips moved tenderly over my skin.

"Oh," said Bo. "It *does* feel different." He laughed heartily, as if the sound came from his abdomen. "It's so soft!" The tip of his tongue jutted out to caress his bottom lip just slightly as his eyes met mine. Was he going to try to kiss me? Was I going to let him?

"Enough fondling the hostage," Rhett said, plunking down on the couch and using a thin plastic rectangle to make the moving images appear on the screen before him.

Bo went paler and dropped my hand as he cleared his throat. "Guys, I don't know if I feel comfortable with this—"

Caspian hadn't stopped massaging my hand, but he did when Monroe appeared in the door, shutting it behind him. "Then you shouldn't have joined up with us. How can we *risk it all* if that doesn't mean risking a little jailtime?"

"Or worse," muttered Rhett. He flailed his little rectangle in the air toward the moving images on the screen. *Alarik.* And Zander—all muscle and dark hair that sat close to his scalp—along with Lila, her short pale hair, her tall defined frame behind him. In parallel, Alarik's top soldier, Normak, stood behind him. Svelte and graceful Normak stood as still as could be, his hand on the hilt of his dagger. Alarik spoke animatedly straight to us—to anyone watching, I supposed. I still didn't understand how these screens worked, but Alarik had made great use of them in his quest to get the humans to take better care of themselves and the planet.

"...unacceptable," he said, His lips pulled back, bearing his teeth as his hand trembled on a wooden stand in front of him. "This Nelian has stayed out of your affairs and only asked to be left alone. I will not rest until she is found again—and let me state this clearly to her abductors: You. Will. Not. Know. Peace." His neck practically bulged, his nostrils flaring as he gripped the stand so hard, he might have broken it.

I hadn't seen my brother so angry before, not even during his arguments with Xerxes over how to best approach our rescue of Earth.

The image changed to a human I didn't know, who touched a hand to her ear and then began to speak into a long black stick in her hand. I picked up her referring to "His Majesty, King Alarik of Nelia" and "special news conference" and "the kidnapping of a Nelian woman by a group of four Natch men."

"Damn it," said Monroe, snatching the rectangle from Rhett and shaking it wildly at the large screen, turning it off. He whirled around to face me. "That didn't take long."

Bo ran a hand up and down his forearm. "They're going to find our digital footprints," he said. "They'll get pictures and names soon enough."

"We've been careful," said Rhett.

"Yeah, maybe *you* have," Bo snapped. "Mr. 'I-Hate-Social-Media.' But I didn't think I'd be joining an underground resistance someday, okay? Even if I deleted all my profiles, I assume someone can recover the data."

"Calm down," said Monroe, stroking his chin as he stared at a point on the wall. "It's not like your old profiles explain where you are now. We're underground—that means untraceable."

"Yeah, but the people we love aren't," Bo said sharply. He cradled both sides of his head. "You guys may not care that much about your parents or whatever, but I have Lacey!"

A woman's name? Despite everything more important going on, I felt my throat grow dry, a strange thought flashing through my mind that I would not share Bo with anyone—as if it were up to me, and as if sharing were not something perfectly natural. I let out a sharp breath to calm my thoughts.

"What did you *expect* when you agreed to this plan?" asked Caspian. "That no one would find out? How can we *use* a hostage if they don't know we have her?"

"Hush," said Monroe. "I'm thinking."

The men went quiet, Bo pacing back and forth as Rhett turned back around on the couch. Monroe's only movement was the subtle stroking of his chin and Caspian shrugged, walking over toward the kitchen and opening the large rectangular box humans used to keep foods chilled. The *frigerfrator*. The snap of the cover off his glass bottle penetrated the silence, then he chugged the contents down, the amber liquid vanishing in a few swallows.

"Let me talk to Alarik," I said. "With a phone."

"What?" Monroe scoffed. He pointed to the blank screen where my brother had been moments before. "You want us to let you *talk* to that elven prick?"

My lips pinched together as I suppressed the urge to correct him—whatever he had called my brother, I could tell it wasn't nice. "I'll tell him I'm okay and he must call off the search. Until you can figure out what you want from them."

"Less press scrutiny would help," Caspian said, lifting his bottle in the air toward me.

Standing, Rhett shook his head. "Figure out what we want to do with her *now* and get this over with." He jutted his chin toward me. "She's not staying here long. That would be suicide."

"Says you," said Bo, moving beside me. "She stays until we're sure Lacey is safe." That woman again. I wanted to meet her—to make sure she deserved my Bo.

I laughed a little. Lust was muddling my mind.

"You think this is funny?" Monroe asked. "It's too soon to

let her go," he said to Rhett. "We keep her for assurances until we're sure what we can get out of her. Until we know what the hell's going on with our powers." He shook his hand in the air as if for emphasis. Nothing happened, of course. "*Dammit!* What the fuck is going on here? How can we focus on negotiations when we can't even *do* anything?"

I ground my foot against the floor. *Good.* They'd be power-less—literally—at my side.

"What do you propose then?" asked Rhett. "We can't hang on to her forever."

Bo was pacing again, grinding a fist into his hair. "What are we *doing*? We're just four layabouts crashing in an attic, stalking Renegades. And now we're powerless. We're *useless*."

His comment shouldn't have stung. It was why I'd let them take me. I wanted them to be powerless. But I... That confused, lascivious side of me didn't like seeing them so helpless.

Focus, I reminded myself.

"And what's to stop them from going back on their promise once we make the exchange?" Caspian clicked his tongue. "We didn't think this through."

Monroe slammed a palm on the table. "So what? What do you propose we do? You think we have a *chance* of making a difference if we don't have something our enemies want?"

"The longer she stays, the bigger our problems," said Rhett. Our eyes met, and he didn't shy away.

No one said anything for a moment.

"We let them sweat a little." Monroe gazed at his flexing hands. "Wait and see if our powers come back."

"What if they're gone?" Rhett asked quietly. "For good?"

"Then we'll deal with it," snapped Bo. He rushed over toward the bookshelf, then came back with a small rectangle —a phone, I supposed, though it was smaller than the one I'd been given—wrapped in that obnoxious, oversized *plastic* packaging my brother was working on outlawing. "Give her a burner."

44

"They still could trace it," said Rhett as Bo attacked the plastic with a grunt.

Monroe's eyes lit up. "Not if we keep it short and destroy it right after." He snatched the package from Bo and pulled out a dagger—one of *my* daggers—from his boot. I gasped as he used it to savagely attack the plastic, then slipped the dagger back into his boot. He let out a little cry as he ripped the phone—burner?—out of there. "Goddammit," he said, sucking on his finger as he tossed the burner-phone at Bo. Bo caught it and Monroe chucked the plastic on the couch beside Rhett. "Cut myself."

"Why do you humans even use *that* to wrap items?" I asked. "It's wasteful, it's hard to open, it hurts you—"

"Enough with the sanctimony, elf." Monroe sucked on his finger once more.

The burner-phone lit up in Bo's hand. "What's the number?" he asked me.

"The… number?" I repeated.

"The elf king or whoever's phone number," said Bo.

They all stared at me blankly. I shrugged. "I tap their picture," I said. "Then they speak."

"*Fuck.*" Monroe shook his injured hand now. He strode across the room to the shelf and rifled around until he pulled out a hard, plastic box with a red cross on top of it. "Well, so much for that."

Caspian put his bottle down on the table. "Your friends' numbers aren't on every phone, *hermosa*," he said tenderly. "Every phone has a number and you have to know it to call it. Someone must have programmed yours with your friends' numbers so you wouldn't have to remember them."

Biting my lip, I watched as Monroe tore through the red-cross-box, pulling out another box and then another small piece of paper and then ripping *that* and pulling out something from which he tore yet *more* papers off before wrapping it around his finger. Humans and their packaging—*seriously*. We'd have made a salve from leaves to pack the wound tightly, maybe wrapped it with thin bandages made from vines.

"So what do we do?" There was an edge to Bo's voice.

"Wait," I said, resting a hand on his wrist. I closed my eyes and tried to picture the name "Aurora Haddix" on my own phone screen, a series of ten numbers below it just a short time ago—though it felt like so much longer. "I can call my friend." I rattled off the numbers to Bo, who nodded and tapped the screen. He handed it to me and all four men went tense, staring at me.

"What do you want me to tell her?" I asked.

All eyes looked to Monroe. He didn't so much as flinch. "Tell them you're here willingly."

"*What?*" said Bo.

Caspian shook his head. "They're not going to believe that, bro."

"It'll buy us time," said Monroe curtly. "Then we'll figure out what to do next. Wait for our powers to come back."

His plan suited me just fine. I pushed the *speaker* button on the small screen.

"Hello...?" Aurora answered. She sounded fatigued, her voice cracking.

"Aurora, it's me," I said.

"Alanna!" she screamed. She started rattling off information to people presumably around her—something about "get a trace" and "tell Alarik" and "tell Zander then—Jayden, just *think* it to him."

"Your name's Alanna?" whispered Bo beside me. "It suits you. We should have asked. I'm sorry."

Caspian elbowed him.

"Aurora, listen to me," I said firmly. "I'm okay. I'm here willingly."

"You're *what*?" shrieked Aurora. "They're just making you say that—put them on the phone! Let them know that my friends and I are going to *kick their asses* into a new dimension, you hear me? You listening? Your brother is going to—"

"*Aurora!*" I snapped, cutting her off. I hadn't wanted the R.I.A. to put two and two together. "Please just listen to me. *Don't* send anyone looking for me. Call off the search. I'll be in touch as soon as I can. Aurora, I *promise* you I can take care of myself. You know I can."

Rhett raised an eyebrow at that, the corner of his mouth twitching upward.

"Okay," said Aurora more calmly. She must have understood I had a plan—that I was keeping these men from being a threat just by being near them. "Alanna, I'll tell everyone, but I don't like this."

"That's enough," Monroe said, stomping across the room and grabbing the burner-phone from me. He jammed his thumb against the screen and then tossed it to Bo. "Crunch it," he said.

Bo cocked his head and squeezed the phone. "Can't. Still as weak as a Typical."

Monroe huffed and grabbed the phone back. He ripped open a drawer by the *stoven* and removed a tool that reminded me of an elven hammer, only it was much smaller. He rapidly smashed the phone again and again, causing the rest of us to jump in place.

"There," he said, tossing the hammer beside the crumpled-up metal. "Now let's get some sleep. We'll talk some more in the morning." He tugged hard on the chain by the electric lamp, bathing the wide, open room in darkness. "I'll take first watch." He dragged a chair from the table toward the door and sat down in it, staring my way. "If you try anything funny—"

"Let's at least refrain from action movie quips," Rhett said dryly. He shivered as he fell forward onto one of the mattresses. They all looked exhausted in the glow of the yellow light from outside. "I feel like too much of a goon already."

"I don't know if I *can* sleep," said Bo. His shoulders slumped forward as he sat down on another empty mattress.

"We lost our powers, we're kidnappers—"

"If you don't like it, there's the door!" Monroe pointed his thumb over his shoulder.

"I *thought* we were getting one of the men," Bo snapped.

Rhett's voice carried across the room from where he lay. "Like that would have made it all right?"

"Guys, please. Give it a rest." Caspian gestured toward his mattress and brazenly reached up to remove my hat. My hair tumbled down over my shoulders. "Never you mind about them. You're safe here," he whispered. "I promise. Even if I have to fight off these bickering *pendejos* myself. Sweet dreams." Hesitatingly, perhaps waiting to see if I would object, he traced his finger in a line down my cheek, his gossamer touch stirring a sense of bliss at my very core, before he stepped back to give me space.

I crawled into his sheets, asleep almost as soon as my eyes shut, that tingling sense of *longing* assuring me I was indeed safe with these men, even if they were my enemies.

CHAPTER FIVE

My eyelids fluttered open to the room beset by sunbeams struggling to penetrate a series of tattered curtains. The form in the chair by the door came into focus.

Caspian.

"Shh," he said in a hushed tone. "I'm on watch." He shifted slightly to look over his shoulder. The chorus of heavy breaths from the corner where the other mattresses were must have told him what he'd wanted to know.

"I'm sorry," he said softly, turning back to face me. "I've been thinking about it all night. I shouldn't have gone along with this. If you want to leave, I'll take you somewhere. Right now."

If I wanted to leave? As if there were a situation he could picture that involved me willingly staying with them. Only there *was*. This wasn't a kidnapping like they thought—this was my *mission*. My way to snap out of my solitude and help my brother and those who had aided me. I could keep these foes powerless this way. And besides, there was the *craving*. I felt it now, the moment I woke, pouring over me in waves.

I shook my head, afraid to speak. Afraid to give anything away.

"Don't you have someone waiting for you?" he asked,

his voice as dulcet as a lullaby. He shuffled over, taking a seat at the edge of my mattress as I sat up to face him. A lock of my long, green hair fell over my face. Reaching over, he snagged it on my pointed ear as he tucked the hair behind it for me. His fingertips lingered on the point of the ear and I reached up to cover my mouth to keep from laughing. I was ticklish.

He grinned as he pulled back. "*Lo siento*," he said huskily. "Look. I don't exactly know what the plan is here. Since the Typical government and police force seem inept or unwilling to handle any of this elf business, we figured it was necessary for Natches to step up to the plate. Turns out we don't know what we're doing, either." He shook with a shiver.

"I don't like what your people are doing," he continued. "I called myself a coward for not stepping up and helping Veras fight the invaders downtown a few months back. So when Monroe proposed we fight back…" He left the rest unsaid, chewing his bottom lip. "But now we have nothing. I quit my job—without notice. We left the house we were renting together behind and came here—Monroe is friends with the owner, thought he could get him on our side. This apartment isn't even finished. The bathroom and cooking range are busted. So we're a group of losers just crashing in a junky pad, and we haven't *done* anything. We've just been training. And then we finally decide to go after the Renegades, we lose our powers." He grimaced. "Didn't even think to train without our powers."

Listening intently, I nodded along. I only understood some of what he said, but the sentiment was there.

"And now we're kidnapping innocent women?" His voice went a little louder and he flinched as one of the sleeping bodies let out a snore. "I don't care if you're Nelian. I feel like a fucking villain right now. I *am* one."

Before I realized what I was doing, I found my hand caressing his chin, feeling the strange rough sensation of the smallest bit of dark hair sprouting out from his cheek. The junction of my thighs ignited at the thought of running my lips against it.

Caspian. Bo. Rhett. Even Monroe. It wasn't one. It was all of them. And in the dawn of that new morning, I accepted the strange prospect of being destined for them all—this group of friends, of wannabe warriors. I wondered what they were like with their full power—a sight I'd never see. Strong, fighting hard for something they believed in. Misguided but not so different from my own kind.

Could I love them, though? As much as nature wanted me to, I didn't have to give in, regardless of how great the call. I'd have to change them to love them—get them to understand. And yet I knew from my time with Xerxes that changing someone at their core was not so simple a task.

As I pulled my hand away, Caspian turned his head just slightly and laid a soft kiss upon my palm. We stared at one another a moment longer, and so lost was I that I didn't notice when something landed on my ankles over the blanket—and I turned to find Monroe standing behind Caspian. Caspian darkened and leaned back.

I reached for the clothes Monroe had tossed on my mattress. They looked exactly like what that woman of the red hair had been wearing, complete with the wide-visor hat. I poked at the little dip at the top of the hat. It was hard, but if I poked hard enough, I could get the material to bend.

"There's a working shower stall beside the staff toilet downstairs," he said, pointing toward the door. "I don't know when it was you last bathed, but you look like you've been camping for weeks. Shower and change. We'll get your clothes laundered."

Caspian shot up. "We're running errands now, are we? And how long do you expect Alanna will be with us?" he asked Monroe, using my name for the first time. "We need to figure this out, Monroe. This isn't what we planned."

"I don't remember you voicing any objections when you helped nab her at the diner," said Monroe. Across the room,

Bo let out a loud yawn as he stretched and Rhett sullenly fixed his sheets across from me.

Caspian shot up, clenching his fists. "I was hopped up on adrenaline." His hands tore through his hair. "But this—this, shit, Monroe. We're criminals. *Me cago en Dios!*"

Bo broke into a coughing fit.

Monroe jabbed a finger against Caspian's chest. "You agreed to be one the moment we decided to go up against the despots and invaders. The plan was always to use a Renegade for leverage. We got an elf instead. So why have you gone soft suddenly?" Spittle practically flew from his lips and he crossed his arms, pulling back. "It's because she's a woman. Because you want to screw her."

"Shut up." Caspian shoved Monroe back a step.

"I could see your boner from across the room!" I didn't know what *screw* and *boner* meant in those contexts, but it didn't sound very pleasant. Monroe laughed—but there was darkness to the sound. "You think I haven't noticed you and Bo both leering at her? You want to talk about treating a hostage with humanity? Don't ogle her." His gaze flicked to me in that moment, his breath catching before he looked at his feet.

"Can you *hear* yourself?" asked Caspian. He padded over to me, offering me a hand. "Come on, *hermosa*," he said, clearly done talking to Monroe. "I'll show you where to go."

I took his hand and he lifted me up, pulling me close to keep me steady.

"Yeah, but are you going to keep an eye on her or fuck her?" Monroe asked.

"Fuck *you*," spat Caspian.

"Hey," said Bo, "that's out of line. We're a team."

"Yeah, a team of nobodies." Caspian flourished his free hand above him. "In case you haven't noticed, we didn't wake up to suddenly find our powers working."

Bo frowned as he flexed his arm.

Monroe growled and wandered over to the table, slamming a fist against it.

"Hot shot doesn't know what the fuck we're doing, does he?" Caspian asked as we retreated toward the door.

I exchanged a quick look with Rhett as we left. The curt man nodded at me, then walked past his arguing companions and headed toward the kitchen.

Perhaps these two coming to blows was normal, like it had been with Alarik and Xerxes.

Caspian hummed an unfamiliar tune as we made our way down the stairs through the darkness. At the bottom, he pulled on a hanging chain that turned on one of those overhead electric lamps, revealing the room full of boxes through which we'd entered the night before. "Back here," he said, leading the way. We wandered through a larger kitchen than the one upstairs, and Caspian nodded at a man who was slicing up tomatoes on a counter. "Morning, Drake. Another rough night last night?"

"Pretty quiet," said this Drake, not looking up from his work. He was rotund, his flesh almost straining against the white, long fabric that covered only the front of his clothes. His chin was dark and scratchy-looking, his thin gray hair under a crisscrossing series of thin ropes, like a hunting net. He looked up. "Say, Bella mentioned something about a *new arrival.*"

"The less you know, the better, *hermano,*" Caspian said to the man preparing food. He opened another door and shut it behind us. Inside was a toilet and a sink, then something like a wall faucet beside it, a drain on the tiled floor, and a long, hanging curtain made of a material unfamiliar to me.

"Here," he said, grabbing my stack of clothes and putting it atop a small, dusty cabinet in the corner on which were stacked rolls of that white *toilet paper sheets* humans liked to use instead of simply rinsing in fresh bowls of water. He tucked his hands into his jeans pockets. "So you know how to work everything?" He winced. "Why am I asking you that?"

He started muttering to himself in a language I didn't understand. I knew there were many more of them here in this world. "It's just... Nelians haven't been here long and they've been cagey about what their own world is like."

He kept rambling and I walked toward the wall faucet, turning it all the way.

"Whoa, whoa!" said Caspian, but I was already soaked, the icy cold water flattening my hair against my head, pasting my shirt to my skin. I removed the shirt and threw it on the ground.

"Oh—okay." He covered his face with one palm, though one eye was wide between two of his fingers, so I wondered at the point of it. Then I flinched and let out a cry, jumping back from the stream. The water had become hot—unbearably hot.

"Let me," he mumbled as he fiddled with the faucet, stretching his arm as far as it would go to stay out of the water. He nodded, then darted his eyes away from me. "Good temperature now." Grabbing hold of the curtain, he pulled it along a long metal pole above his head so it hung between us —me on the side of the stream, him on the other. "I'll get you some soap," he added.

I removed my jeans and threw them on the floor alongside my shirt. I stared up at the stream and positioned myself beneath it. It *was* a nice temperature. Warm and soothing, no longer threatening to scorch me.

"Here." Caspian's hand stuck through at the edge of the curtain, holding a bar of soap. "I've got a towel for you when you're done, too. Oh, and some shampoo."

I took the soap and stood there, staring at it, before his hand stuck through again and handed me a bottle. I frowned at that plastic, heavy in my hand.

"What's a *shammm-poo*?" I asked.

He chuckled. "Soap for your hair. Only keep your eyes closed when you use it. It can sting."

Putting the soap down by my feet, I flicked open the top

of the plasticky bottle and sniffed. A strong, soapy scent met my nostrils and I sneezed.

He laughed again. "You all right?"

"Yes," I replied. I shook the bottle upside down until the white, goopy soap came out into my other hand. Frowning, I filled my entire palm full and then put the bottle down, working the goop through my hair. The thick soap produced more bubbles the more I scrubbed. I pulled my hand away. It was *covered* with bubbles.

"Caspian, I am doing this wrong." I ripped aside the curtain and he let out a small cry, jumping back a few places until his back hit the wall. I pointed to my soapy head. "I am a bubble now."

His wide eyes crinkled as his muscles grew slack, his shoulders rolling back as he removed his shirt.

My throat constricted at the sight of his smooth, brown skin, the shapely muscles in the flesh.

"You're doing fine," he said. "You might have used a bit much." He walked closer and cleared his throat. "You can't just keep showing off your goods like this. I'm *trying* to keep my boner contained, okay?" He spun me around and directed me under the stream of water.

Boner. There was that word again. "What's a boner?" I asked. Caspian's hands worked through my long, green hair. "And what do you mean, goods? I'm selling nothing. Nelians —we do not sell. Our *goods* are shared with everyone."

He was shaking so hard—his mouth eliciting just the slightest sounds of laughter—that I could feel his unsteady limbs as his hands worked through my hair.

"Well, that's not a surprise," he said, "about the Nelians. You must be so proud of your people."

"I am," I said. I winced as some of the bubbles hit my eyes and I remembered Caspian's instructions to keep them closed. "We do what is best for our Mother Nelia—what is best for all of us."

"It seems like you do," he said, and I wondered if he was

thinking about what I'd told him—if there was hope of changing his mind after all. "But Earth isn't Nelia. Your people can't just command us to live like you."

"That's not what we're doing," I said, turning around. His eyes darted downward, toward my breasts, my nipples growing erect as the wave of desire between us crashed over me. "We understand things are different here. We just want to save your planet—and save your people."

"I can see your intentions are good, *hermosa.*" Caspian's hands withdrew from my hair and he stepped back. "So you can use the bar of soap on the rest of you, right?"

I grabbed his wrist. "You did not explain the goods and the boner."

Caspian's cheeks darkened and his usual confident demeanor seemed to have vanished. Then a slow smile crept upon his lips. "Alanna, you're showing off your *goods* right now and it's giving me a *boner.*" He looked down at his jeans. I followed suit.

His organ pushed hard against the firm material of the jeans, bulging forward, like it wanted to pop out.

When I looked up, his eyes were darting from my breasts to the hot and moist place between my legs. I let him go. "I know what this *boner* is," I said, lifting my nose high in the air. "I'm no virginal maiden. We just don't call it by such a name. There is no *bone* in our men's genitalia."

He cackled so hard he actually stumbled, catching himself against the wall. "There's no bone in ours, either." Straightening slightly, he scratched his chin. "You know, I'm not sure *why* we call it that. Because it gets hard like a bone?"

"We call it an erection," I said, reaching for the soap and lathering my body up, starting with my arm.

"You can call it that here, too." He let out a hearty breath as he moved forward to grip the curtain once more. "*Hermosa,* you can call it whatever you want. I just want to thank you for giving me one." He started tugging on the curtain and I reached out to stop him.

"You are dirty, too," I said.

He took a look down at his jeans, splattered with water from my shower. "Yes, I suppose I am. I'll shower after you."

"*Now*," I said, rubbing the soap through the dark green hair below my abdomen. "Do not waste the water when we can bathe together."

"Alanna, you don't know what you're asking me," he said. The spark of fire that I'd only ever felt with Xerxes before last night burst up from my mons to my heart, causing my fingers and toes to tingle.

"Yes, I do," I said. My hands latched on to the top of his jeans, my fingers moving inside, feeling the warm moisture of the hair around his *boner*.

Part of me knew this was wrong. So wrong. He was my brother's enemy and I was here to stop him. But I wasn't the one who'd decided I *needed* him. It was nature itself.

"*Dios mio*," Caspian mumbled, stumbling back. "Look. As much as I would *love* to shower with you, it would take everything in me to put some space between us, so please just let me shower after you."

"I don't want space," I said. I turned around and bent slightly, putting both palms on the wall of the shower above the faucets. The stream of water caressed my rear. "I want your *boner* inside me," I said, looking over my shoulder. "Please."

His breaths grew shallow and a trembling hand moved through his dark, sleek hair. "Alanna, are you sure? You're asking me to have sex with you? What am I even saying? You're our hostage. I can't touch you."

"You can," I said. "Please. It's been so long for me. Too long." I traced a single finger from my lips and down my neck to the space between my breasts. "And I... I feel the need with you."

"The *need*, huh? You know, you don't have to seduce me. I'll get you out of here right now. Just ask."

"I'm *asking* you to come inside me."

57

Caspian blinked rapidly. "You're not thinking straight. What about birth control? We'd need a condom."

I didn't know exactly what he was talking about, but I had an idea. "I will not become pregnant," I said. "Nelian women decide when they want a child. And I do not have the desire to have one." I wondered if that would make him reconsider, but he said nothing.

Fumbling with those metal buttons keeping his jeans up, I struggled to get him out of his pants. I watched his erection grow. His phallus was indeed like a bone—girthy, *solid*. It made me stumble back, my vulva ablaze as I felt the moisture from inside me soak the area between my legs.

"This isn't right," he whispered as he neared me, his hands reaching for my face but hesitating, his fingers curling.

His nearness without his touch caused me to beat my fist against the wall behind me, my *need* to have him so great, this *need* he was denying me.

"Please," I said. "It's right. It's what I want. Is it not what *you* want?"

His palm finally touched me, cupping my cheek. "More than anything, but you're our prisoner and—"

My lips moved up to smash against his, the heat inside me soaring, my need too great to talk anymore. His tongue burst inside my mouth and I met it, my own dancing with his, as I grabbed his head in both hands and pulled him closer, closer, closer.

His *boner* rubbed against my bellybutton and my knees went weak at the thought of it being so near.

"Inside me," I breathed, then I let his face go, stroking the erect phallus instead, my finger shivering at the thick, smooth feel of his shaft, so unlike the skin of a Nelian.

"We can't go back from this," he whispered, rubbing his forearm over his lips. Letting out a cry, he grunted, stumbling back as I went to my knees and wrapped my mouth around his thick *boner*, so hard. I let my tongue move gently along the skin, *tasting* him as the shower water rained overhead. His member shuddered inside me as his fingers went gently to the back of my head, but I didn't pull away, drinking his seed as it shot down the back of my throat.

I wiped my own lips, the salty taste of him lingering there —so different from what I'd known before.

He panted as he gazed down at me, then he laughed. "*Dios mio*, woman."

"I don't want to *go back*," I said. "Please." I moved my hand down my belly, weaving my fingers through my green curls to find my pleasure spot.

"*Carajo*," he mumbled, then he reached toward me. "Let me. It's only fair after the little slice of heaven you just showed *me*."

I got the meaning of what he'd said. Taking his hand, I stood, and he pulled me to him roughly, triumphantly. Kissing my lips, he let his hand wander lower, sliding along my slit, moving in practiced circles at my point of pleasure. I moaned between his kisses, as the soft but determined touch woke its magic, my limbs hardly able to stop shaking.

He grew a *boner* again, and it danced across my abdomen as his fingers worked, then dipped lower to slide up inside me.

"Ready?" he whispered into my ear.

I nodded and he laid a gentle kiss on the tip of my ear, pulling his hand out to spin me around and grab me on either side of my hips. My hands shot out against the wall to catch myself as he lined my rear up beneath the warm, inviting stream of water.

His erect *boner* slid inside me and I moaned, rocking with the movement. I could hear him breathing, my own mouth saturated with the steam from the shower. He pulled out partway and then slid in again and I let out a frenzied cry. Beauty. Nature. This was just what I needed—just *whom* I needed inside me right now. "More!" I said, breathless.

He repeated the maneuver again and again, the slap of his soft thighs against my Nelian skin like the beat of a song. I mumbled louder and louder, not even sure what I was saying any more, and at last he pushed harder—the hardest yet. As he erupted inside me, I stumbled forward, my limbs threatening to give out beneath me as I exploded in wave after wave of bliss.

Panting, he caught me, one hand reaching up to cradle one of my breasts, his thumb working in lazy circles around my nipple. I didn't know how much more I could take—but I knew I never wanted it to end.

A hard pounding at the door startled us both, and Caspian pulled himself out, even as he laid a sweet kiss on my shoulder, my neck, my ear.

"Hey! About done in there? Not that I want to *disturb* anything, but you're using all the hot water."

It was Drake.

Caspian laughed and stepped back, directing my body into the water stream. "Almost done!" he shouted. "Sorry!"

He bent over to hand me the bar of soap, tossed aside and forgotten. "We should get back," he said, his breaths heavy.

I nodded, taking the soap and running it quickly over the length of my body. He closed the distance between us and laid a kiss atop my head.

"Thank you," he said. "*Mi corazón.*"

We stayed together in each other's arms until the water became very cold indeed.

CHAPTER SIX

"Do you need a blanket?" Rhett asked. It was the first thing he'd said to me the entire time we'd been alone together in their living space.

I shook my head from where I sat atop one of the mattresses. My heart still thundered from the release of my passions in the bathing room. But I'd been right—that feeling, that *need* hadn't gone away along with Caspian. I felt it here, alone in this place with Rhett, too.

And he'd been the one I'd spent the least amount of time connecting with, except maybe for Monroe.

I walked to the couch where Rhett was seated, reading a book. We had those on Nelia, too, but they were bound differently—organically. That made them scarcer than they seemed to be here. "What is that about?"

Rhett examined the cover and interior of his book, as if he'd never seen it before. "Oh," he said. "Nothing special." The book looked worn, its spine cracked, its pages yellower than the pages of the other Earth books I'd seen before. But that made it feel more natural somehow.

"*Pride and Prejudice*," I read slowly, still not overly confident in the different words I'd encountered in this Earth tongue so similar to ours. But I think I knew those. "It sounds informative," I said. "I know some Nelian men who suffer too much pride." My brother and Xerxes, each assuming they knew best. Prejudice... I knew that word now. There was much of it here on Earth, and Aurora had explained that, to be fair, we Nelians were prejudiced against Earth people.

Rhett chuckled despite the serious expression masking his face, the slightest smile curling his lips. It made his eyes brighten, his muscles relax—which made my toes tingle. "I guess I know a few Earth men like that, too. It's not very *informative*. It's a story. A love story." He pulled at the collar of his crisscross-lined shirt and put the book down in front of me.

"I like love stories," I said quietly, reaching for the book. Its cover felt smoother to the touch than I'd expected. There were drawings of two Earth people on it—wearing clothes the likes of which I'd never seen before, the woman's hair up in a pile above her head.

"You can have it if you like," he said.

"Thank you." I flipped through the pages. Most of these words I seemed to know. I'd just have to read slowly.

"It's by Jane Austen," he added, clearing his throat. "She lived about three hundred years ago."

I bolted upright. "She's one of your scribes? A great sage to stand the test of time?"

Grinning, he scratched the back of his neck. "Something like that."

"So this is a tale from a different time," I said, caressing the book against my bare abdomen. I was dressed like Bella, so the short, checkered red shirt was tied beneath my breasts. "I like her hair," I added. I tugged on mine. I had the *cowgirl hat*, as Caspian had called it, over my hair to cover the tips of my ears.

"I wonder if we should have asked them for hair dye." Rhett stared at the lock of hair I twirled in one hand. "If you're going to be here a while." He fidgeted and then stood. "You hungry?"

As if in response, my stomach growled. I clutched it and nodded.

He padded over to the kitchen and opened the *frigerfrator*. "Hmm," he said as he rummaged around. "Not much. I'll have to ask downstairs. Want anything specific?"

I shook my head *no*. Then I thought better of it. "*Pan*cakes. Coffee."

He snorted, but the mirth was clear on his face as he shut the *frigerfrator* door and stared at me. "Well, I think they have coffee. I'll see what I can do." He shuffled across the room. "Stay here, okay? Don't let anyone see your hair or ears."

I clutched my cowgirl hat tightly and nodded, but Rhett seemed unsure. "The back door downstairs is deadbolted," he said. "And you'd have to pass by me to get to the front."

"I will stay."

Rhett's lips went into a thin line. "Hmm." I didn't know if he believed me or not. It didn't seem like he was willing to threaten more.

If I walked downstairs and walked right out the door, would he even stop me?

Only Monroe had remained so *certain*, so confident in his decision to keep me here.

He was gone for a little while. I'd taken his spot on the couch and had shimmied and squirmed my thighs as I'd taken in the *warmth* of him, the fresh, almost woodsy *scent* of him. What I imagined to be the *feel* of him.

I knew I'd just been with Caspian, and perhaps humans were far less likely to understand the love between one and many at once, but I couldn't help it. I'd never thought I'd feel this way again, and I was going to *relish* the feeling, even if I fought to keep it contained.

I read some of the story Rhett had given me and was laughing on the second page—this great sage Jane Austen was very charming in her words, even if I didn't understand it all.

But after a while, I dropped the book, cursing my foolishness. This wasn't the time for that, for melting into Rhett's lingering aroma. Time was moving forward, and Caspian, Monroe, and Bo were away from me, away from my aura.

If they thought to test their powers while away, they'd find them returned.

They'd know the cause of their problems soon enough.

I hadn't been able to stop them from leaving, though. I hadn't even tried—hadn't known what to say to try to convince them without letting them know why I didn't want them to go. I wasn't used to this kind of *battle*. I could fight a man one on one—even take a group of them. But pretending to be helpless and not here for my own reasons? I'd been lost.

Nelians didn't lie. But I hadn't told the truth.

I searched the room for a burner-phone, another one in that atrocious plastic packaging. But there wasn't one. I couldn't call Aurora again and explain my plan in more detail —and how it was probably about to be thwarted by my own inability to deceive.

My heart was thundering with the conflict of emotions. Part of me just wanted to *stay*, to hope the other men would come back and not have had cause to discover their powers had returned, and then we'd go back to... I snorted at my own stupidity. As if the five of us would just spend time up here. Would live up here together. What did I want? They wouldn't give up on trying to get my brother to listen to them.

I would just have to hope this kept working. I would stay and take away their powers as long as I could. But first I had to tell my brother about my plans, to assure him that no harm would come to me. I'd find a phone downstairs. But just as I reached the handle, the door opened and instead of my R.I.A. captor, there stood Bella.

"Hey, can you help out?" She coughed into her hand. "Got to earn your keep, sugar." She hacked again. "I just can't do it today. And you're dressed for the part." I realized she, too, was wearing the outfit, but she didn't have the hat on today and she'd draped a large cloak—or *coat*, I thought they were called here—over her body.

Scrambling to tuck my hair up under the hat, I wished my hair could be styled up like Miss Elizabeth Bennet's.

"Don't sweat it, sugar," Bella said. "The boys told me they had a Nelian *guest*."

"Rhett told me to stay," I said.

Her eyebrows narrowed. "Yeah, well, I went home last night and saw a TV report about a missing Nelian woman in the company of four Natch men. So I asked Rhett about it just now and he shrugged. Said if you were here willingly, he wouldn't mind if you helped out some then, right? He just shrugged again." She studied me, her hard stare punctuated by tittering coughs. "But then again, the news reports this morning that the crisis was averted and we weren't to worry no more about missing Nelians and kidnapper Natches."

So Aurora had convinced Alarik to let it go. A lightness spread in my chest. Good. My brother knew better than anyone what I was capable of. When I wanted to leave, I would.

When I wanted to leave.

"You all right here, hon?" Bella asked quietly.

"I truly am well, thank you," I said.

"Because that *sure* would be a coincidence, another Nelian woman gone in the company of four Natch men," continued Bella. "And I don't usually ask the boys for *details*, but I know they ain't exactly operating in the light, the way they skulk about."

Carefully tucking all of my hair inside the hat, I stood and made my way to her. "I am well, thank you."

She huffed. "Okay, then." Sneezing, she wiped her nose against her sleeve, which made me flinch. "You got a name, Ms. I-Am-Well?"

"Alanna."

"That's a mouthful." She frowned. "Have the boys downstairs just call you 'Lana,' okay?"

I cocked my head but nodded. "Where is Rhett?" I asked, hesitating at the door.

Bella sniffled and pushed past me. "Downstairs. Making you lunch." She winked at me. "Drake tells me you worked up quite an appetite this morning, yeah?"

Flushing, I followed her down, shutting the door behind me.

"So you and Caspian..." She bumped her elbow against my arm as we reached the room full of boxes. "Don't blame you. He's fucking gorgeous. They're all fine specimens. If I owned this place, I wouldn't turn them away, neither." She coughed again. "Sorry," she said, sniffling. "Hope you got immunity built up for Earth viruses."

My brother had examined that very issue and found that Earth bacteria and viruses had posed us little danger. "I will be fine, thank you."

She tittered. "So where are all the other boys? Rhett's about as talkative as a mute statue, as usual."

"They took my clothes and theirs. They mentioned *groceries* and *laundry-mats*."

She arched an eyebrow as we approached the kitchen. "They left you here to go on *errands*?"

I shrugged.

"Right." She put a hand on her hip as she sniffled again. "I suppose the less we know, the better."

"Hey," Rhett said, looking up from the *stoven*. He had a small, flat paddle thing in his hand and he used it to flip over something brown and round in front of him. The *pancakes*.

Bella nudged me with her elbow once more. "He had to rustle up some ingredients for pancake batter for you all special, sugar. Though we don't have any maple syrup."

I made a note to ask someone about *may-pul*. I knew about syrup. We harvested it from the trees in Nelia. Hmm. Bella was right. Some sweet syrup would have tasted good on pancakes.

"What's she doing down here?" Rhett asked.

"Helping out," said Bella, coughing into her arm. She glared at Rhett. "What? Are you keeping her prisoner up there?"

Rhett's face flushed and he cleared his throat, flipping the pancake without another word.

"Let me show you what to do while he's finishing up and then you can get to work once you've eaten, okay, Lana?" Bella guided me past the kitchen to the front of the place, the area that had glowed and echoed with strange music last night.

"'*Lana*'?" Rhett said quietly behind me. I looked at him and he fidgeted. "I like it," he added.

I smiled.

Drake gave a hearty laugh when Bella and I joined him behind the *bar*, she'd called it—I had to ask whether that long table or the whole place was known by that name and she answered that they both were. How confusing. Drake mentioned something about "making myself comfortable" in his bar—and how I'd "clearly already done that this morning." I nodded. For the first time in months, I truly was comfortable.

"Do you know how to take orders, sugar?" Bella asked, then she proceeded to explain what I was supposed to do. "Thanks for helping out," she said once finished. She coughed again. "Ask Drake if you have any questions."

Rhett came out from the kitchen then, a plate of pancakes in each hand. "I don't think this is a good idea, Bella," he said, putting the plates down on the other side of the bar and sitting on one of the tall chairs in front of it. His feet dangled slightly off the floor. I was confused as to why people would make chairs like this. He patted the seat beside him. "Monroe won't like it."

Bella sneezed and went around the bar. "Yeah, well, Monroe doesn't have to know." She jutted her chin toward me. "Or should I be worried? Is she not a *friend* of yours who can help out?"

Rhett mumbled something.

"That's what I thought," said Bella, sniffling. "You'll do great, sugar," she said to me. "Now eat your breakfast before the lunch rush comes in. See you, Drake!"

Drake waved goodbye. "Rest up, honey. Regulars will miss you."

"And here I thought *you* would be the one who to miss me most." She blew him a kiss as she left out the front door, and he chuckled.

I wasn't sure what a "lunch rush" was, but I was certain to find out. Cutting into the pancakes, I shifted to stare at Rhett out of the corner of my eye. His profile was stern, but his features were so fragile and alluring, I ached to run my hand along that smooth cheek. We ate in silence a long time while Drake made clattering noises in the back.

"This was delicious," I said, downing my last bite. "Thank you."

Rhett grunted and nodded, then put his own fork down. "I made do with what we had," he said, shuddering. "Frankly, it could have been better." He jumped off his tall chair, grabbing his plate and mine. "Ah, let me get you that coffee."

I fidgeted in my seat as I waited. He returned not too long later with two of those glass cups that steamed. Our hot drinks were served in clay, which enriched the flavor of our teas. Coffee was so *strong*, though, I didn't know if clay would add any flavor.

"Cream or sugar?" He slid back beside me and sent the coffee my way.

"Cream," I said and he fumbled into his pants pocket, producing three of those little white cups I knew contained the creamy stuff.

I poured it into my drink with skill and know-how, if I did say so myself.

"So," Rhett said after a while, "I'm not sure if the others could tell, but did you and Caspian...?" He flourished his hand in the air.

"Did we what?" I asked, blowing on my coffee and taking a sip.

His chin dipped downward as he rubbed the handle on his cup. "Have sex?"

Oh. I nodded. "Is that okay?"

A faltering smile pasted on Rhett's lips as he looked at me. "I should be asking *you* that. I know Caspian wouldn't force anything on a lady she didn't want, but..." He took a long sip of his drink. "He shouldn't have done that."

"Why not?"

"Because you're with our enemies, for starters. And we dragged you here." He seemed to be trying to avoid saying anything explicit, as if labeling me a *hostage*, as they'd called it, would make his guilt more palpable.

"I came willingly," I said.

"Hmm," said Rhett. "That strikes me as strange." He stared hard at the steaming cup. "You know, I'm supposed to be able to lift this." He lifted the cup in the air. "With my mind, I mean. I'm telekinetic."

Telekinetic? That was a new word for me. But that was fascinating. Moving cups with your mind. We didn't have Nelians with that power—most could summon the vines, the twisting plant life that wormed its way into its surroundings. My brother had that power. A small number could summon portals that led to this other world, to Earth. A rare few had different powers entirely—like Xerxes. Like me.

I'd taken powers from the moment I'd been born, confusing my entire family—my entire people, until they'd figured out what it was I did. I didn't even consciously do it.

"Do you carry glass cups with you then?" I asked, taking a large gulp of my coffee.

"What?" he asked, his breath hitching as he chuckled.

"So you can lift them. With your mind. And throw them at people?"

He clutched the edge of the bar as his stomach shook uncontrollably, his laughter growing louder and louder, causing me to flinch back. I'd never seen such a wide smile on his face.

It made him even more breathtaking.

"Sorry," he said at last, exhaling a loud sigh. He wiped a tear from his eye. "I was just picturing me with a case of mugs, chucking them at people with my mind."

Mugs. I kept forgetting that word.

"No, Lana," he said, using the name Bella had given me. "I mean, I can lift *anything*." He pointed around him. "It's easier to lift small things, that's true, but I can lift anything that's not tied down." He bit his lip. "Actually, maybe if I tried hard enough—if I just had some kind of power boost, I could lift even that."

I finished my coffee quickly. I was *not* telling him about Aurora's ability to boost powers. Besides, her succubus lips were promised to her four special men.

He scratched the back of his neck. "So I can use whatever's around me. No need for carrying anything. It's not often there's nothing around I can launch at an enemy. Not that I've had a *ton* of experience with that yet." He flexed his fingers and stared at them. "At this rate, I don't know if I'll ever get my powers back again." He looked askance at me, as if waiting for me to say something, leaning back slightly as if he unconsciously knew to put space between us. But this wasn't enough space. This whole building wasn't enough space.

My breaths went shallow as I cradled my *mug* and tried hard not to stare at Rhett, tried to calm the rapid beat of my heart. Some part of me knew he was figuring out the truth.

The front door opened, a peal of laughter filling the room. Drake darted out from the kitchen, wiping his hands on a cloth and grinning widely. "Welcome, gents. The usual?"

"I better go," I said, shifting my dangling feet so I could stand up from the too-high chair. "Bella told me what to do when people came in."

Rhett's hand gripped my wrist. "I don't like this." His voice seemed tense.

Some of that loud, echoing music rung out throughout the room as Drake stepped away from a big lit-up box that rested near the front door, the men who'd walked in seating themselves in a corner. "Rhett, I need you back in the kitchen," said Drake as he passed us by.

I let a small smile flutter across my lips. "I'll be fine."

Sighing, Rhett let me go and headed toward the back. "I'm just a room away," he added before he disappeared.

Tugging on my tiny shirt, I made sure my outfit was just right—"*Always look tidy, sugar*," Bella had said—and I straightened my hat before I approached the three men at the round table with a cushioned seat wrapped around all but a small portion of it.

"Welcome to Drake's," I said. "Can I take your order?"

The men stopped speaking all at once as their heads turned. One, a wide-set man with a checkered shirt and a *baseball cap*, let his jaw drop.

"Hello there, little fine thing," said the man seated closest to me. He was far too skinny and his orangish skin was marred with deep wrinkles, though I wouldn't have guessed he was *that* old. "You're new?"

I nodded and threaded my fingers together in front of my bellybutton. "They call me 'Lana' here."

The third man—neither as thin nor as fat as his companions, his long hair entirely missing on top and greasy besides—guffawed. "What do they call you other places, hmm? Sexpot?" The other men snickered along with him.

I didn't know what a pot had to do with sex.

"Well, Drake already knows what we want, Little Miss Fine Thing," said the wrinkled man, stretching his arms high above his head, "but we didn't know you were on the menu."

His arm came back down and his fingers slipped behind me, pinching my butt cheeks hard enough that I could feel it through the thick, short jeans pants.

I let out a yelp just as the door swung open—slamming so hard against the music-making box, the melody skipped a beat.

CHAPTER SEVEN

YANKING THE WRINKLED CUSTOMER BY THAT SAME ARM THAT HAD pinched me, I rolled quickly, stretching his limb so much, he rolled out of his seat, cursing and screaming the whole time.

The man in the doorway was Monroe, and he flexed his fingers as he stomped over, Caspian and Bo both with arms full of sacks a few steps behind him. "Why did we come in the front—?" started Bo, but Monroe would not be deterred as he made his way straight for me.

"Goddammit, girlie, what the hell is wrong with you?" asked the wrinkled man I'd removed from his seat. His face was red and there were tears in his eyes as he massaged his arm with his other hand. "I was just being friendly, bitch!"

I did not like the sound of this word—*bitch*. I glared at him.

"We need to talk," barked Monroe. The man with the bald top scrambled to help his friend out of the way without a word. Monroe meant business. "What are you even doing out here?" His voice grew louder with each word.

"Helping," I said.

The wrinkled man snorted. "Losing Drake some regular customers is more like it. Where's that sweetheart Bella? Send her out here." He made a motion at me in the air like a feline. "Less bite to that pussy."

I flipped around, ready to kick him in the groin, but Monroe caught me mid-spin, flattening me against his chest.

His breath was warm against my forehead, his scent exhilarating. My muscles relaxed as I let myself melt against his sturdy chest, my heart dancing out of my throat.

"Come with me," he snapped. "*Now.*"

"Monroe," Caspian said, "take it easy now—"

But Monroe had grabbed me by the wrist, dragging me back through the kitchen past Rhett and Drake in front of the *stoven.*

"I'll chat with *you* later," spat Monroe. I was practically skipping now, the way he dragged me. "Drake, you might want to go out there and smooth things over with the regulars."

Drake raised an eyebrow at me, but I was distracted as Monroe spun around, still clutching my wrist, twirling me behind him. "And you two, stay out of this," he said to Caspian and Bo.

Bo's nostrils flared. "We're a team, Monroe, even if you call the shots. We—" But Monroe had already dragged me through the box room and then up the stairs. I let him take me. There was a thrill to being able to submit—to him at least.

But Monroe was clearly in no mood for love right now.

He flicked his hand up in a strange way, the muscles in his face going tense. Then he laughed, but there was no joy in that sound. He kept laughing and his muscles loosened. He rubbed his hands over his face and took a deep breath. "I just almost shot lightning out of the roof. Goddammit, woman— elf, *whatever you are.*" He stared pointedly at me and flung his hands out to either side. "You did this to me."

I clutched my hands behind my back and shuffled a toe along the floor. There was no denying I felt a raging, lusty *need* to be with him, just as I did with the others. But I was afraid if I voiced that now, I'd ruin my chances of ever being with him.

"But I *knew*, I knew as soon as I got near you again, I'd lose my powers." Closing the distance between us, he snatched my elbow. "Tell me that's why. Caspian, Bo, and I all got our powers back in town—a little over an hour after we left."

I bit down on my lower lip. They knew. I was foolish to ever think they wouldn't find out.

He let me go, stepping back slowly. "That's why you agreed to go with us—to take our powers away."

"Yes," I said. "I nullify the powers of everyone who has them—Nelians and Natches alike." My breath caught in my throat. Maybe I shouldn't have told him that much. "But that's not the only reason why I stayed."

He let out a growl. "Really? You decided to make the whole of R.I.A. powerless after we attacked your friends just for the fun of it?"

I stepped closer to him and put a hand on his shoulder, but he flinched and moved away. The rejection stung. "You're right. That was part of it. I know from experience that violence isn't the answer."

"Alanna, you have no right to tell me that!" It was the first time he'd used my name. The sound of it on his tongue sent a thrill down my spine. "After all the Nelians have done—"

"I'm sorry," I said. "We wanted to save your planet. Your people. But I'm not a part of that now."

"Why are you here?" he asked, pacing the room. "Not here"—his hands flailed around him—"but on Earth? If not to help your king rule over us?"

"I'm exiled," I said. "I banished myself."

"Why?" he asked, coming to a stop. "What did you do?"

I shrugged, biting down on my lip to stop the tears from falling. "I was tired of... this." I gestured around me. "Making those around me feel powerless. Being useless."

He sneered. "Seems like it turned out to be a pretty damn

useful power to me." He stared at me. "Can you stop doing that?"

"Doing what?"

"Biting your lip. It's... *Fuck!*" He pounded the table with his fist. "I can't be distracted here."

"I'm not trying to distract you—"

"Sure. Only make me powerless. Helpless."

I swallowed. "That's why I made sure to leave those I loved behind."

"Caspian is acting weird," he said. "Did you fuck him? Downstairs this morning?"

My thoughts became fuzzy. "Why are you asking me that?"

He slammed his fist on the table again. "Did you or did you not have sex with Caspian?"

"I did." I jutted my chin, ignoring the way the cowgirl hat angled downward over my eyes as I did. "There's a bond between him and me—I'm not sure humans understand such a thing."

He let out a short, sharp laugh. "I'm sure Caspian fell for your nonsense hook, line, and sinker. But listen to me—you lay off my friends, okay? Whatever little machinations you have going on here, I'm not falling for it any longer." He cracked his knuckles. "You need to leave. I was an idiot for ever taking you to begin with."

I ground my shoe into the floor. "No."

His jaw dropped. "*Excuse me*? I'm setting you free."

"I could have walked away anytime I wanted," I said, crossing my arms over my chest. "I'm not leaving."

Monroe laughed again and walked by me, heading for the door. He swung it open so hard, it practically shook off its hinges. "Your clothes are cleaned. Change into them. Get in the truck with Rhett or Bo and get the hell out of here. But stay away from Caspian." He slammed the door, causing a small sprinkle of dust to fall down on the wide *visor* of my cowgirl hat.

RUNNING MY FINGERS OVER THE FABRIC OF THE BASEBALL CAP Kouta had given me, I thought about how I had to hide beneath it anywhere I went if I didn't want to attract attention. That was part of why I'd preferred living alone where no one else could find me.

If I didn't belong here, though, and I didn't belong in Nelia—where did I belong?

"You looked cute in the cowboy hat," said Bo. He cracked his neck this way and that as we drove down the nearly-empty road in the R.I.A.'s pickup.

My stomach went cold. *Cute* was a word we used for children and little animals on Nelia. But I couldn't be greedy. Just because I felt a demanding, incessant calling toward him didn't mean I had to act on it. Besides, I… I'd lost that chance. My great plan to keep the R.I.A. away from my brother had lasted all of one day.

"Cowgirl?" I asked.

"Cowgirl what?"

"Cowgirl hat? That's what Caspian called it." I pretended I had it on my head, grasping the air around my head. "The hat with the round-the-whole-way visor."

"Round-the-whole-way visor?" Bo looked away from the road long enough to stare at me. He laughed. "A brim. That's a visor." He pointed to the hat in my hand. "It's longer—only sticks out the front of it."

Chewing my lip, I nodded and stuck the cap atop my head. I would never grow accustomed to all these terms.

"It must be hard getting used to everything here," he said.

"Yes." I stared ahead, taking in the fields marred by poles and *power lines* and dwellings spaced so incredibly far from one another.

"So what's it like—Nelia?" he asked.

"You want to know?" My senses sharpened in that moment. If I could convince him of the beauty of Nelia, perhaps he'd understand that was all my people wanted for Earth.

"Yeah. Just because I don't want Nelians *interfering* here doesn't mean I think they shouldn't *live* here or anything." His gaze darted quickly in my direction. "And maybe humans could visit their home if things were better between us."

"I'd love for you to see it someday," I said quietly. "It's beautiful—lush trees, dense forest. The entire planet. And my people, we coexist with it, taking only what we need, tilling the soil and giving back where we can. We make our things from cloth and wood—only taking from the trees at the end of their lifetimes, to make room for the new."

"That's exactly what I pictured." His lips twitched up into a smile. "It sounds amazing."

Though my heart fluttered to hear his compliments, I gazed out at the world around us. Even without an abundance of metals and plastic, there was still the touch of humans everywhere, from this road to those wires overhead. "But you don't want this world to be that way?"

Bo barked. I hadn't heard the sound from him before. "No! For one thing"—he patted the wheel under his hands— "I'm a fan of quite a few human innovations."

"My br—that is, some of my people have grown to appreciate them, too." I cleared my throat. "That's why we're trying to *work with* what you have. To decrease the damage your technology does. Without eliminating it."

Bo made a *hmm* noise as he came to a stop at one of those red signs, though there was no one else around. "I could agree with that, but there has to be a better way than brute force—or the threat of it."

"It's better than forcing the plants to grow in the cities?"

"I suppose it's better than that. I can give you that much," he said, grinning. "So there are only trees there, huh?"

"Trees and small fields we've claimed to grow our food

and materials. They're not like the fields here. Not so vast and wide."

"Well, that's not all we have here—trees and fields. There are many different kinds of environments in this world naturally."

"That's true," I said. "I've seen images of many beautiful places on Earth."

"Which ones have you been to?"

The city was growing closer now, appearing on the horizon as more cars joined us on the road from roads that led off in different directions.

"Here," I said, nodding ahead. "And there," I added, looking over my shoulder and nodding behind me.

He practically choked on a chuckle. "You came to Earth and went right out to a field?" He nudged my shoulder. "There's so much you're missing out on, sweetheart."

Heat reached my cheeks. "I wanted—I *needed* to be alone."

He frowned. "That doesn't sound good. What happened?"

I shrugged and watched as the buildings grew larger, closer. The sight of so many metal and glass and plastic things… It made me want to jump out of this car before we got to the city.

"You okay?" His hand rested over mine.

I realized I was clutching the door handle. "I'm not," I admitted, pulling it back.

"Say," he said, his shoulders straightening as he gripped the wheel once more. "Where would you say you've had the most fun on Earth so far?"

"Drake's Bar," I said without even thinking about it.

"Surely not."

Tears threatened to spill from my eyes. "It is true." I sniffed, then I started shaking at the thought of putting it all behind me, of leaving these men I'd found, once and for all.

"Oh, sweetheart." He pulled the car off the road and onto one of those private spaces of pavements that surrounded a building. There was a line of people in front of the structure decorated with a giant, white, swirly, fluffy cloud-like thing with a triangular brown base. It was probably food. Humans certainly liked their food-making places.

Bo turned the truck off. I looked around. I'd thought he was going to take me farther into town, give me one of his burner-phones to call Aurora to pick me up. He laid a hesitant hand on my shoulder. "You were serious?"

I nodded.

He reached across the seat and embraced me. I settled my face against the soft material of his shirt, rubbing my cheek against him and feeling my muscles relax.

"Your happiest memories shouldn't be being with us," he whispered. "We're no good for you, sweetheart."

"You're wrong," I whispered back.

He pulled slowly back, though his grip lingered on my shoulder. "Or do you just mean because you weakened us?" He beamed. "I can't believe we didn't figure out it was *you*. A power to nullify powers? I'd never heard of one before."

"It's not a power. It's a poison. You'll be better off without me." It was the truth, no matter what my heart said.

Besides, we were still enemies.

"According to Monroe, maybe," he said. "But..." He leaned back and jutted his chin toward the line of people. "Tell you what. Before I drop you off downtown, how about we make sure you have some fun? Some *normal* human fun."

I wasn't about to contradict anything that might let me spend more time with one of my men.

My men. As if they ever could be.

But I would pretend they could a little while longer.

CHAPTER EIGHT

"VANILLA IS THE DULLEST OF FLAVORS," BO SAID, POINTING TO what he'd called an "ice cream cone" in my hand. "But *someone* insisted on trying the one that looked like that old, chipped, ice cream replica on the sign."

We were seated on what he'd called a "picnic" table, a wooden table and bench that reminded me of the furnishings back home. "Here. Try some of mine." He reached across the table to hold his green ice cream near my lips.

I shivered—and not from the coldness of the treat. With my tongue, I licked his ice cream slowly, locking eyes with him all the while. I wanted him to miss me as much as I would miss him.

The tips of his ears went red as he sat back down.

"It's delicious," I said, smacking my lips.

"Pistachio," he said. He cleared his throat and then stuck one end of the cone in his mouth, pulling it away with a crunch. "The flavor, I mean."

Staring at my own cone, I felt the delicious vanilla ice cream roll onto my fingers. I licked them off and then stuck as much of the cone as would fit in my mouth and crunched into it. It tasted cold. And weird.

"Whoa, whoa, sweetheart, you're eating the paper." Bo

quickly tossed the rest of his cone into his mouth and grabbed for my cone, his fingers brushing against mine. I let him pull it out and he peeled a thin layer of paper off the cone. "It's edible," he said, "but you're supposed to take it off." He offered me the cone again and I crunched it all down, delighting in the chill that ran down my spine. Then I took the paper from him and ate that, too.

"Whoa, whoa—" he started.

It didn't taste nearly as good as the ice cream cone, that was for sure. "If it's edible, you shouldn't waste it." I eyed the paper he'd taken off his own cone.

He chuckled and crumpled it up. "No way, sweetheart. Grass is edible—most of the time. But people don't eat it."

He had a point there. I stared out at the expanse of grass behind him. At the edge of the town, this ice cream place had one foot in the human world and one foot in nature, trying to wedge its *metal* and *plastics* and *bricks* into the expanse of field beyond.

But I liked it, this ice cream, this picnic table—being here with Bo—so I stuffed those feelings down.

This was a good place. I was happy here.

My fingers were sticky, but I still had the rest of my paper to chew.

"Here," said Bo, shaking his head with a twinkle in his eye. He joined me on my side of the picnic table, sliding in beside me. Our thighs bumped against each other and I swallowed the rest of the paper, gulping.

He took my sticky hand between both of his, directing the fingers up to his mouth. "Do you mind if I...?"

"If you...?"

He wrapped his mouth around my fingers, letting his tongue slide up and down.

Oh. "No, I don't mind at all."

His lips lingered a moment longer and then he let go. Even behind his facial hair, the flush of his skin was noticeable. "Alanna, I have no right to ask you, but do your powers affect every Natch around you?"

I opened my mouth, but before I could speak, a young woman in the line for ice cream let out a startled cry. "It's not working!" she shrieked. Her dark hair was woven beautifully in many small braids, which clacked against her face as she started jumping in place.

Everyone's heads turned her way.

She jumped up and down and spun around. "Dave, my powers aren't working!" Her face was drained of all color.

"Em, quiet," said the pale young man in dark clothes beside her. I couldn't hear everything else he said, but he moved to put hands on her shoulders.

"Powers?" muttered a man with two kids from two picnic tables over. "Damn fucking Natch freaks."

Clenching my fist, I stood.

"Hold on," Bo said quietly. "Where are you going?" He nodded toward the family. "Comments like that aren't too rare. Just let it go."

"I could take him," I said, digging my nails into my palm.

"I have no doubt about that, sweetheart." We both stared at the man and he stared back at us. He was big, his arms hairy, his facial hair all scraggly and unkempt.

"What are you looking at, freaks?" he said. *He* looked like the freak to me, the way he was causing his small, delicate children to slink down into their seats across from him.

A strand of my green hair fell out from under my hat.

The man's jaw dropped as his ice cream fell from his cone to the picnic table. "A Nelian? Here? Fuck!" He jumped up, tossing his cone to the grass and grabbing a child under each arm.

People turned their attention to me now, forgetting the panicked Natch in line, whispering amongst themselves. One pointed at me. "She has green hair!"

"What's her hat hiding?" said another. "Pointed ears?"

"Come on," said Bo, taking my hand in his. We scrambled to the truck and he got it started and moving, putting the ice cream place, where I'd been happy for a few minutes, behind us.

I stared at the crowd as we left them behind. Everyone was looking at us, except the few rushing to their cars in an attempt to escape me before they'd realized I'd left.

And then there was the young woman who had panicked, her lover wrapping her in an embrace, rocking her back and forth. The loss of whatever power she had had truly frightened her.

"Sorry about that," Bo said. "I tried to take you somewhere fun and it turned into… that."

"I had fun," I said. It was true. I laid a hand over his on the wheel and squeezed. "Thank you."

He flipped his hand to take hold of mine, then brought it up to his lips to kiss it. "I'll never get over the feel of your skin." His thumb ran in smooth circles between my thumb and pointer finger. "It's so beautiful."

I had to bite down on my tongue to stop myself from asking him to be my lover, if only for a day. We were about to part, and besides, I'd have to tell him about Caspian first. It wouldn't be right otherwise.

"I know everyone was terrified back there," he said, "but you've never used your vine powers around me—do you take your own powers away too?"

The corner of my lips twitched. "I don't have command over the vines," I said. "My powers *are* nullification. That's all I do." I didn't tell him that being unconscious—even in sleep —stopped my powers for a time. They'd slept beside me last night but hadn't discovered the truth, hadn't tested their powers after I'd been asleep and the lingering effects had worn off. Even though one had been awake "on watch" at all times. I hadn't realized how fortunate I'd been in that regard, that they hadn't discovered me sooner. But in any case, I wasn't a sound sleeper. My fellow Nelians would have to be *forceful* in their methods of making me achieve unconsciousness. My head hurt just thinking about it.

"Your nullification powers took that woman's power away. Back there."

"Yes," I said. "Anyone near me, and for a while after we've parted, so I've been told."

"About an hour—maybe a little more, based on our discovery earlier today." Bo rubbed his jaw and then the back of his neck. "I know Monroe wanted me to drop you off. Put what happened behind us."

"But?"

"But I have a favor to ask you."

Anything that meant spending even a minute more in his company. "You don't even have to ask."

"Please don't think I'm using you." Bo tucked his hands in his jeans pockets. "I guess I am. I'm sorry."

"I don't mind," I said. "I want to help you."

"Is that something someone usually says to their enemy?" he whispered, his grin so wide, he could no longer hide it.

"You're not my enemy," I whispered back.

His arms trembled slightly as his breath hitched. He looked away, pointing to the words above the door of the building we stood in front of. "So, there's someone I want you to meet. Then you're free to go."

I read the two words slowly, but though familiar, they didn't make sense to me together. The building was worn, decayed almost, like a tree rotting of disease, its bricks pale and crumbling. Strangely, though, some plant life had grown between the cracks, the beautiful, delicate vines twirling upward and latching between the stone. It was almost as if the bright green plant life were trying to breathe life into the decay, just as my brother and Xerxes both had always thought it could.

"This is where my sister is," said Bo.

My blood ran cold. "What is this place?"

"Second Hope. A kids' home for Natches. The ones without parents or guardians—and the ones whose parents can't handle their powers."

"Your sister…"

"Has parents who can't handle her powers. Assholes who gave up on her."

I laid a hand on his shoulder. "I'm sorry."

"I'm over it—they left, moved several states away. I stopped speaking to them the moment they decided to abandon their daughter. But I don't know if Lacey will ever get over it." He swallowed.

Lacey. So this was the name he'd mentioned. Not a lover. My mind filled with relief and self-loathing. I should have never been jealous—I'd had no right.

"I don't know what I'm doing here. With you," he said. He paced back and forth before the entrance. "I know I shouldn't have brought you—"

"I'm glad you did."

"But you don't understand." He was wringing his hands now. "I couldn't take Lacey, either. Not with the R.I.A.—but not before it, either. I've been a legal adult for seven years, but I needed money. A better-paying job. A place for the two of us. And then I threw all that effort I'd put into trying to adopt her away for Monroe's wild ideas."

I didn't know what made someone a "legal adult," but I understood the meaning. He could have been her guardian, but something had kept him from it.

"It seems that here, on this planet, there's much that goes into raising a child," I said. "You do not share resources freely. Some prosper while others suffer—and others just manage to get by." On Nelia, no one did without. It was something I didn't like here—though our focus was to heal the planet first. And these R.I.A. men didn't even like that much—what would they say if my brother instructed their governments to share resources with all their peoples? "I can see why a young man could not provide for a child."

A tear trickled from of the corner of Bo's eye. "I should have made it work—somehow. But her powers. They're *useless*. Her limbs can stretch, but she has to focus to keep them snapped back into a default shape. It even hurts when she lets go and lets them loosen. She's suffering, Alanna. Always in pain."

Useless powers. Like mine. Only hers caused her physical pain. I stepped up the crumbling staircase and grabbed the door.

"Alanna, wait—" Bo said, but I was already inside, looking for this sister for whom just having Natch powers was pain.

Bo shuffled up behind me as I approached a seated woman who was looking at one of those big screens that they had to type on oversized letter boards to search for the knowledge the *internets* provided.

"Can I help you?" she asked. She sounded very bored.

"We are here to see a sister," I said, but before I could say more, there was a jumble of voices down the hall.

Bo took my hand in his, his gaze locked in the direction of the commotion.

The woman who had greeted me stood up, her attention fixed in that direction as well. "Excuse me," she said, then rushed down the hall as other adults in plain, pale-blue clothes appeared out of doorways.

"What's going on?" asked one woman.

"Why are children out of their rooms?" snapped another. She had those *eyeglasses* hung on a chain around her neck. I didn't understand what good they would do there. Maybe I didn't understand their purpose.

Laughter and screams of joy—followed by a scream less joyous—rung out from the open doors around them.

"Come on," Bo said, tugging me down the hallway.

Every room we looked into had children jumping and

dancing, though some were crying. A few more adults rushed past us to check on the children.

"My powers are gone!" said one child.

"Look! I have a normal face!" said another.

What we were seeing were these children with powers they couldn't handle being stripped of those powers. Because of me.

I felt suddenly taller, stronger, my shoulders tossing back as this sense of *purpose* started dancing within me.

At the end of the hall, a little girl I could only guess to be about eight or nine of these Earth years shuffled slowly out of her room.

She had on a wrinkled, white dress with ruffles at the bottom and at the edge of her sleeves. Her yellow hair was precisely the same shade as Bo's, her skin just as rosy, but there were dark circles under her puffy eyes. She clutched her dress with both hands at her thighs.

"Bo...?" she said. "Bo, I... I don't hurt..." Her eyes rolled up and she collapsed.

CHAPTER NINE

"LACEY!" BO DASHED FORWARD AND CAUGHT THE LITTLE GIRL IN his arms before she crashed to the floor. I scrambled to see if she was okay.

Her eyes fluttered open and then she laughed, a happy sound marred by the echo of sadness and pain—a sound so much melancholier coming from a child. Her hand reached up to touch her brother's cheek. "Where have you been?" she asked.

"I know I missed my scheduled visit yesterday—"

"You didn't *call* me. I was scared you would never come back," she said.

"I know," he said, laying a kiss on top of her head. "I'm so sorry. I should have at least called. Something happened." I wondered how long they'd been tailing the Renegades and if that was what had kept him away before they'd attempted to take a hostage. "But it's okay," he added. "We're okay now."

She straightened in his arms. "What happened to me?"

"Are you in pain?" Bo asked.

"No." She laughed. "No, I'm not!" She sat up and she must have been dizzy because her head lolled slightly.

"Whoa, slow down," said Bo.

"But I'm not in pain anymore!"

My hand covered my mouth to suppress a gasp. Tears brimmed at the corners of my eyes. This would be the first time my own powers had done actual good. For these Natch children, their powers weren't an advantage—they were an illness. A poison. And I had the power to cure them with my mere presence.

Only I… I couldn't stay here forever, could I?

"Who's this?" Lacey asked, turning around. A small smile flit across her face. "Your girlfriend?"

Bo's eyes widened. "This is Alanna." I noticed he didn't say anything about me not being his "girlfriend." I'd picked up that this word meant something akin to *lover*.

Lacey gasped as I removed my hat and held it in front of me. "An… elf…" She broke away from her brother's grasp and tried to reach for my pointed ears.

"Excuse me. Who are you?" said a woman behind us. She was the one who wore her eyeglasses like a necklace.

Bo put himself between his sister and me and the woman. "I'm Bo James, Lacey's brother." He extended his hand.

Her lips pinched into a straight line as she ignored his proffered hand. "You look familiar…" She affixed those eyeglasses over her eyes and then gazed over a board with a clip that she cradled in one arm, flipping the papers attached to it. "Your scheduled visit was yesterday."

Bo licked his lips as Lacey slipped in to embrace me. I patted her back.

"I know," he said. "I had an emergency. I couldn't call to arrange another visit."

"All visits must be *pre-approved*. If you have to cancel a visitation, you have to call to arrange another." She took off her glasses and let them fall. Children were shrieking in delight all around us. How could she be so stiff, so unmoved? All of the adults here were grim as they scrambled after their charges.

"I know." Bo licked his lips again. "But—"

The woman gasped and dropped the board to the floor.

"A Nelian!" she shrieked, and the orphanage fell silent in shock. She looked over her shoulder. "Call the police!"

"Wait!" said Bo. "You don't understand. She's different. She's the one making it so the kids can't use their powers." He turned to look over at Lacey. "I'm sorry, baby, but it's only temporary. It'll last about an hour after Alanna leaves and then the powers will come back again."

Lacey looked up at me. "You…?"

But the woman and the other adults rushed children back into their rooms, *protecting* them from me.

"Wait," said one man. "I don't think the police can help us —what if it angers the Renegades and the Nelian king?"

"Asking an unauthorized visitor to leave our private property would anger them?" The woman with the eyeglasses necklace massaged her temples. "Did anyone check them in?"

The woman who'd been seated at the front of the building approached. "No. They said they were visitors and then I heard noises—"

"So they're not authorized to be here," the eyeglasses woman said. Her entire face seemed tight and sour, like someone was pinching her all over. "You'll have to leave. Now. I won't have these children in danger."

"They're not in danger," I said.

Lacey tugged at my sleeve. "Please don't go. Don't let her make you go!"

Bo bent down to her level, his knees on the shiny, white floor. "I'm sorry, Lacey, but we have to leave for now."

"*No!*" she screamed, wrapping her arms around him.

"I'll come back," he said, stroking her hair. "I promise. I'll always come back."

"Liar!" she said. "You didn't come yesterday—"

"That was a mistake," he said. "Lacey, please—"

"Out!" shouted the pinched-faced woman. "Out right now before I call the authorities!"

Lacey latched on to my leg. "Don't make her go! She's doing this!"

"Doing *what*?" demanded the woman.

"It's not *hurting* anymore!" Lacey shrieked. "Don't kick out the pretty elf princess! Please!"

A lump caught in my throat. I didn't know how she knew I was a princess—I wasn't sure even the R.I.A. knew that about me.

"Chuck, escort them out," said the woman with the eyeglasses necklace, her eyes lifeless and cold.

"Ma'am, I don't have my powers, either," said a tall man with no hair at all on the top of his head. He was staring at his arms.

"You have hands, don't you? Just *grab* them and escort them out."

The bald Chuck went to do just that.

"We'll go." Bo dodged Chuck's grasp and wove his arm through mine. "But you don't understand what you're doing here." He whipped me past the crowd, the curious children peeking out open rooms. Some of their jaws dropped while others just stared without blinking until we were out the building.

"I have to go back!" I said once we got outside. "I have to stay. They'll get their powers back all too soon once I leave."

Bo ran both hands through his hair, clutching it so tightly, it looked like he was about to rip it out by its roots. "You can't —they'll call the cops."

"I don't care, whoever these *cops* are!" I gestured behind me. "Didn't you see what I did in there? The children—"

"Of course I saw!" Bo rounded on me, but the vein pulsing at his temple relaxed, his features softening. "I'm sorry. I shouldn't have yelled at *you*. But I never should have brought you here. Now Lacey has hope, and you... You won't be coming back." He stared up at the sign above the doorway behind us. *Second Hope*. Only there seemed to be no hope at all in there.

"Bo, you don't understand." I clutched his bicep. "This is

the only place where I… Where people have been *happy* to be around me."

"You can't come back."

"I can. I *will*."

"How?" he asked. "You can't *make* them let you in—"

"I *can*."

His mouth suddenly seemed to grow dry. "You're going to rely on your dictator to force your way in here. I shouldn't have shown you this place."

"Of *course* you should have! Bo, why can't you understand that we aren't your enemies!"

Bo's jaw was agape, but he closed it as the door opened behind us. The eyeglasses woman and Chuck stepped outside.

"The police are on their way," said the woman in a clipped voice.

Bo grunted. "Let's go."

Bo and I drove in circles. In silence and in circles. There had been plenty of places where I could have made my way back to my brother and the Renegades, but I said nothing as he kept driving around.

I would go back to Second Hope. With or without Bo. But I wanted it to be with him.

I just needed to check in with my brother to get it all arranged.

There were still areas of the city blocked off from the aftermath of Nelian efforts, though it had been months since we'd done any of that. Men suspended by ropes on little cages worked to repair the damage of the building where Xerxes had almost died.

The memory didn't pinch quite so tightly in my chest anymore.

Bo's phone kept buzzing, but he didn't answer it. Finally,

he pulled over, deftly maneuvering the large *beeacal* between two other cars. It was a wonder he even managed to fit it without hitting either one.

Digging his phone out of his back pocket, he glanced at it, then tossed it onto the backseat. I jumped.

"Your phone was making noises," I said, looking over my shoulder.

Bo leaned an elbow on the wheel in front of him, his leg bouncing. "It's just the guys. Wondering why I'm not back yet."

Ah. It must have been those word messages, those *textings*. I preferred the speaking calls.

"They'll worry," I pointed out. I kept glancing at the phone, wondering if I should say something to it.

"Let them," he said. He'd parked us in front of what looked like another little *diner*, this one all brown and full of people holding paper cups. At least they were paper and not plastic—oh, there were some with those, too, sucking on green cylinders of plastic to down their drinks.

Bo tried to smile. "I have to let you off here," he said, reluctance clear in his expression. "You can call your friends to pick you up."

"I'll go," I said. "But only if you promise to meet me again. Lacey and Second Hope—"

"Are *my* problem." Reaching into his back pocket again, he pulled green paper rectangles out of a folded black pouch that looked to be made of leather. "Here's some cash if you want to buy some coffee while you wait for them." Ah, yes. I knew this *cash money*. I hadn't had to use it yet, though, as I'd never been into a place that required it alone.

"You need me." I snatched the cash money.

"Maybe." He leaned forward, sticking his hand behind my seat and fumbling in a pouch there. He was incredibly close, his shoulder nudging against mine, sending a jolt of electricity through me. He seemed to notice as well because he pulled back very slowly, the warmth of his breath lingering on my skin. "But I can't rely on you. Not after what we did to you."

"I *came* with you—"

He smirked. "Because you're clever, taking advantage of a bunch of fumbling dolts clunkily making their way through a felony. But there's no way Monroe will want any of us to see you again."

"Monroe doesn't get to decide what *I* do—"

"Here's the phone you can use," he said, handing me a giant plastic package with a small phone inside it. "I'm sorry again about everything."

I dropped the package almost as soon as my hands gripped it, my nose wrinkling. "I don't like this plastic," I said. "It's wasteful. It cuts."

He scrambled to take it back from me, as if I'd complained of it actually causing me pain. In some ways, it did. "Let me get that for you." He tried tearing it with his hands. He grunted. "Dammit. I wish you could see me with my super strength. This would be child's play. I guess I won't tease any of the other guys for ever having trouble opening jars again."

"I will never see," I said, biting my lip.

Letting out a grunt, he gave up on the package. "I'll record it and show you a video sometime."

"I'd like that," I said, but then both our smiles dropped. We weren't supposed to be friends after this. He'd made that clear.

"Alanna…" he said. "You're right. I don't want to let you go."

I understood. "You've seen what I can do for your sister. I was happy to do it. I would do it again gladly."

"With you around, I could take Lacey back home with me. She could *function*. Maybe get some homeschooling, so you wouldn't have to go to school with her, and we'd work on her handling the pain when you weren't there because I wouldn't ask you to be joined at the hip—"

"I would hope not," I said. "That sounds very painful."

He held his stomach as he shook, then he stared at me, the light dancing in his eyes.

"But I have no home now. No place to bring Lacey." He had a blank look on his face. "All because I've been drafted into this… this…" He didn't explain more.

"I would do it," I said, clutching the cash money tightly in my hands. "Stay with you—with her, to make her feel better. I've never felt so *needed* before."

"Impossible," he said quietly. "Alanna, you're the most beautiful, kindest woman I've ever met. I already need you—and it's not just because of the hope you offer my sister." He reached over and caressed my cheek. I leaned into it, feeling the roughness of his palm massage against my flesh. "By taking my powers away, you make me empathize more with a Typical, make me think harder about what I'm doing—and why. For whom."

We stared at each other silently for a moment longer.

"I'm sorry we had to meet this way," he added quietly.

"I'm not," I said. "Because I don't know any other way we could have met."

That made him laugh, but he sighed and pulled away. "There," he said, nodding toward a nearby building. "That's a hotel. Ask to use their phone. Then you won't have to deal with this monstrosity." He picked up the package and tossed it behind him. He adjusted my hat, tucking a loose strand of green hair beneath it as I gazed at this *hotel*.

It was a nice, extravagant building. I liked the hanging plants every few feet. I wondered if I could be comfortable in such a place, full of metal and plastics and shaped stone. "Come with me," I said, my voice cracking.

He frowned, but then nodded. "Okay." Once we were both out of the pickup, he took my hand in his and we crossed the street together.

CHAPTER TEN

"What does a *hotel* sell?" I asked as we entered. Bo held the door for me.

"They don't really *sell* so much as *rent*," he said. "They let people use their rooms for rest"—he scratched his cheek—"and *relaxation*, I guess? It makes more sense to stay in one in other towns when you're too far to rest at home."

I went up to the man behind a tall table—humans really liked their people greeting you behind tall tables—and slapped my cash money on the hard surface between us. "One room for rest and *relaxation* please."

The man adjusted the eyeglasses on his face and raised an eyebrow. "That's not enough cash," he said. "Do you have a credit card or—?"

Bo took out more cash money from his leather pouch and placed it on top of mine. "Is one night okay?" he asked me.

I nodded. Just one more night of pretend, of delaying me having to go back… Go back to what? What would I do? I still didn't want to go back to Nelia—my people were much happier without me there. But I didn't want to join the Renegades or Veras, either. I'd just be a hindrance to them.

Bo and the man spoke as the man typed at one of those

letter boards. I walked around the room. There was a tiny waterfall in the middle. I crouched and stuck my fingers in the pool beneath it. My nose wrinkled as the scent of tangy metal assaulted my nostrils. I thought they were called *coins*. Another kind of money.

"What are you doing?" Bo asked. "That's dirty. Here's the key." He held out a plastic rectangle, and I felt the saliva build in my mouth as I fought the urge to spit. I did not like plastic most of all.

He seemed to understand and tucked the rectangle into his pocket. Arm in arm, we walked toward the back of the big room and he pushed a button beside a set of sleek metal doors. I tried to pry the doors open with my fingers, but I couldn't find the handle—there was only one big crack.

"Wait, wait!" he said, pulling my hand away gently. Right after, the doors slid open and he led me inside, but it was only a small box.

"This room is not very relaxing," I said as he pushed a button on the wall. "The room out there was much bigger." I let out a small cry as the earth shook beneath us, my heart practically jumping out of my skin. My fingers dug into Bo's arm.

His face was reddening, his lips clamped tightly together as his head shook slightly. "Never been on an elevator?"

The door slid open again, and the room outside had changed.

"What powers are these?" I asked, before thinking better of it. If someone's powers were responsible, I'd have stolen them. Words failed me as I stepped out to find the room had changed into a long hallway with countless doors on either side.

Bo took my arm again and explained about *elevators* and how they were like quick staircases that didn't require effort, and how this was the third floor of the hotel. Gripping the visor on my hat, I pulled it down low over my eyes, embarrassed at my naïve behavior, but he didn't seem to think poorly of me for it at all.

"So this is it," he said, stopping in front of a door. He took that rectangle out of his pocket and slid it into a slot above the door handle. With a click, a light went green and Bo opened the door, gesturing for me to go in.

He flicked on one light and then another, though I'd have been fine with pushing those curtains aside and just letting the sunlight in. At the center of the room, one large bed was decorated with a strange, folded towel and a plastic-wrapped hard circle. I lifted it to my mouth, inhaling the strong scent of mint even through the crinkly plastic. Perhaps this flexible kind of the stuff was edible. That would be a better use of the material than just tossing it away, since it'd take lifetimes to disintegrate.

"There's a phone you can use here." He pointed to a table beside the bed.

I put the mint circle in my mouth and then spit it out. "Not good."

He laughed and picked it up. "It's a peppermint." He peeled away the plastic and popped it in his mouth. Oh, of course. They wasted that stuff everywhere.

I gazed at the thing he'd called a phone. "That's not a phone," I said. I pretended I had a phone in my hand and lifted it to my ear, then pushed its imaginary screen. "A phone is small. It does not have these… ropes."

"Cords and wires?" he asked. He picked up part of the contraption. "This is an old-fashioned phone. Not that long ago—like twenty or so years, even less—this is how you had to call someone." He put it in my hand and gestured for me to hold it up to my ear.

There was a ringing in my ear and I yelped, pushing it away. "It rings!"

He nodded. "That's normal. It's called a dial tone." He pointed to the keys on the other part of the old phone. "Just dial your friend's number and she'll probably pick up. Tell her you're at the downtown Griffin Inn, Room 309. She'll come get you."

My chest hitched. "No." I handed the old phone to him.

He raised an eyebrow and put it back. "They must be worried—"

"*No,*" I said again. "I don't want you to leave. I don't want to go back."

Bo cupped one hand around my cheek, the other around my waist. "Are they unkind to you?"

I shook my head, leaning into his palm. I felt so at home here. "They are kind. But I don't belong with them. I belong with you—with the R.I.A."

"Monroe would beg to differ. Alanna, Caspian was acting a bit *weird* this morning. Usually he shoots the shit, but he seemed almost lost in a dream." He visibly swallowed. "Are you and he…?"

"I took him as my lover this morning." I slid a hand through his beard.

"Oh," he said. He took a step back, breaking the contact between us. "So that's why you don't want to leave us. I'll talk to him without Monroe around. We'll work something out. Maybe. And then, if you still want to help my sister—"

"It's not just Caspian," I said, stepping closer to him. "Bo, do you…? Do you feel the love between us, too?"

"Between you and Caspian?"

"Between you and me." I took both his hands in mine. "In Nelia, people are not bonded to one consort or another. It is possible to feel attraction to one—or to a number."

His face twitched. "All at the same time?"

I nodded. "Though that is not the way for everyone." Lifting his hand to my breast, I placed it where my heart beat. "We can only rely on the *feeling,* then we know. We know who's just a fun sexual experience and who can truly bring us peace, bring us happiness down to our very core."

His face grew redder. "And you and Caspian…?"

"Me and Caspian. Me and Rhett. Me and Monroe," I admitted, voicing this for the first time aloud. "Me and you."

"Whoa." Bo shook his head and then his smile dropped. "You're serious. Sweetheart, if anyone deserves a whole bunch of lovers, it's you, but that's just not that common here—"

"Do you feel it?"

His lips went thin. His hand started moving and I let it, his palm cupping my breast through the thin fabric of my shirt, hardening my nipple against the gentle circular motion of his thumb. "I do," he said in practically a whisper, as if he were afraid of anyone hearing it.

"I am yours," I said. "I always will be." My thoughts flashed darkly to Xerxes, but I pushed it aside. "But you must know that you're not the only one who can claim me." I focused instead on Caspian, on the feel of him inside me. On Rhett and his gentle, quiet acts of kindness, the way his eyes tried to ravage me when he thought I wasn't looking. On Monroe, on the fragments of something more beneath his wild, driven purpose.

On the caring man who'd brought me for ice cream, who'd shown me a beloved sister in pain, who'd given me a purpose.

His lips smashed urgently against mine as he fumbled to take off my hat and toss it somewhere behind me. My hair fell over my shoulders and he pulled back, gently running his fingers through its strands and up to the tip of my pointed ear.

"You like that," I said, feeling the heat on my face. My ears hadn't been anything special on Nelia, but here, he made me feel like they were special.

"I like all of you," he said in a husky, throaty growl. He gripped the bottom of my shirt and lifted it up. I raised my arms to make it easier, then tossed my head, whipping my hair across one shoulder as he threw the shirt on the floor.

"Exquisite," he said, his breaths growing shallow. He

placed his lips on my bare shoulder, then worked his way up along the side of my neck, the feathery kisses sending a shiver down my spine even as they felt warm against my flesh. "You taste of sunshine," he said between kisses. "Of morning dew," he added. His lips met mine again. "Of paradise." He deliberately maneuvered me to the bed. I lay back, my head hitting the strange folded-up towel.

"*Ah,*" I groaned.

His kisses continued probing, moving to my temple. "Here, beneath me, you look almost fragile," he said. "Though I know better. I will be gentle with you." His mouth lowered to my ear. "But I will still ravish you."

My limbs trembled as he stood back and removed his shirt, revealing the thick, defined muscles that were so much bigger than those of the Nelian men back home. There was so much *hair* there, too—not too long, just perfectly shaping the top of his chest and then in a thin trail down to what led below. I reached up, desperate to run my fingers through it. Bo removed his pants first, though, and the *boxer pants* he had beneath them, revealing his generous phallus, thick and swollen, and my back arched as heat rushed between my legs, desperate for its entrance, demanding I get these jeans off me so I could feel flesh against flesh.

He leaned over, his hands on either side of me, and he breathed deeply as his eyes roved. He dove to take a nipple between his lips and he bit—enough to make me cry out, but it didn't hurt too much, just enough to make the blood flow. He feasted on my nipple with his tongue.

"Yes," I said between breaths. "Give me more."

He lifted his head from my chest. "I'll give you more," he said. My hands darted upward, grabbing for him, feeling the luxurious softness of his chest hair between my fingers. "I'll give you so much, you won't be able to keep up."

I smirked up at him. "I accept the challenge."

He leaned back, standing at the foot of the bed as he grabbed my ankles and yanked me toward him. "Off," he said, and his fingers fumbled to unlatch my jeans, my thighs squeezing together at the nearness of his hands there, and then he had them loose, pulling them down my legs. "I need those legs apart, sweetheart," he said, his voice gruff.

I grinned wickedly at him. "You'll have to spread them apart yourself."

"I accept that challenge," he said, and his hand went to work between my green curls, sliding between the lips of my vulva and moving up and down, causing me to cry out. My legs twitched, and he yanked the pants fully off, the loss of his finger at my apex too much for me to bear.

I reached out for him and he grinned at me, then he yanked my legs even farther so my rear rested right at the edge of the bed.

Guiding my legs over his shoulders, he got down on his knees. "My delicate lady," he said, shifting his face to kiss the inside of one of my thighs. "Of the lovely green hair." The corner of his mouth twitched and he moved his head down, the very top of his scalp the only thing visible to me.

My eyelids clenched closed as the blood from every-where in my body rushed down to my groin, Bo's tongue at work between my folds. I shuddered with each circular movement and slide of his tongue, his thumbs moving closer and closer to my canal. Slick wetness flowed from inside me as sweat coated my skin. He came up for a breath, and our eyes met once more, our heavy breaths in tune with one another's. His hands shifted upward, one finger entering inside me, stretching me. I had to lean back and close my eyes once more, trying to scream "yes!" but finding my breaths too heavy.

He went to work again, my shaking legs slipping from his shoulders as he penetrated inside me, tasting me as no one ever had before, sending me positively buzzing as his tongue made wild movements to and fro.

"Yes!" I finally squeaked out. "Yes! Please. More."

He pulled out his tongue, and a sound choked my throat at the loss of him.

"No! Please!" I whispered.

But he was already standing, one hand wrapped around his length as he stroked it up and down, staring down at me, his chest thrusting out as his eyes roved over me.

"*Bone* me," I said, twisting this way and that as the *need* overtook me at my core.

He chuckled. "With pleasure." He crawled onto the bed, his erect *boner* dancing in delicate circles around my belly and moving lower. He bit my other nipple and I let out a yelp, and then he let go, flicking it with his tongue as he guided his erection between my legs. It slid silkily between my folds, dancing around my apex.

"Inside," I breathed. "Come inside me."

He didn't have to be asked twice. Pulling back and repositioning himself, he thrust his hardness inward with such force, I shuddered, clutching the scratchy blanket beneath me in both hands. He pulled out a little more and then plunged in again, leaning forward so his chest, sleek with perspiration, hung over mine. I moaned. "Harder," I begged. "Faster."

He obliged, the rhythm of our bodies a dance on this prickly blanket in this beautiful, relaxing *hotel*. I didn't care that I wasn't out amidst the trees, the wood and the cotton of home. My hands grabbed hold of his arms. Here, I was home.

He let out a cry as he delved deeper once more, the hardest yet, and I cried out with him. The thumping of my heart crafted its own melody in my head, the beat rising to its climax, louder, harder until at last... Release. I felt him spill inside me, and I shuddered. A mewling sound escaped my lips.

"Dammit," he said through heavy breaths. "I forgot the condom."

Whatever that was, and he was the second man to mention it, it wasn't needed. "I'm fine," I said, taking his face in one hand to look at me once more. "I will not get pregnant."

He nuzzled against my cheek. "I hope you're right about that." He kissed me on the lips. "Because if you did, I might just up and marry you and take you far, far away."

I didn't know why he seemed to think that would be a bad thing.

CHAPTER ELEVEN

I woke to the scent of musk, to the warm and rising chest of the man beside me. We'd made love multiple times until we'd collapsed together on the bed, exhausted, only rousing so Bo could pick up that old phone and make someone appear at the door with food. Then we'd eaten and done it all over again. Now, a thin sunbeam was penetrating the room through the curtains.

I teased my lips against Bo's shoulder and then his cheek and carefully disentangled myself from his limbs and all the blankets; the scratchy top one had somehow made it to the floor. Padding across the plush carpet beneath my bare feet—even human floors were covered in fabric—I gripped the curtain and pulled back, watching the sun rise over the horizon for a while. The sun here was so like our sun on Nelia, even if the land it touched was so strange, so altered.

But, like Bo had said, not all of this planet had ever been covered in lush forest. I imagined this part had once been like the field in which I'd hid myself away: tall grasses, the occasional tree.

That, too, had a serene beauty, but if I were being honest with myself, I was much happier here, amidst all the metal and plastic... and Bo.

"If anyone's looking up right now, you're putting on quite a show for them," came his gruff voice from behind me.

"They would not look at me. Your planet puts on the better spectacle. Every morning—every evening."

"We'll have to disagree on that." He was leaning on one arm.

I climbed back on the bed, pressing my lips to his.

"See?" he said, pulling back. "Now time for an encore..." The mirth on his face vanished as he pulled back. "Oh, shit. It's tomorrow—I mean, today."

He jumped out of bed, found his pants, and dug through the pockets. "The guys are going to be livid—dammit! I left my phone in the truck."

Sighing, he crossed the room to the old-fashioned phone, bringing that one part to his ear and then pushing numbers. I lay on my stomach on the bed, leaning my chin on my palms and just admiring his body on full display.

"It's me—yeah, I know. Listen. *Just listen.* What?" Bo's face went pallid. He turned to me and looked about to say something, but then he spoke to the phone instead. "Okay, okay. Yeah, about that... She's still with me." He winced and held the phone away from his ear. I could hear the muffled sound of Monroe's voice. "I'll get her to talk to them. Okay. *Okay!*" He let out a heavy sigh. "I'll be in touch." Then he slammed the phone down.

What had happened?

He paced the room with wide, anxious strides. "They've been trying to reach me all night—their powers returned and they went back on the trail of the Renegades."

My heart went cold. My friends and these men whom nature called me to... I couldn't choose which ones I wanted to make sure were safe. It was like Alarik and Xerxes all over again.

He stopped pacing. "Are you a princess? The king's sister?"

I sat up, clenching the white sheet in my hands. "Yes."

"Jesus, Alanna, you could have told us that." He snatched his clothes off the ground and began dressing.

"Does it matter?"

"It explains why the king is extra pissed about us having you."

"My brother would care about any Nelian who went missing," I said, tossing my hair back.

"Yeah, but believe me, I know, if anything happened to Lacey, I'd be a *lot more* driven to make sure she was okay than I would be if anyone else I knew got captured." He let out a deep breath. "Sweetheart, they got Rhett."

"What? Who? How?"

"Your Renegade friends." He tossed his hands in the air. "Or Veras because they're traitors and allies of their supposed foes, I don't know. I can't keep up these days." He pulled his hair in two big clumps, one for each hand. "Caspian, Monroe, and Rhett followed a report of Renegades stepping in at some office, where a Natch was having a bad day yesterday and going a little haywire. They had to borrow Drake's car since I had the truck. Veras showed and they calmed the situation and the R.I.A. split up, each tailing someone else. Then they used Rhett's phone to send Monroe a video of Rhett strapped to a table unconscious."

I grabbed the old-fashioned phone, searching my brain for that number I'd used to reach Aurora.

"Wait." Bo pushed a number first. "You need to hit this to dial out."

I didn't bother asking what that meant, just pushed the numbers.

"Hello?" It was Aurora.

"It's Alanna," I said.

"Alanna? Thank god!"

"Aurora, I told you I had everything under control—"

"Apparently not if one of these M.I.A. dudes was tailing us!" Someone shouted something behind her. *"R.I.A.* Whatever."

"I was with another one of them," I said, swallowing. "Please tell me Rhett is okay."

"Oh, is that his name? Because he's not been very cooperative—all he's done is try to rip the furnishings out of the wall and chuck them at us." The anger was palpable in her voice. "We've had to sedate him, but yeah, he's *fine.*"

"Please let him go," I said.

"Not until you get your ass back here." She seemed to be talking to someone else, then back to me. "Your brother wants to talk to you."

She didn't let me answer before it was Alarik's voice on the line. "Alanna! Tell me you're all right."

"I'm *fine,*" I said. "I told Aurora this. Please, Alarik. Please understand that I'm fine."

"If this piece of sediment has harmed even one hair on your body—"

"He *hasn't*! Please, Alarik. You're not listening to me." I took a deep breath. "I feel the bond with him. With all of the R.I.A."

That made him go silent for a moment.

"Roots and sediment, Alanna, do you do this on *purpose*? Fall in love with the most inconvenient men possible, people who want to see me fail or even return to the soil?"

"It's not like that, and you know it. I don't have a choice. Did you with Aurora?"

Bo tapped a finger to his lips as he stared down at me.

"No, by mother, I didn't." Alarik sighed. "So what do you propose? We just let you all go on your merry way, just give you a friendly wave the next time one of your lovers tries to follow the mother of my children home to break into the place where she sleeps?"

"When they're with me, they don't have their powers." My voice cracked as I looked at Bo, his face a perpetual mask of worry as he chewed on the tip of his thumb.

"Then all they'll have to do is leave you at home—or

distract you with their lovemaking, like I assume is what happened last night."

"That's not *precisely* what happened—"

"No. No. I won't allow it."

"You won't *allow* it?"

"You've separated yourself from Xerxes. It can be done. You don't have to give in to the urges—"

"I'm not *asking* you for permission!"

Alarik ignored me as he murmured, speaking to someone nearby. "Aurora says her phone tells her you're at a Griffin Inn."

"I am," I said.

"We'll come get you and we can discuss this in person."

"Bo's with me," I told him.

"Who's *Bo*? If he's one of these men, he can't come."

"Well, he's going to," I said. "Or I'm not coming, either."

"Really? When one of your *lovers* is right here?"

I swallowed. "Don't threaten me, brother."

Alarik spoke in murmured tones again. "This isn't a threat, and it's not a negotiation. You come back, then perhaps we'll let this thorn in my side go."

"*Perhaps*?"

"Meet us in front of the building." There was a click and then that ringing in my ears again. I handed the old phone to Bo, relaying the message.

"Get dressed," he said, "and I'll update the other two, tell them where to come meet us."

Bo's palm was sweaty in mine, but I clutched it harder and kept looking for the Veras car—*van*, Aurora had called it—to appear. Bo had been even more nervous ever since he'd finished speaking to Monroe. He'd said there'd be no way Caspian and Monroe would appear before our ride pulled up, and he'd been right.

The van pulled up and stopped right in front of us, the side door sliding open and Alarik unabashedly strolling out, Aurora right behind him. His angular features were narrowed tightly in concern, his long, green hair flapping behind him as he rushed forward. He wore his standard Nelian clothes, all natural browns and greens, made from form-fitting leather hides. Aurora wasn't suited up in her skintight Veras battle outfit; instead, she wore a loose, dark jacket and pants of a matching crinkly material, her long, brown hair tied back behind her head.

"Holy shit," said Bo under his breath. "The king himself."

Alarik took me in his arms, yanking me away from Bo. I couldn't see my brother's face, but I could easily imagine the look he was giving Bo over the top of my head.

"Are you okay? Did those dirt-eaters hurt you? What do you have this on for?" Alarik yanked my hat off my head, letting my green hair tumble to my shoulders. "You need not cower among these people," he said louder, this time to the humans walking on the concrete path behind us. The humans picked up their feet, rushing farther away.

"Stop it," I said, pulling away and snatching the hat back. "I don't cower. Maybe I just don't want them to run in fear." I put the *baseball cap* back on, not bothering to tuck my hair back into it.

"There's no need for you to walk amongst these people." Alarik grabbed me by the wrist and tugged me after him.

I pulled back. "I'm not going without Bo!"

Alarik whirled on Bo, his grip on me still tight. "If he wants his friend alive, he'll stay put! And be thankful I don't strike him down where he stands."

"Hey," Bo said. "Stop manhandling her!" He stepped closer and Alarik reached for the dagger at his hips.

I didn't know what *manhandle* meant, but I spun around to free myself from my brother's grasp, standing between him and my human. "Don't you dare."

He let go of the dagger's hilt and snatched my arm again. "Then come."

"Alanna," said Bo, but Aurora moved toward him as my brother and I brushed past her toward the van.

"Change of plans. Hang back," she said to Bo. He did. She jogged to catch up to me. "Sorry. I tried to keep your brother calm—"

"I'm not arguing with you about this," said Alarik as he pushed me toward Flayme, who pulled me onto the seat beside him. He was wearing his deep blue Veras outfit, which fitted to his strapping form. "Let's go." My brother pounded on the wall of the van.

"Where's Rhett?" I asked.

"Not here," Alarik snapped.

"You *said* you'd let him go—"

"I said *perhaps*."

Alarik helped Aurora into the van.

"No!" I said, not ready to leave Bo behind.

"Easy, Your Highness," said Flayme beside me, grabbing my arm. I elbowed him in the abdomen and he let out a grunt.

Alarik and Aurora climbed back in. "Drive," said my brother, and the Veras member with the short, angled dark hair who sat before the wheel—Chastity, her name was—took off before Aurora even pulled the door closed.

I spun on Alarik, who sat behind me. "You lied to me! How could you even *think* of lying?"

Flayme was still grunting beside me and Aurora shifted uncomfortably across Alarik's lap to sit across from him. "You okay, hon?" she said, massaging his bicep.

"Never better," he said between clenched teeth.

I glared at Alarik. He held his hands up in surrender. "There was no way we'd let another of our enemies into our hideout."

"Alanna, I know you're upset," Aurora started.

"You don't understand at all!" I pounded the back of the

chair. "You lied to me. Like a human. You didn't trust me and you lied to me."

"We'll let you free your enemy lover—*this* time," spat Alarik. His nose went up in the air. "But it's only a matter of time before they do something like Xerxes, and then what are you going to do? If you keep loving the wrong men, your heart will always be broken."

I slapped him across the face. Tears threatened to fall and I had to bite down hard on my lip.

Aurora gasped. Alarik shook his head at her but kept his eyes pinned straight on me.

"You would strike your king?" His words were slow, cautious.

"I would strike my brother, who is cruel," I said. "You have a human lover. You share her with human men. That is a bond *you* have, but you would deride me for wanting to bond with humans."

"That's not the issue," he growled. "The issue is they *stand against us*." He fluffed a hand in the air. "Not that they pose a significant threat, mind you, but I certainly wouldn't want my own flesh and blood *consorting* with them."

"You don't understand!" I snapped. Chastity let out a quiet "yikes" from the front of the van. "They're scared—they don't like the idea of people being forced into things."

"If I don't force them, they'll kill their own planet!" said Alarik, his tone rising. "Which would kill them, too! They're such children!"

"Hey, speaking of," Flayme said quietly beside me. He ruffled his short, yellow hair. "Can we keep it down? Stress isn't good for babies in utero." He nodded toward Aurora.

Almost as if being reminded of something she'd forgotten, Aurora sat back in her seat and cradled her stomach, staring down at it.

Both my brother and I went quiet.

I spoke first. "I know this, brother. But I understand how

they feel. I was trying to change their minds, reach some sort of compromise—but they have to trust me first."

"How?" Alarik sneered. "By having sex with them one at a time?"

"Alarik, that's not fair," said Aurora, leaning her head on his shoulder. "You know I couldn't have fought what I felt for you, even though I wanted to—even though you were my enemy." She turned to me. "But, Alanna, you asked me to trust you could handle yourself, and I did—and it took a lot to keep your brother calm, I might add." Alarik moved to speak, but she shushed him. "What are these men after?"

"They…" My tongue felt dry. "They think you're a dictator."

Alarik snorted. He was more familiar with the word, apparently, than I had been. Were the R.I.A. not the first to call him such?

"They're not *entirely* wrong," Flayme said under his breath.

Alarik narrowed his eyes on him, but Aurora silenced him with a look. "That aside, then. Do they want to kill him? Your own brother?"

"No!" At least, I'd never even considered it. Why hadn't I? Because I'd believed in them? Because I'd believed my own nature wouldn't lead me astray? They'd never *discussed* killing him in front of me. "They wanted to make him leave the governments alone."

"How?" snapped Alarik. "With what army?"

"They thought *we* had an army, waiting in Nelia to attack if the *corpornations* didn't comply with your plan."

"We do." Alarik's face softened as he took in Aurora's and Flayme's anxious expressions. "But I have no intentions of using it. The *implication* should be enough—"

"They thought that with a *hostage*, you would back off. But they… They thought I was useless once they discovered that I was the reason they'd lost their powers." Useless. To my enemies. To my lovers.

Alarik sniveled. "Amateurs."

"Sure. But you and Zander never gave them the time of day until they took your sister," Flayme pointed out. "*That* got your attention. Guess even amateurs get things done right once in a while."

Alarik didn't need to say anything. His look alone sent Flayme cowering backward.

"If I paid attention to *everyone* who disagreed with my vision for this planet's survival, I'd never have a free moment to do anything else."

"All right, all right." Aurora patted his knee. "Well, it's over now. *We* have one of *theirs* if they try anything else."

"You can't *keep* Rhett!" I said, aghast.

"Will *nothing* satisfy you?" said Alarik, his voice rising. "Need I remind you they intended to keep *you* until they got what they wanted?"

"I could have left at any time," I said, straightening. "I'm used to fighting without powers. They aren't."

Aurora began rubbing her temples. "Can we discuss this later?"

"Starlight, are you feeling unwell?" Alarik asked. "I told you to stay behind—"

"And I told *you*, you don't get to tell me to stay or go anywhere. I'm pregnant, not an invalid."

Alarik growled, but he crossed his arms and said no more.

"If you're all done squabbling," Chastity said from the front, "I thought you should know we're here."

"Here" was the place where Veras was headquartered. The Renegades had called it the "old community center," but I'd never asked what that meant. We came to a stop and I tried to open the door.

"You have to unlock it first," said Chastity. Flayme slid past me, all bent over and awkward, in order to get it open, and I jumped out, rushing past him.

Running into the building, I looked this way and that—I'd never been here before. Two other members of Veras were seated on a couch. Aurora's best friend, Roulette, and the woman's lover, Ice-Blast. I forgot their other names. "Where is he? Where is Rhett?"

"The prodigal princess has returned," Roulette said. She unwound her arm from behind her lover's back, running a dark hand through her bright red curls. "Should have known." She flexed her hand and stared at it. "It's like my power battery ran out."

Ice-Blast flung his arm out, too, but nothing happened.

Roulette giggled, tickling the dark stubble on his tanned cheek. "You could have blasted the TV into ice cubes if that had worked."

He ran his face up the side of hers, almost as if inhaling her. "I could think of something else we could be doing besides watching TV."

"Where is he?" is all I asked.

She cocked an eyebrow. "With Wade and Jayden in Wade's lab." Her head jutted slightly down a hallway, so that was where I went just as the others entered behind me.

I heard voices down the hall and saw a light through an open doorway. I ran through it, clutching to the side of the door as my feet almost kept sliding down the too-sleek flooring.

"Rhett!" I cried, rushing to his side. I grabbed his restraints, trying to tear them off. They wouldn't budge, so I started ripping at the thin cords with round white circles at the tips that they'd stuck all over his flesh.

"Whoa, whoa, princess, that's some delicate equipment." Veras' resident genius, Wade, stood and tried to push me back, but I kneed him in the groin.

He let out an *oof*. "That's some delicate equipment, too," he said between seething breaths. He clutched a nearby table.

"Is that a junk joke?" asked the tall man with fair hair and eyeglasses from behind me. That was Jayden, leader of Veras and another of Aurora's lovers. "She must have totally sapped your intelligence, Wade."

"Funny," said Wade, ruffling his shorn black hair. He was not laughing.

Jayden put a hand on my shoulder and I whirled around to smack him across the face, but he caught my arm before it made contact. "We're not your enemies," he said quietly.

He was right. Breathing hard, I let go. The doorway filled with familiar faces.

"Well," said Wade, straightening up and clearly trying to make his voice even, "with Her Highness around, we can rest easy about him telekinetically rearranging my lab." He waved a hand at Rhett on his table. "He should be waking soon. Get the restraints off him. I've got enough data."

Aurora slid into the room and asked me to stand aside as Jayden and Chastity freed Rhett. I had time to study him and noticed the bandaged cut at his temple, the bruise on his knuckles.

"We had to subdue him," Aurora said softly, as if recognizing what was on my mind. "We were gentle, Alanna. We've never wanted bloodshed—you know that. Veras never attacks first."

There were things slightly askew around the room—like Rhett had been trying to rip the place apart and someone had hastily tried to put it back together.

Aurora went strangely quiet, her face blank. "I almost forgot you made it so Zander can't reach me." She let go of me and tapped her temple. Her other lover was a *telepath* who could speak to those he loved through his mind—he could speak to everyone on Earth and even in Nelia, apparently, when Aurora boosted his powers. But not to me—and not to anyone recently in my presence. "Let me go call him and update him." She glanced at me as she dug her phone out of her pocket. "You okay?"

Chewing my lip, I nodded, unable to look away from Rhett, even as he slept peacefully on the table, free from all restraints. "Please let me be alone with him."

Alarik's eyes narrowed, but Jayden nodded. "Come on,"

Jayden said, gesturing for everyone to follow him. "Let's give them some space."

Everyone filed out, Wade limping slightly. I supposed I needed to apologize to him. My mind was foggy, my instincts too protective of these men with whom I'd bonded. I glared at my brother, the last to leave the room, as I slid a chair beside Rhett and grasped his hand.

Alarik gripped the handle on the door. "This bonding portends disaster," he said. "Because if you choose any of them, you'll be choosing to walk away from me. From your kind. From your family."

Then he shut the door behind him, sending a piercing pain to my heart.

CHAPTER TWELVE

At last, what felt like an eternity later, Rhett's eyes fluttered open and he jumped up with a shout.

"It's all well," I said. "I'm here. You're safe now."

Rhett stared at his hands, then at me, then looked around the room. "What happened?" His voice was rough. "I was caught trailing them on forty-sixth, and then I went down, and the next thing I knew, I was strapped to a table. I used my powers to try to get free, and then everything went dark again." He looked around the room, seeming to take in evidence of his earlier skirmish with *telekinesis*—with throwing everything around with his mind. Someone had tried to set things right again, but there were still the shards of glass, the plant tumbling out of its vase. "And now you're here—which explains why my powers don't work again." He flexed his fingers. "What happened to Bo? What about Caspian and Monroe? Are your friends holding them captive too?"

"They're fine," I said. The sight of his heaving chest just then left me short of breath. "Bo and I lost track of time—"

"You were *together*? What happened to him dropping you off?"

I gestured around me. "So you could just turn around and

attack my friends? You're fortunate I wasn't there. I would have negated your powers."

"Theirs and ours." He grunted and rubbed a hand over a red patch on his arm where some of Wade's "delicate equipment" had been affixed to his skin. "Maybe it'd be an even match."

I tossed my hair back over my shoulders. "I could have taken the four of you without powers myself." It was simply fact.

He chuckled. It was rare to see a smile on his face, and it melted my resolve. "I have no doubt about that."

His shaking fingers moved to grab my hand, which rested on the table beside him, but he hesitated. "Caspian has fallen for you—hard."

My core warmed at the thought, though I knew I needed to talk to him—if I ever saw him again. Our lovemaking seemed so long ago now.

"I am drawn to him, too," I said quietly. "But not just him."

The corner of Rhett's lips twitched. "Oh, yeah? Is that what you and Bo were up to yesterday?"

I opened my mouth, about to tell him the same things I'd told Bo just last night: that the five of us belonged together.

Rhett just shook his head and chuckled some more, swinging his legs off the side of the table. He patted his pockets. "Where is it…?" He spotted his coat on a chair in the corner. Beside it was a book. He grabbed it and handed it to me. "You forgot to take this with you."

I recognized the cover immediately. "*Pride and Prejudice*. You mean I can keep it?"

"I was carrying it around in case I ever ran into you again. Part of me didn't think I really would—was dismayed that I never would—but here we are." He smiled softly.

Cradling the book against my chest, I ran a hand through the tips of a lock of my hair, picturing it like Miss Elizabeth

Bennet's. "Thank you." I had an idea. "Will you join me for dinner?"

He arched an eyebrow. "Do you also wine and dine your prisoners?"

I shot to my feet. I didn't like the sound of this word *prisoner*. "You don't have to stay here. I'll *make* them let you go. But I would like to dine with you before then."

"So it's almost dinner already? How long have I been out?"

"It's been only one night since I saw you last," I said, my fingers nervously dancing over the book cover. "Please? Just wait and then you can go."

"I don't have a choice," he said. "But you don't have to ask. I'd always love dining with you."

My insides purred and I nodded, heading out the door.

"HOLD STILL," AURORA SAID, SPRAYING THAT WRETCHED, FOUL-smelling liquid again.

Clutching my hands into fists in my lap, I sputtered and shut my eyes.

Roulette chuckled from behind me on her bed. "I think you can lay off the spray, Rora. Any more and her hair might be stiff forever."

The horrid sound stopped and I coughed some more until that *hairspray* dissipated into a mildly foul lingering scent. Opening my eyes, I took in my reflection in the mirror. With countless metal *pins* and softer *hair ties* and too much foul spray, Aurora had arranged my hair in what she called an *updo*, something similar to Miss Elizabeth Bennet on the cover of the book in my lap.

"Given the soft, straight hair I'm working with, she needs a little stiffness to get it to stick." She nodded at me in the mirror.

"That can't be good for the babies, either," said Roulette,

getting off the bed to grab the can. She frowned as she stared at it. "Yeah, let's get rid of this."

I didn't want to ask. The smell of it made me feel like I was tearing a hole in the protective layer around the planet. All because I'd wanted to do something meaningful before I said farewell to Rhett.

I'd convinced Aurora and the rest of Veras at least to let him go—with a "warning," so to speak. But even if I *could* go with Rhett, even if he'd wanted me to, I wasn't sure if I should.

"Are you sure about this?" Aurora asked quietly. "You think you can really sleep with him and then just... say goodbye?"

"I don't know if we will sleep," I said.

"That's the idea, right?" Roulette tittered.

"I just want to spend some time with him," I said. "Before we part." I swallowed. I'd have to go to Second Hope on my own if I couldn't stay with the R.I.A.

My brother couldn't fault me for finding my purpose.

"Alanna, I know it's hard. But, bumbling as they may be, these guys just don't agree with us." Aurora tapped her abdomen. "If they try something like *kidnapping* again, if they try to hurt Alarik or Zander or any of us—"

"I know," I said. "You don't have to say anything more." Besides, the R.I.A. wouldn't want me near them regardless. They were *useless* around me. Well, I wasn't going to be useless. Not if I could help the children like Lacey.

Chastity appeared in the doorway, knocking on the open door. "So Wade let that R.I.A. guy talk to his friends—briefly —and he thinks they're satisfied he'll be on his way tomorrow morning." Her lips turned down as she stared at me. "You sure about this, princess?"

I nodded. I didn't know how much she knew, but she was observant, that one. "Then the Renegades will pick me up again and I'll no longer be a bother," I said. "You'll all have your powers back soon enough."

"You're never a bother, Alanna," Aurora said.

Chastity raised an eyebrow at that and turned on her heel. It was all right. I understood she must have felt vulnerable without her abilities. And I knew that in combat not too long ago, I'd been responsible for that being a genuine disadvantage.

"That's enough with the hair." Roulette tossed the can into a bin filled with crumpled *tissues* and little bits of junk. So much waste. I fought the urge to comment about the metal can and foul spray being headed to their giant piles of junks they kept all around the globe, like simply stuffing all the waste together was a method of dealing with it.

"Now for the real highlight of the night." Roulette opened a sliding door, then rummaged around through hanging clothes. There was so much in there. "You can probably fit… This!" She pulled out a bright red, silky smooth gown, holding it up in front of herself. "I know it's not Regency, but you'd have to go to a costume shop for that."

"Regency? Costume shop?" I posed.

"People don't dress like that anymore," Aurora explained. She helped me to my feet. "You need help with your shirt so you don't mess up the 'do?"

I cocked my head.

"I take that as a *yes*." Roulette tossed the red dress on one of the beds behind her and she and Aurora both took a side, rolling my shirt up as I raised my arms, being very careful not to disturb my *updo 'do*.

"You, um, want a bra, hon?" Aurora asked.

I shook my head. I had been offered this thing before—the *panties*, too, but I had no need for them.

She shrugged and asked me to step out of my pants.

"Someone likes going commando," said Roulette.

Going commando must have meant something about my naked form.

They both helped me slide into the dress and then Aurora fussed with the hair once more. They buzzed about, Aurora tapping my cheeks with some pink powder that made me sneeze, Roulette offering me a pair of smooth, shiny leather shoes—only they were wobbly and affixed atop a little platform at the heel. Ridiculous.

Still, I managed to balance in them and looked at myself in the mirror. It was not quite like Miss Elizabeth Bennet, but it was close enough.

Besides, I hadn't read the full book yet. Perhaps she put on these wobbly shoes later. All I knew was that the book was well-worn and that Rhett seemed to enjoy it.

I wanted him to enjoy me.

Flayme let out a whistle as we exited the room and headed down the hallway. Aurora slapped him gently across the chest.

"Sorry, angel," he said, wrapping his arms around her and nuzzling her cheek. "You know you're the only one for me. I was just admiring your… makeover skills."

"Yeah, yeah." She turned around and yanked him toward her, planting a kiss on his lips. "You can look, but don't touch, okay?"

"Look at what?" Flayme asked dreamily, his gaze boring into hers.

"Once they get started, you can sew a whole quilt before they stop." Roulette gestured for me to follow. "Let's get you to your dinner."

She led me to a quiet room, darkened, the soft bits of sunset streaming through the open window the main source of light, the candles burning from the middle of the table another. It was a small table—large enough for only two, and there were two beds pressed up against each other by the wall. This was clearly a shared bedroom transformed for the evening.

"Sorry," she said, wincing. "The boys did their best." Her lover appeared from behind her and slipped an arm around her, kissing the top of her head.

"We don't have a dining room," he said, a trace of the

musical accent that Caspian spoke with to his words. "And the kitchen is so wide and open. Rou was insistent you'd want some privacy."

"I know Kouta's a better cook, but Jayden can whip up something nice when he tries," added Roulette. She gestured to the table. "A vegan meal. Stir-fry noodles. I guess your brother likes it, so…"

"It's beautiful," I said, turning around and beaming at them. "And it smells delicious," I added, taking in the gentle aroma of simmering vegetables. "Thank you."

Ice-Blast winked at me. "Now to see if telekinetic boy put on the suit Flayme lent him."

He stepped back farther into the hallway, glancing over his shoulder. "Ah. He did."

Both Ice-Blast and Roulette stepped aside as Rhett appeared in the doorway.

In the gentle flickering light, the brightness of the hallway behind him, Rhett looked like a creature sent from someplace beyond these dirtied lands. The human word that came to mind was *heaven*.

He tugged at the loop of fabric around his neck. "I haven't worn a tie since I was twelve," he said. "What's all…?" But then his wandering eyes found me and his jaw just stayed open.

"I wanted to have a nice dinner with you," I said. "To thank you for the pancakes." Stepping forward, I took that smooth, silky *tie* in my own hands. I liked having something to grab a man by. Rhett tumbled closer.

"That's my cue," Roulette said with a giggle. She slipped out, closing the door quietly behind her, leaving me alone with my man.

I knew this was our first and last chance to be together.

CHAPTER THIRTEEN

RHETT SWALLOWED AND STEPPED AWAY, GENTLY EXTRACTING THE *tie* from my grip. "Lana, you certainly don't have to *thank* me." He pulled one of the chairs out from the small cloth-covered table. "Though I can't say I don't appreciate all this effort."

I went to sit at the other end, but Rhett caught me gently by the elbow, directing me to the seat he'd pulled out instead. "Tonight, you get treated like a lady. It's the least I could do after…" His face darkened, his lips thin.

I took a seat. "Thank you. I feel like a Miss Elizabeth Bennet already." I frowned. "Though I don't think the men have been very gentlemanly to her just yet."

"You haven't finished the story," he said. A smile fluttered across his face. "Though you're not wrong." He stared at me, long and hard. I felt myself flinch at his gaze. "Is that what your hair is? Like a Georgian woman?"

I offered him a blank look. "An Elizabethan woman?"

"That's something else entirely." He seemed to swallow his laughter. "Oh, but the important thing is—damn, it looks good on you. Though you looked amazing from the moment I saw you." He flinched, fiddling with his shirt sleeves a moment.

I decided to fill in the space with plating the vegetables and the long noodles. "Stir-fry," I said. "This is quite similar to a Nelian meal."

He picked up his fork. "I'd like to try a Nelian meal sometime." He took a bite. "This isn't bad."

"I didn't make it," I said, suddenly embarrassed that I hadn't thought to, instead focusing on my now-crunchy hair. I could still smell the foul scent of it. It threatened to ruin the meal.

We ate in silence a bit longer, my tongue unable to express anything I'd wanted to say.

"It's soothing," Rhett said after a while, pushing his empty plate forward. "Being around you. You don't demand that I talk non-stop—it's part of why I hate being alone with someone usually." He swallowed. "At least in a group, there are other people talking."

"I like solitude," I said. "It's less draining. There's no one I'm hurting when I'm alone."

"You don't hurt anybody, Lana." He got up and sat on the bed in this rearranged bedroom, taking my hand in his and directing me to sit next to him.

"When we do talk, you make me laugh," he said. "You impress me with your thirst for knowledge about this place that must be so foreign to you. I thought…"

"You thought what?" I pressed. His fingers were so smooth over my knuckles, so relaxing.

"I thought your people were a lot different." His eyes met mine. "I'm sorry for taking you. For not understanding you."

"I have some things to tell you."

He looked as if he'd sit there a year, waiting for me to be ready to speak. I wasn't used to that in the men I'd been drawn to—not that I was complaining about their take-charge attitudes, mind you. But this was… different. Nice. He was right. It was so quiet in this room with him. So soothing.

"I'm the Nelian princess," I said first—the others knew now. He had to know.

His fingers stopped moving for a moment. "No wonder the king was so angry," he said. "I thought there was something *personal* behind it."

"You're not mad I kept it from you?"

"Why would I be? It was smart." Releasing my hand, he leaned back on the bed. "We're your enemies. Don't let an enemy know how valuable what they have is."

"Are you still my enemy?" I rubbed a hand down my arm.

"I don't want to be," he admitted. He sighed. "I really don't want to be. But I can't just walk away from what I believe in."

"I didn't ask you to. I just want you to understand where we're coming from."

He swallowed visibly as he took me in. We fell into silence once more, the last sunbeams of the day dying as the candle flickering became our only source of light.

"Lana, are you attracted to Caspian or Bo?" He sat up straighter, tugging at his tie once more. "You had sex with Caspian, I could tell that almost immediately. But you were also gone for so long with Bo, and I know how he looks at you."

How did you know? I wanted to ask. But I wouldn't be anything but direct with this man who could steal my breath at a glance. "Yes. I had sex with them both. I love them both."

Rhett let out a little chuckle, but it was hollow, sad. He finally succeeded in removing the tie. "I won't even ask. Just lament that I got in there too late."

"You didn't." Standing, I took the silky tie from him, playing with it between my fingers. "On Nelia, it isn't odd for a person to have more than one lover at a time."

Rhett bobbed his head, lightly snatching the end of the tie as it dangled between us. "So it would seem."

"And there's this *attraction*. This bond that we feel with the person or people whom we are simply *meant* to be with. We don't question it when it happens. It just does. It's undeniable—to everyone around us even. That is, to other Nelians

128

at least." I wrapped his red tie around both sets of my fingers.

He yanked on the tie, causing me to stumble forward, his knees knocking against mine as I stood before him. "And what happens if a Nelian tries to fight it?"

I let out a little moan. "It's difficult," I whispered. "*Painful.*"

With another yank on the tie, Rhett's free hand settled on the small of my back. "Are you in pain, Lana?" he whispered. "Around me?"

He felt it, too.

"Rhett, I've felt that *need*, that attraction to all four of you," I said. "Please tell me you won't fight it. At least not tonight. It's our only chance."

Rhett stood, pulling harder on the tie, yanking me against him. His *boner* was solid against my abdomen. "I won't," he whispered, cupping my cheek. "If you don't want me to, I won't."

I showed him my hands, the silky red tie still woven around them. "I'm yours."

"Do you trust me?" His voice was throaty, raw. "Despite everything I've been party to—kidnapping you, attacking your friends?"

"I do."

Rhett's hand slipped from my face to my back, finding that hard, cold, metal *zippa* at the back of the fabric and moving it down, slowly, the sound ringing out around us. I was in awe. In my few short experiences with *zippas*, I'd never been able to *unzippa* one with one hand. The dress fell from my shoulder and he unwound the tie from my hands, then pulled the dress down until it hit the floor.

His eyes widened.

"I am always *in commando*," I explained.

He turned away slightly, a fist against his mouth, his eyes sparkling as his body shook.

I traced my finger over the collar of his shirt, into the small gap at the base of his throat. He caught my hand, his lips back in a thin line, his chin slightly raised. "Lie back," he said, gesturing to the two small beds behind me.

I did, but not before running a finger up that haughty chin.

He grinned just slightly, playing with the tie between his hands, back and forth, up and down. "Look at that ass," he said, twitching his head just slightly.

I twisted sideways so he could get a better look.

"I don't know which side I want to fuck first," he said.

"I'll let you choose."

"Put your arms over your head and lie on your stomach."

I did, though I wasn't sure why.

He crawled over me, his jutting bulge dragging up across my legs to my rear before he gripped my wrists together. "I'm going to tie you to the bed," he said, wrapping the red tie around my wrists and looping it through in a knot. "Any objections?"

"You don't have to tie me down to keep me on this bed," I said, my voice cracking.

He paused. "I won't if you don't want me to."

"I didn't say *that*."

Chuckling, he continued what he was doing, looping the other end of the tie around the bedpost and tying another knot.

I looked over my shoulder at him, my essence pooling as he stood at the foot of the bed and removed his shirt. "We need a safe word," he said.

"What's that?"

"A word you say while we're being intimate that will make me stop what I'm doing—immediately. A word you wouldn't usually use while having sex."

I bit my lip. "I don't imagine I'll want you to stop."

"Even so," he said, running a supple finger up the back of one of my calves. I shivered. "It's only okay if you know I'll stop if you need me to—untie you if you need me to."

"Pancakes," I said, suggesting a word that made me feel warm and relaxed.

Swallowing laughter, he nodded as his hand went to the *zippa* of his jeans. "'Pancakes' it is. Now, don't take the word lightly. Only say it when you want me to stop."

I nodded and twisted my body so I could get a better look as he removed his pants. The tie holding my arms went taut at the movement, my muscles straining, but it felt good—the resistance. The tightness.

Rhett revealed his *boner*, the glorious, plump, stiff appendage extending out from beneath a shock of dark curls. My thighs squeezed together, my apex growing slippery. I wanted to touch it, to feel it beneath my fingers, my tongue— but I couldn't. I was his *captive*. The thought sent a rush through me, but I swore I wouldn't shout out my special word "pancakes" because even if I wanted to grab hold of that chiseled organ, I wanted to see what he had in mind.

Rhett slipped one leg and then the other out of his pants, flicking his shoulder-length black hair behind his back. I ached to run my fingers over the muscles of his smooth, tanned chest. I squirmed more, squeezing my legs harder and harder, swimming in the moisture between my legs. A little moan escaped my mouth.

The side of his mouth tugged up in a smile. "I haven't even done anything yet."

"I want to touch you," I breathed.

"No, the touching's all for me this evening," he purred. He crawled onto the bed, gently shifting me onto my stomach once more. His fingers danced over either side of my rear and I gasped again, pulling on the tie holding my arms up. The strain sent a rush through my entire body.

His fingers slid down the length of my thighs and back up again, his thumbs slipping into the crack between my butt cheeks and titillating the wrinkled skin around my anus, gently applying pressure to the cheeks to pull them just far enough apart for his thumbs to go to work.

I moaned some more, gasping for breath as my legs squeezed tighter, trying to contain the vibrating energy coming together there.

"I wish I had some of my toys," he said in a low voice. "Your pretty ass would feel so good with some beads about now."

I didn't know what he meant—*beads*? On my ass?

"*Inside* it," he whispered, his face moving in to kiss up my back, his hands still playing around between my slick butt cheeks. His thumb poked through and I gasped.

"Remember the word?" he asked.

I nodded breathlessly, and he stilled, as if waiting.

My toes curled as I embraced the thrill. It hurt just a little, but it felt so incredibly *good*, I couldn't believe it.

He pushed his thumb in farther, letting the other hand travel down and between the lips of my vulva, trailing through the slick, glistening wetness to my apex and massaging in a gentle circle.

"Oh, *roots* and *sediment*." I groaned, my legs convulsing, my arms straining as I yanked on the tie, practically threatening to rip the silk apart.

Rhett chuckled—a deep, throaty sound. "I love everything about you," he whispered, his fingers still going to work. "Your incredibly soft, pliant skin. Your lean, muscular frame. Your breasts. This *ass*." His words grew more and more breathless. "Your kindness. Your strength. Your cunning. Your malapropisms."

I didn't know what that last word was, but I didn't care. Blood was rushing to my head—to my genitals, everywhere. I couldn't stop the sounds of pleasure coming from my mouth.

"I want to come in," he said. "In your fine, soft ass." Breathless, he raised my hips and shifted my legs so my weight rested on my knees and elbows, moving slowly, as if waiting for me to say my *safe word* at any moment. I wouldn't. I wouldn't do that, wouldn't put an end to *this*.

"Has anyone ever done that with you, Lana?" he whispered.

My heart threatened to pound right out of my ears. "Come?" I asked. "In my *ass*?" Xerxes had never ventured to try such a thing. "No."

"Remember the safe word?"

Yanking down on my arms, I nodded, my clitoris positively shaking in anticipation. "Come inside me."

He took hold of both of my butt cheeks again. The slight pain caused a burst of energy to rush there, making my limbs go numb and achy.

Glancing over my shoulder, I watched and *felt* as he buried his alert, taut erection into my anus, the initial stretching a shock of pain that caused me to cry out.

He froze, his black hair slick with sweat over his shoulder.

"Go on," I said, my breaths out of control, tears in my eyes, but not wanting this to end. "Go! Please! Go!"

He penetrated more forcefully and my head grew dizzy, the pain warping into intense pleasure the likes of which I'd never known possible from such a place. Sliding inside me, he stopped, his testicles pressed flush against my butt cheeks. We stayed that way for a moment. He pulled back out slowly, then thrust back in. I moaned.

His fingers went back to work, this time his thumb heading up my tunnel as his pointer finger brushed up against my apex. He was inside me in so many places and I couldn't stand it. I kept screaming out his name, moaning the word "yes!" more times than I could count.

But there was nothing—not the penetrating ache of the new experience, not the fact that someone could be listening nearby—that would make me say "pancakes."

He ravaged me a few more times, hard, slow, and somehow both gentle and firm at once—and then I felt him release inside me, in a new place inside me, and my vision went blurry as I screamed out once more.

My sounds died down and I focused on the hard breaths

coming from him as he slipped out. He laid his soft lips atop one of my butt cheeks. "You're a goddess, Lana."

I knew that was a compliment of the highest order, even if it wasn't true.

He slipped out from between my legs and I turned over, sore all over—particularly my rear, my arms, and my legs— but still abuzz with an intense *need* to have him back inside me.

"Kiss me," I breathed. I didn't ask him to untie me just yet.

He crawled up beside me, his face level with mine, his limbs entangled around my body, and pressed his lips to mine—hard, hungry, and full of an intense focus on devouring me once more.

CHAPTER FOURTEEN

As I'd hoped, we didn't sleep at all. A knock at the door startled me. My arms were down—draped across Rhett's abdomen, my cheek resting on his chest—but the tie was still looped around one of my wrists. His abdomen's muscles were so very well defined, the dips and bumps calling to my fingers despite the repeated knocking at the door.

Sunlight streamed through the curtains, the candle fizzled out on the table, its wax dripped in streaks down its side. For the second night in a row, I'd welcomed dawn in the arms of one of my lovers, rested with the feel of him beneath my cheek. I didn't want to go back to meeting the dawn alone.

"Alanna." It was Aurora's voice. "I'm sorry to disturb you, but it's almost time—the time we said we'd rendezvous with the R.I.A."

I shot up in a flash. Rhett was leaving today. I wouldn't go with him—I would never see him, Caspian, or Bo again. I would never have a chance to tell Monroe how I felt. I was toxic, poison to them. For their own wellbeing, I needed to stay away.

The Second Hope children needed me. They were the only ones who did. Maybe if I visited Lacey, Bo would be there one day. It was the most I could hope for.

Rhett arose so silently beside me, I didn't even notice him leaving until he put a gentle hand on my arm, then bent to put his cheek on my bare shoulder. He didn't need to say anything. I *felt* his desire to stay with me, to wish our differences away. But I understood he could never speak that aloud.

"Alanna?" Aurora called.

"Coming," I said, the single word catching roughly in my throat. "Thank you." Brushing my lips over Rhett's knuckles, I gave his hand a squeeze.

He moved his lips to meet mine lightly at first—then harder, greedier. "Farewell, my sweet Georgian princess." Then he pulled away and got up, slipping into his clothing, his eyes never once leaving me even as he made his way to the door and opened it, leaving me behind.

AFTER A SHOWER, THE ACHE THROUGHOUT MY BODY, particularly between my legs, dulled considerably, though it was still there, a quiet reminder of last night and the euphoria I'd felt, the new world he'd shown me.

It had been difficult to wash the stiffness out of my hair, but I'd used the *shamm-poo* as Caspian had taught me and got it back to how it was meant to be, vowing to never try an *updo* again, at least not one that required such unnatural spray. Some clothes Aurora had left me awaited me as I exited—comfortable, skin-tight pale pink leggings and a smooth, silky creamy white shirt with buttons down the front, ruffles at the edges of the sleeves, and little flowers embroidered into the material.

Alarik was in the hallway when I exited, his arms crossed over his chest as he leaned against the wall, like he'd been standing there waiting for me. He rarely stayed away from Nelia for so long, as I understood from what I'd known of his behavior in the past few months—even if he had his regular nights with Aurora.

I went to move past him and he stood in front of me. "Where are you going?"

"To say goodbye to Rhett," I said, moving to squeeze between him and the wall. "And to see the others."

His arm jut out in front of me. "You think I would be foolish enough to let them come here? Where the mother of my children sleeps? Our hostage doesn't know where he was —and Veras took him away blindfolded."

"I'll go with," I insisted.

"They're already gone."

My chest tightened. "Where are they taking him?"

"Just to the other side of the city." Alarik growled. "Did you think I would take him out back and kill him? You know I'm not that heartless." His eyes narrowed. "But if they *ever* try something like that again... They're lucky they're even allowed within the same city as you."

I clutched his arm, threatening to rip it out of my way if I had to. "You'd think you'd want your enemies exposed to my powers."

"Not at the cost of them stealing your heart." His nose wrinkled and he let me pass, but he grabbed me by the wrist. "Don't forget what happened with Xerxes. Your *powers* didn't stop him."

I yanked free of his grip. "Oh, I'd never forget—you'd never let me." Turning away, I fought back the tears in my eyes.

MORE THAN A COUPLE OF DAYS HAD PASSED, BUT I HADN'T KEPT track of them. I hadn't gone with the Renegades when they'd come to take me back to a new spot out there somewhere, out in some remote, desolate field. I hadn't yet spoken to my brother about Second Hope.

My insides were cold. Hollow. I should have been satisfied I'd found a purpose—a way to be useful to this planet, even if for just a small group of people—but I'd barely been able to summon the strength to move.

Chastity had lent me her room, going to stay with friends —"only a comm away if needed," she'd said, "and besides, that way I can keep my powers if we need them in a pinch." Aurora visited me often, but I forgot what she spoke of. One time she'd asked if I needed anything and I'd told her *Pride and Prejudice*. She'd laughed but brought me the battered-up copy Rhett had left behind.

It was slow-going at first, but I continued where I'd left off, reading it until the end.

And then I read it again. Aurora had given me back my phone, and I'd used it to look up some of the things I didn't understand.

And then I found a *moving picture* of the book on my phone and I watched it.

And then I sat there in the dark, thinking about them— my men.

My door was usually left slightly ajar, the whispers of those in the hall reaching me.

"She can't stay here forever," said Jayden. "Aurora, I'm sorry—but we can't keep not having our powers this long. Wade got so jittery, he packed up and went to his boyfriend's. He can't use his computers, any of his equipment so long as she's here. He says it was like he was hit by a dumb truck, whatever that means—he's getting dumber already."

"And I suppose the fact that sex with me doesn't boost your powers at the moment is bothering you as well?" Aurora asked dryly.

The sounds of kissing carried into my room, making my heart squeeze tighter. "You know that's not the case. Sex with you is the most amazing thing I've ever experienced. I never even needed it before you. And your powers have nothing at all to do with it."

138

"I love you," she responded quietly.

"You are my everything," he said, followed by kisses again.

Sex with Aurora made Natch and Nelian powers so much stronger, as I'd been told—and even kissing her resulted in a short boost. Wade had intelligence as his power, and some sort of limited invisibility. I'd forgotten. I'd had no need of knowing how to combat any of the powers since I'd never see them in person while awake.

"Alarik doesn't think it a good idea for her to go back to Nelia," he said. "Not with Xerxes there—and because, well, she'd just have to be out in a cabin alone anyway, or she'd take away most of their powers. They've only got the one village."

No one wanted me here. No one wanted me there. And I couldn't blame them.

What good would I do for the Second Hope kids with those cold-eyed people standing guard over them? I couldn't stay with them forever. Bo was right. If I asked Alarik, he might help me, but he'd use force and then there would be more people like the R.I.A., more people who thought of my brother as a *dictator*. And I still wouldn't be able to stay with the kids. Not without a Nelian guard to help me force the issue.

Sometimes even the right thing could turn into a wrong thing if done through force. I could see that now. I didn't completely agree with it, but I understood why someone else might.

"Zander found her another camping site." Jayden let out a little yelp. "Did you just pinch me?"

"Stop being so heartless," Aurora snapped. "Fine. We'll find her a place in the country—but not another damn tent."

"She *wanted* to camp in nature," he replied to the echo of Aurora's footfalls.

I didn't hear more about that for a while. There were other conversations, too—professions of love between Roulette and

Ice-Blast, the arrival of my brother again and consultation with Zander, who'd stopped by, on what their plans were next when it came to saving the environment and protecting Natchkind.

There was a knock on the door. "Hey, Your Highness." Torynt stood there, his hands in his pockets. "Glad to see you're all right."

I shrugged from my place on my bed, clutching my legs tighter to my chest.

"Though you don't look all right." He slipped into a chair. "Did those creeps do something to you?"

"Those *creeps*"—I got the general meaning of the word— "are my beloveds."

Torynt shook his head rapidly, blinking all the while. "Beloved*s*?"

I nodded.

"Damn, what did you all get up to in the couple of days you were gone?" He ruffled his yellow hair. "You are super hot, princess, so I can't blame them—but you know they're our enemies, right?"

"I have heard all the lectures," I said, raising a hand to stop him. "I have all the bad feelings one can have."

"I didn't mean to make you feel bad about it." He scratched the back of his neck. "My own boss is sort of like sleeping with the enemy? Part-time? Part-time sleeping with the part-time enemy? Is Aurora's Zander's enemy anymore or not?" He sucked in a quick breath. "Damn, you ladies have got *game*. I just need some tips on assembling a harem of my own."

"Harem?"

"You know, like, multiple people having sex with you— and only you?" He asked that last bit as a question and I nodded, though I supposed I couldn't be sure. He continued. "I mean, like, are they all together with you at once, enjoying each other as they enjoy you or—?"

I cocked my head. "You ask some very detailed questions."

"My bad." He laughed. "Anyway, either way, I'd say you got yourself a harem of baddies, princess. Or a harem of resistance rebels seeking justice, I suppose, depending on one's point of view."

"They're not bad," I said, clunking my chin hard atop my knees.

Torynt nodded thoughtfully. "I suppose they do keep their targets rather confined to me and my friends, unlike some *elves* I know. Or at least how those elves used to be." He leaned back in his chair, scratching his chin. "Actually, are they a harem of heroes? Are we the bad guys here...?" He shrugged. "I've been doing what I've been doing since before Zander even turned Renegade. I used to be Target Number One of this here group of wannabe heroes, all the mischief I caused. Whatever. Things change. Foes become friends, friends become foes, and everyone's fucking everyone but me."

He stood and put his hands back in his pockets. "If I were you, I wouldn't let something like *sides* stop you. Follow the example of your big bro, right? Sleep with the enemy. Make it fucking work—your pussy might be just the negotiating tool we need to get those fuckers off our backs."

His words were crude and not entirely clear, but I understood him well enough.

And he was right.

Heart soaring, I jumped to my feet. "Tell everyone I left willingly, okay?"

His eyes twinkled. "And I'll keep them off the scent as long as I can. Need a lift? Boss is *spending the night*, so to speak. I can drop you off and be back before anyone's the wiser."

"You have an hour," I said. "But we will make the most of it."

CHAPTER FIFTEEN

"This place?" Torynt asked, leaning over the wheel to get a better look at Drake's Bar. "This is like one of those dives you only see in movies about cowboys and motorcycle gangs, princess."

Half of that I didn't comprehend, but I exited the car. "Thanks so much," I said, shaking my phone in the air. "I'll let Aurora or my brother know what I'm up to as soon as they notice I'm gone."

"Should I stay?" he asked. "Make sure everything goes all right—give you a ride home if they're not even there?"

"I'll phone you if I need you. I can walk and then take a *boos* back if I need to. Kouta taught me what to do."

Chuckling, Torynt waved and shifted the car's stick at his side. "Go get 'em, Your Highness."

His car exited the parking lot, kicking up dust that made me cough in its wake. Once his car disappeared from view, everything went quiet around me, the hum of the cowgirl-hat woman above me, the dull beat of the music from within echoing in my head.

Opening the door, the music blasted in my ears, the man's voice somehow sad and aggressive all at once.

"Welcome to Drake's, sugar—oh. I didn't expect to see

that face of yours so soon." Bella approached the door, a rag in her hand. She looked over her shoulder and saw the other couple of customers looking, which caused her to remove her hat and park it atop my head. "Let's get you to the back," she said, sliding her arm through mine.

"Is that Lana?" asked Drake as we brushed past him at a fast pace through the kitchen.

"Hello," I said in a cheery voice. The smile he gave me warmed my heart, like he was welcoming me home, despite how little time I'd ended up spending here.

"You finish up those orders," Bella barked at Drake, yanking me into the room with boxes. She pulled on a thin, metal rope hanging from the ceiling, dimly illuminating the room.

"The boys aren't here anymore." Bella crossed her arms. "And they told me if anyone—*anyone*—came looking for them that I was to call the police for Drake's and my safety. You threatening to use those elf plant powers on our little establishment?"

"I don't have that ability," I said. Bella looked like she didn't believe me. "It's the truth."

"Should I still be worried?"

I shook my head. "I never wanted things to be this way. I'd never hurt them—never."

Bella frowned. "Could you say the same about them? That they'd never hurt you?" She sighed. "I had an inklin' something shady was going on when they showed up with you."

"I came willingly."

"Because you and Caspian...?"

I opened my mouth and shut it again. I didn't know what to say. I still had to explain myself to Caspian, and though both Bo and Rhett had accepted that I had room in my heart for more than just one, they'd both chosen their cause over me.

And then there was Monroe. I'd never convince him to give me a chance.

But I was determined to try.

"You don't have to explain to me," she said. She gestured up the stairs. "Look—well, I won't call the police. I don't think things have to come to that. The boys left a lot of stuff up there. If you want to look around, see if you can figure out where they went, you're welcome to."

I embraced Bella and put her cowgirl hat back on her head.

She squeezed me back and then pulled away, gripping me by the shoulders. "But if they ask, I had nothing to do with it." She sniffed. "I hope they get a chance to ask, though. It'd be a shame if I never got to see those handsome faces again. Too bad they were always so busy with… whatever they were doing to date anyone, apparently." She pinched my arm. "Until Caspian met you, anyway."

Drake called out Bella's name from some distance away.

"Coming!" She turned to me. "Let me know if you need anything."

I thanked her and headed up the steps, feeling my way through the dark. The door was unlocked, though I still hesitated to step through.

The men had left practically everything there. It didn't look like they'd abandoned the place at all. I walked to the window first, pushing aside the curtains to let a little light in. The beds—or what passed for them—were still unmade and there were boxes of food still left on the counter. It felt like they had all left in a hurry—had they feared retribution from my friends?

I hadn't told them the location of the R.I.A's hideout. Though Torynt now knew.

From my pocket, my phone buzzed. I played with the screen—there was Aurora's name and number again—until she started speaking. "I'm fine," I said, interrupting her. "I asked Torynt to take me out."

"Torynt?" She mumbled something to other people around her, then moved back to the phone. "He's not really my first choice for an errand buddy. Sorry," she said to someone else who'd spoken up—probably Zander. "Alanna, are you looking for the R.I.A.?"

I wasn't going to even try to hide it. "Aurora, how would you feel if you were kept from your men—any one of them? All of them?"

There was silence on the other end of the line. "You've been through a lot," she said after a while. "But, Alanna, how can this possibly work between you? Those guys may be small-fry, but they are our enemies. They oppose everything we're fighting for. A clean environment. A healthy Earth. What about Xerxes? You felt the pull to him but decided to end it."

"Xerxes and I had our time," I said. After being around my four other men, I was more certain of it. "But I want my time with my humans. I need to at least try to make this work. They're not as bad as you think. They're not trying to hurt anyone. We should stop fighting and listen to each other."

"It's not that simple, Alanna."

"It was for you."

"Alarik isn't going to like this."

"I don't care."

Another period of silence. "All right then. But call me the *instant* anything goes wrong. Because something will."

"I will."

We said our goodbyes and I slipped the phone back into my pocket.

"Have you heard of Stockholm Syndrome, *hermosa*?"

Whipping around, I came face to face with Caspian, who shut the door quietly behind him. His face lit up with a smile, but he ran a shaking hand through his dark hair. "*Lo siento*. Didn't mean to eavesdrop. Certainly didn't expect to find you. I slipped in through the back. Monroe didn't want Bella or Drake to see. Just wanted us in and out and on our way." A hesitant smile graced his lips. "I've never been so thankful to volunteer to get off my butt and do the busywork."

"What is… *busywork*?"

"In this case, just grabbing a few things we didn't mean to leave behind." Caspian crossed in front of me, a stiffness to his step as he grabbed a large sack with handles and those metal *zippas* from between the shelf and one of the mattresses. He tossed it on the mattress and stared at me.

"You're a princess," he said.

"Does that matter to you?"

"Well, no, but…" He scratched the back of his head, then closed the distance between us. "I can't believe fucking *royalty* had sex with me." His hands slid in easily around my waist, and I breathed in the musk of him—earthy, from his leather jacket, with a touch of something sweeter.

I laid a careful hand on his chest, my eyes darting downward. "You have to know that my heart is drawn to others as well as you. I should have told you right away, but I didn't know it would be possible for the others to return my affections as well. I'm sorry."

"Yeah, you had sex with Bo and Rhett." Caspian let out a little growl and yanked me even closer. "The idea of you with other men kind of turns me on," he said. "Only I wish I could have watched."

Heat surged to my face as I rested my cheek against his shoulder. I felt so comfortable here in his arms—whole again for the first time in however long it had been. "I care for them both," I said. "And you. It's not simply a matter of enjoying their *boners* inside me. It's deeper than that."

Caspian rocked me back and forth, his own cheek resting atop my head. "I know," he whispered. "The way they talk about you… Monroe is livid."

Something caught in my throat at the idea of Monroe never being mine. Slipping back from the embrace, I caught a sole tear escaping from my eye.

"What is it, *hermosa*?" Caspian asked, his voice soothing. He reached up to catch another tear from my other eye.

"It's... nothing," I said. I could not be so selfish as to want the love of so many. But I didn't see how I would ever be allowed to love Caspian, Bo, and Rhett if Monroe was the man they most looked up to—and he was the man who looked at me with nothing but distaste.

"It doesn't change how I feel about you," said Caspian. "You being with them. I've never loved *anyone* before the way I love you."

His lips on mine were soft, searching—then more desperate, hungry.

I gave in, letting my tears dry with the rush of blood to my head, to my apex.

"I was wondering what was taking you so long."

Both Caspian and I pulled back quickly, as if children caught with the sweetcakes our parents had forbidden us to sample.

Monroe stood in the doorway, his arms crossed, his brow narrowed. He stared at me, hard—a look of venomous hatred etched into his features.

CHAPTER SIXTEEN

"I just have one question," Monroe said as Caspian opened his mouth to speak. The glare his leader shot him quieted him immediately. "Did you know she was going to be here?"

"How would I have known that?" asked Caspian. He yanked me possessively toward him.

"I don't know. Maybe because you've all been taken in by this *succubus* and you're going around behind my back." His tone was even, carefully controlled, but his arms were shaking as he ran a palm over his scalp.

My shoulders quaking, I wiped the last of the tears away. "I had to see you," I said. "All of you."

"Yeah, so you can render us impotent," Monroe snapped.

"Oh, *impotent* is a poor choice of words, *mi hermano*," said Caspian, a twinkle in his eye as he looked down at me. "She renders men anything but."

"Are you hearing yourself?" Monroe paced away from us, going to stare out the window, his back to us.

Bo and Rhett summited the steps, Bo's face going from solemn to joyful in an instant when he took in the sight of me. He crossed the room and took me into his arms, spinning me around a short distance off the ground.

"Okay, okay, buddy," Caspian said, laughing as he stepped back. "You almost clocked me there."

Bo put me down and crushed his lips against mine. "I'd gladly be knocked out by you any day," he said as he pulled away.

Rhett tugged at his shirt collar as he sent a fluttering smile my way.

My heart soared to be so near all of them, that bond that demanded I give all of myself to them flaring to life, sparking something inside me that had been missing for days.

The jubilation was short-lived.

"You've lost your wits—all of you." Monroe paced quickly across the room. He started yanking things off piles, from shelves—clothing and papers and little things I didn't recognize—and tossing them in the sack Caspian had left on the mattress. "Well, I don't need a single one of you. I'll save our society myself."

"Monroe—" Bo started, his grip on me slipping somewhat.

"*Hermano*," said Caspian.

Rhett shifted his weight from one leg to the other.

Monroe hastily pulled on that *zippa*, shutting the sack and flinging it over his shoulder. "Save it," he said, pushing past Caspian, who'd tried to step in front of him. "You're all on your own."

"Wait," I said, stepping out from beside Bo. "You have to listen to me."

I couldn't be responsible for the four of them drifting apart. I wouldn't be. Monroe just had to understand.

He gazed into my eyes for a moment, his brow softening, his lip trembling just slightly.

Then his face hardened. "I don't have to listen to a Nelian, thanks." He moved to step around me.

"Hey," Rhett said, speaking up for the first time. He stopped Monroe with a hand on his chest.

Monroe looked down at it and then to Rhett and back again. "Move the hand or lose it."

Rhett shook his head resolutely. "You need to listen to her."

Monroe dropped his sack to the ground with a loud *thunk*. "Are you even hearing yourselves?" he asked. "We gave up everything to do this—and now you're all letting some woman—some *elf*—derail you from your purpose."

Bo and Caspian looked away at that, Bo taking a few steps toward the window.

"Listen to her," is all Rhett had to say once more.

The room quieted.

Monroe was listening, his legs slightly parting.

Now I just had to figure out what to say. There was so much.

I opened my mouth.

"Guys," Bo said from behind me. "We have a problem."

The four of us joined him at the window, peering down the barren road to almost as far as we could see. Two figures were there, one staying put while the other made her way closer to the bar.

One human—one Nelian.

"That's Teleport," Caspian said, stiffening. That was the Renegade member Lila's code name, though the humans with whom I surrounded myself didn't usually refer to her as such. "She's hanging back." He looked over his shoulder at me. "Almost like she knows you're here."

She might have by now—Torynt didn't exactly stand up to pressure well.

"Is that how far you have to stay to be unaffected by your nullification?" Monroe asked, his arched eyebrow taking me in from head to toe. He always seemed to be studying me, taking in new information.

I nodded.

"Who's the other one?" asked Caspian, pointing to the woman farther back.

"It's a Nelian woman," said Rhett.

He was right. I recognized her the closer she got. That green hair affixed in a bun framing that waxen face could only belong to one Nelian. "Flora!" She was one of the elves who helped take care of the royal residence.

"Is she here for you?" Bo asked.

"Well, she's not here to sell us Girl Scout cookies," Monroe muttered. He seized me by the shoulders. "Is this a trap?"

"No!" I didn't fight to get out of his grip, although I could have. Instead, I had to push down the savage, feverish charge that coursed through my body at his touch.

"She's going to lose her powers, too, if she's coming closer," said Rhett. "She won't be able to attack with those vines. How in the world did she get here?"

"Watch for other Nelians," I said. "She couldn't have come alone." I bit down on my lip the instant I said it.

The elves who had the ability to open portals were not so widely known. There had to have been some witnesses outside of Veras and the Renegades, but there was still a lot of speculation as to how my people traveled from one world to the next.

That was not information you readily served to your enemies, even if you were in love with them. But Lila would have only been able to bring her so far—she could only teleport as far as she could see—so there was an open portal somewhere nearby.

Monroe's fingers dug into my flesh as he stared out at the approaching Nelian. Yet rather than him being overcome with anger, it was more like he was anchoring himself with me.

"We need to get out of here," he said.

Bo took hold of my hand. "I'm not going anywhere without Alanna."

Monroe let go, wiping his forearm over his lips as he locked eyes with me.

I wanted to believe he didn't want to go anywhere without me, either.

But I also knew there was no point in running, not until I knew what Flora could possibly want.

Squeezing Bo's hand, I gave him a wavering smile and passed it on to Caspian and Rhett. "Go," I said. "I have to talk to her—see what she wants. But you don't need to be here."

"Why is this woman here instead of your brother?" Monroe asked.

"I don't know," I said. "But she's not a warrior—she's a…"

"Friend?" Caspian finished for me.

"I don't have a lot of friends," I replied.

Monroe was bouncing on the balls of his feet. "We need to keep her from bothering Drake and Bella."

"I'll go right now," I said, reluctantly letting go of Bo. "You… do what you need to do."

I was halfway down the stairs when I felt a throng behind me—the comforting, cushioning presence of the men with whom I felt a bond.

I couldn't stop a smile from appearing on my face, though I knew they couldn't see it.

Exiting through the propped-open back door, I marched around the parking lot and headed to the road, the R.I.A. a few steps behind me. I glanced back as we marched on. Monroe was in the lead, sticking an arm out to stop Bo or Caspian whenever one tried to slip in front of him to get closer to me. Rhett, ever the quiet soldier, hung back, not pressing his leader just yet.

Flora began running almost as soon as she saw me. I picked up the pace.

"Princess!" she called, embracing me. I flinched, startled by her affection. She was a kind woman, a good servant to my family, but she, like most everyone on Nelia, did not appreciate being in my presence.

She pulled back and checked over her shoulder. "We have to go," she said. "I asked the Renegades to help. We didn't tell your brother what we were doing, which meant we couldn't get help from Aurora—so Tianah and Renaya are keeping a portal open some distance back on the other side. We have to go quickly before they lose control of it." Tianah was another Nelian who helped at the royal household; Renaya a warrior.

"Slow down," I said. "What are you talking about? What's going on?"

The R.I.A. was behind me now, each of their brows furrowed as Flora looked their way. "Will they help you?" she asked.

"With what?" Monroe asked. I'd been about to ask the same.

Flora leaned closer to my ear, but her voice was loud enough I knew the alert R.I.A. could hear her. "It's Xerxes. He abandoned the heart of Nelia, left our planet's only community without the king's permission. If you don't find him first, who knows what your brother will do? Xerxes has been given enough chances. He might…" No one had ever been *killed* by another Nelian on our planet, but no one had ever betrayed their ruler, either. Flora straightened. "A few of the others from the castle and I, we don't want the poison of Earth to spread to Nelia. We don't want Xerxes killed—it's barbaric."

"Alarik wouldn't…" I couldn't finish my thought. My heart sunk to my feet. Alarik might not *intend* to kill Xerxes, but if the two of them engaged in another conflict, I couldn't say for sure that both would survive.

"Who's Xerxes?" asked Caspian. His shoulders twitched and he seemed ruffled, as if he sensed there was something there—a history between Xerxes and me.

"What do you want *me* to do?" I asked.

"You can find him. Xerxes might listen to you. Might come back to the heart of Nelia." Flora pointed behind her at Lila, still some distance away. "I'll knock you out. This teleportation Natch will take us to the spot where the portal is waiting—"

"Who's knocking whom out?" Bo asked, stepping forward.

I tensed. They would know the way around my powers now, too. But I already knew I had little intention of keeping it from them forever.

"I have to go," I said, meeting each of their eyes in turn.

Flora looked to me. "We could use help," she said. "Too many of our people are starting to think it'd be better off if Xerxes were exiled to Earth, despite your brother's decree that he stay away from humans. Then there are those who are starting to think it might be better if he were... dead." She shook her head, and I found my knees shaking at the idea of Xerxes dead—even if he'd been so callous and had betrayed my brother. Nelians didn't kill. What had happened to our people? "It's a poisonous thought spread from prolonged contact with *this* planet," Flora continued, as if I'd voiced my thoughts aloud.

"We'll go with you." It wasn't Caspian, Rhett, or Bo who'd spoken. It was Monroe.

"You would come?" I asked. "Why?"

Caspian, Rhett, and Bo all seemed to be waiting on an answer as well.

"I'm not letting some elf prisoner be exiled to *our planet*," Monroe said. "We have enough elves causing havoc here." His stare affixed pointedly on me.

I wasn't going to argue if he was offering the R.I.A.'s help. "Then let's go."

Flora nodded. "Then I'll leave it to one of you to render her unconscious."

The men exchanged a look.

"When I'm unconscious, the Natches and Nelians around me don't lose their powers," I said. "It's necessary for me to travel from one world to another."

"I don't care the reason," started Bo. "I don't feel comfortable—"

But Monroe took a step forward and chopped his hand hard against my neck in one clean stroke. Things went dark quickly.

CHAPTER SEVENTEEN

THE SOFTNESS OF THE MOSS BEHIND MY HEAD. THE FRESH SCENT of leaves and pine needles on the air. Halfway between sleep and wake, my mind wandered with the sense of being back in time, of sleeping between trees some distance from the heart of Nelia, to give the rest of the world the space it so desperately needed from me.

"It's flickering," said a familiar, deep voice. The voice didn't belong here, in my past, in my solitude.

"She's coming to, then, I assume?" said another voice— gravelly. Sexy.

My eyes fluttered open to see Caspian, his hand held out in front of him as he sat on the ground beside me. It was shifting, mutating into something like rock, and then it suddenly snapped back into his flawless human hand.

I'd never even asked what his Natch abilities were. I was so used to everyone being powerless around me.

"Hello, *hermosa*." That hand went tentatively to my neck. "Are you all right?" He glared over his shoulder. "*Someone* almost got his ass kicked for treating you so roughly."

"I knocked her out in the most humane way possible," said Monroe. He stood behind Caspian and was wiping a familiar dagger on the side of his boot—*my* dagger. He'd never given them back after I'd left. "And I caught her, didn't I? Carried her, too. Saved the three of you lovesick droolers from arguing over who got to do it."

He'd carried me? I must have been truly lost in the bond between us if that was what I focused on just then—but I felt as if his scent still lingered on me—earthy and strong. Besides, I *had* needed to be knocked out—otherwise, my powers would have canceled out the portal leading home— and he might have been the only one of the men willing to do it.

I stood on shaky legs, bending my neck this way and that to get the stiffness out of it.

Rhett slipped in to support one side of me while Bo moved in to catch the other. "Take it slow," Bo said.

Monroe took one look at us and shook his head, but the lump at his throat bobbed noticeably as he looked away.

"Where's Flora?" I asked, searching for a sign of her—for any Nelian. The exact patch of the forest came more into focus. We weren't far from the small cabin my brother and Xerxes had built me, a place where I could retreat and give the other Nelians a break from my powers—and take a break from their unspoken disdain toward me for taking their powers from them. I had a room in the royal residence in the heart of Nelia, but I'd never much liked spending time there. Even when my parents had been alive, it hadn't felt like… home.

Alarik and Xerxes had been the only ones who'd tried to make me feel like I wasn't unwanted. Even my parents had only *tried*. I wasn't sure they'd succeeded. But they were gone now. Taken by Mother Nelia through a wild boar attack and the ensuing grief.

I hadn't understood how Mother could have died of the grief of losing Father until I'd formed bonds of my own.

"She and the other Nelians left us here," said Caspian. "Said they didn't want your king to know they'd gone to you for help. Who the fuck is this *Xerxes* and why is this mission supposed to be a secret from your own flesh and blood?"

"Xerxes is…" Somehow, I couldn't figure out how to tell them everything just yet. "He and my brother disagreed."

"Disagreed?" Bo asked.

Nodding, I took my phone out of my pocket. I was about to swipe its screen, to see if Alarik had discovered what we were up to and sent a message, but I remembered there were no flying space machines to connect voices here on Nelia. Slipping it back into my pocket, I took a step forward and held my hand out. "My daggers please."

Monroe stared at the dagger he held in his hands a minute before handing it back hilt-first, then untying my double-sheath belt from his waist and handing it over as well. How long had he been wearing that? Had he stopped back at the bar to put it on? "I was just sharpening them for you," he said, pointing to a nearby stone with marks on it.

I raised a brow. Our daggers were made of stone, a sleek, shiny kind that humans might have mistaken for metal. We didn't typically sharpen them on other stones.

"Thanks," I said, tying the double-sheath around my waist. I patted it for my second dagger and found it still there. Then I took a few steps in this and that direction, trying to get my bearings. "We're close to my cabin," I said. "Flora and the others must have assumed Xerxes would go there. But they wouldn't have known exactly where to find it."

"Before we go any farther, enlighten us," demanded Monroe. His jaw set. "Your elf friends weren't exactly forthcoming. Who is this elf and how, exactly, did he *disagree* with your tyrant king?"

I let the comment about my *tyrant* brother go. Though the meaning was clear enough. "They'd argued over…" I hesitated.

"How to invade our planet?" Monroe asked.

I nodded. "It came to a head a few months ago. Thanks to Veras and the Renegades, my brother won."

"That last big attack." Bo seemed thoughtful. "A lot of people lost their homes—a whole condo building had to evacuate."

I bit my lip. Xerxes had pushed harder, attacked without finesse, and it was a miracle there'd been no casualties.

"Xerxes wasn't thinking clearly," I said. "My brother is more delicate with these matters."

"Sure, because he became a dictator," Monroe muttered. He looked to the other men for affirmation, but they each dodged his gaze in turn.

Being with me was conflicting for them, I could tell. I hoped the next part didn't make it easier for them to walk away from me.

"I have to tell you all," I said. "There was only one person I felt a *bond* with before I met all of you. Xerxes."

Caspian let out a little grunt and shifted his weight from one leg to the other. Bo took my hand again, and Rhett watched me silently, waiting.

Monroe started pacing and mumbling to himself. "*Of course*. Because you couldn't just be a Nelian—a princess. You have to be a traitor's fuck buddy, too."

"It's not like that," I said. "It's over. I stayed away from Nelia partially to stay away from him. To me, our love was gone. Bond or no, I could never act on it again. He'd hurt my brother too many times."

Could these men reach that point? Go against my brother too many times? Would I have to step away from them as well? I remembered how I'd felt when parted from them. It was deeper, more painful than what I'd felt after leaving Xerxes and Nelia behind. And that had been enough to make me never want to be around anyone else again.

Monroe's expression was stony. "Fine. So what do you intend to happen when we find him? He's *not* coming to Earth—"

"First we're finding him," I said, stepping forward. I looked left and right, then started marching in the proper direction. "And making sure he doesn't cause more trouble—*and* stopping my brother from doing anything rash should he find Xerxes first."

The leaves rustled behind me as the R.I.A. fell into step. "What usually happens when there's a jailbreak?" asked Caspian.

"Jail… *break*?" I asked. I swatted an insect, careful not to kill it but eager to get it away from my apparently appetizing flesh.

"Busting out of jail? Prison escape?" offered Caspian.

"What's a jail?" I asked.

The footfalls behind me halted abruptly.

"What?" I asked.

"Where were you keeping your prisoners?" Rhett asked.

I'd heard that word before. "What are prisoners?" I asked, putting a hand on my hip. They were really confusing me—though I knew I had much to learn about their world. "Are they like hostages?"

The R.I.A. exchanged quizzical looks. They seemed as confused as I was.

"Wasn't this Xerxes being held prisoner?" Bo asked gently. "Because he led a coup against your brother?"

"*Coo*…" That word Veras and the Renegades had used to describe Xerxes' actions, too. "We've never had a *coo* before," I explained. "Xerxes was the first Nelian to act that way. To go against the king."

"What about those who steal from others? Who hurt them?" Monroe's brows were narrowed, his eyes quizzical. "Who kill?"

"Steal…" That was a word I'd studied. The taking of things that belonged to others—though *belong* was a different concept on Nelia. Kill, I knew. "Killing isn't the Nelian way. Not when it can be helped."

Monroe scoffed. "Don't tell me this is some utopia. That you're all perfect little angels."

Angels… I'd heard one of Aurora's men call her that often. It was certainly a complimentary term.

"We don't hurt others," I said. "We only hurt the wild boars, and only if there's no choice."

"Wild boars?" Bo asked. "*That's* your biggest worry?" He turned this way and that, as if he could spot one. He was looking too low—at about the level of our knees.

"Okay, so you don't have criminals, and Xerxes just ran away from… what?" asked Monroe. "Was he just living amongst everyone?"

I shrugged. "I don't know. I wasn't here. But I know my brother had guards keeping an eye on him."

"Great," Monroe said. "Wonderful prison system you have going on here. We find him and send him back and he'll just escape once more." He brushed past me and started whacking at branches along the way, even though he didn't know which way to go.

"Be careful," I said, jutting forward and sliding around him. "There's a cliffside up ahead…"

Trees shook some distance away. I grabbed hold of Monroe's bicep and squeezed hard—enough to get him to stop.

"Is that a boar?" Bo whispered.

"It might be," I said, just as quiet. "Everyone, get behind me." I got both daggers ready, gripping the hilts above the blades.

Caspian snorted slightly, positioning himself to the side of me. "How much trouble could a little old boar be?" Bo and Rhett joined him, standing beside Monroe on my other side.

The breathing of the creature grew louder, the branches cracking as it moved near.

"Man, that thing is *loud*." Bo's jaw dropped.

The giant beast—the top of its head reaching halfway up the nearest tree—broke through the foliage, its nostrils flaring.

"That's no little boar," Rhett said.

"Run! Get out of here!" I shouted to my men. With a battle cry and daggers raised, I leapt into the beast's path.

CHAPTER EIGHTEEN

THE CREATURE SNORTED, CHARGING STRAIGHT AT ME. Hollering, the four men ran to the animal. It towered over them, nearly twice their height and as long as one of the *beea-cals* they rode on their home planet.

Roots and sediment. They were supposed to hide, not fight. I dove, sliding on my knees. The boar cried out as I made a gash in its leg. Was that enough to deter it?

It was not.

"Get out of its way!" I shouted, but Caspian and Bo dove to tackle the boar on each side. Rhett and Monroe remained straight in its path.

Cursing once more, I jumped to my feet, running back and reaching for the creature's tail, the dagger in that hand flat against my palm so I could grip the spindly flesh. It took two tries, but I managed, making it cry out again.

As I yanked and lifted myself up, Caspian and Bo each took hold of one of the creature's legs. Gratitude and pride flooded me, but that was quickly replaced by panic as Bo tumbled, bouncing to the ground, letting out a moan I could hear even over the creature's snorts.

Caspian strained to crawl upward until he found himself

on top of the boar. "Alanna!" he screamed, shifting himself to crawl toward the creature's rear end.

"Pull me up!" I reached for him. He gripped my forearm tightly, straining to lift me. Clutching him, I moved to get my balance and search for Bo. He was moving some distance back amidst some bushes—my heart slowed its rapid beating somewhat to see him okay—but he was so far. The boar would take us to the cliff's edge at this rate.

I slammed the dagger into the beast's hindquarters. "We have to jump off!" I shouted to Caspian over the creature's squeals. With a squish, I yanked the dagger from its flesh. As I did, Caspian jumped off with a grunt, and I moved to roll off the other way, but the boar made a quick change in direction and I rolled back up against its neck.

"Alanna!" Monroe was in the path of the boar now, and he was grinding his feet into the dirt, seemingly determined to take it on.

What was he going to do—stare it into submission?

"Move!" I shouted, letting out a scream as I went rolling again. My hand went to my leg and pulled away to find blood. No time to worry about that. "Monroe, move!" I screamed, yanking on the boar's ear. The creature squealed and made another sharp turn.

After a few heart-pounding moments, I felt a hand on the small of my back. I whipped my head around, still holding on to the boar's ear for dear life.

"How did you—?" I started.

Monroe pulled himself higher, grabbing hold of the boar's other ear, his eyes glancing off the side and to the edge of the cliff. "We're both going to fall with it at this rate," he shouted over the squeals. "When there's a nice patch of bushes, jump off."

"Not… leaving you!" I grunted through clenched teeth.

"I'll jump right after," he shouted, his own voice shaking.

The creature *was* taking us closer to my cabin, which meant it was going farther from the heart of Nelia. The other men were behind us, no longer in harm's way. Now was as good a time as any to give up the fight.

"Up there!" I called, spotting a patch of bushes between the trees. "In five… four… three—"

But a whistling sound cut me off. The beast roared back, letting out a pained cry as it stood on two legs. My dagger slipped from my grip as I tried in vain to grab the boar's ear with both hands. Monroe and I went rolling off, Monroe quickly circling me in his arms, and we came to a tumbling stop—Monroe letting out a cry of pain as he landed hard against a tree trunk. The boar collapsed sideways with a thud that shook the ground, its cries softening to shallow breaths.

There was an arrow stuck in its chest, near its heart.

"Well, that's enough meat for several days," said a too-familiar gruff voice that sent a shudder down my sore spine. "Though a waste since it's just we two."

Another whoosh of an arrow and the beast twitched one final time before going still.

Monroe's heart pounded against my cheek. His shirt was ripped in several places, my skin tingling as it rested flush against his.

The sleek creak of an arrow being drawn near my head drew my attention.

"You were right," said a raspy voice that seemed vaguely familiar. "It's your beloved. Come home to Nelia at last." Thorn, one of Xerxes' most loyal defenders, stood over us, his arrow pointed down at Monroe and me.

Xerxes stepped forward. His tall form towered over his shorter friend's, his green hair pulled tightly at the nape of his neck, except for a tendril that curled around his broad, brown shoulders. *"Alanna,"* he breathed. His dark eyes sparked to life.

My blood ran cold at the sound of my name on his lips, my heart torn in half between wanting to flee and wanting to fall into that comfortable embrace of his.

Monroe pulled me tighter to him.

CHAPTER NINETEEN

At the threat of arrow point, Xerxes and his friend insisted on Monroe and me having our hands tied before us with vines. "Shame I can't produce some more," muttered Thorn as the arrow tip trembled. As if he'd have been able to finely control it to the point where it could be used as restraints. Only Alarik had achieved such finesse with his vines, and that had only been because of Aurora's power-boosting Natch ability.

"I can't probe this human's mind, either," said Xerxes. "Not when she's around." He was referring to his rare Nelian ability—not to create vines or portals like the majority of our people, but to *pull* the truth from someone. It had never been of much use in our world before we'd begun our rescue of Earth. We did not lie. Though perhaps we kept the truth from being spoken aloud at times when it was unkind.

The corner of Xerxes' mouth lifted up into a smile just slightly as he stared at me, weaving the thin vine he'd plucked from a nearby tree around my wrists. His thumb traced a gentle circle at the bottom of my palm. He hadn't been half as gentle with Monroe, who was crouched on the ground, wincing with pain from his fall off the boar.

"This isn't necessary," I said, my voice hoarse. "We'll go with you. We're here to find you."

Xerxes raised an eyebrow. "So the mighty king sent the princess to take me back home?"

"My brother isn't the one who sent me," I said, swallowing. "Flora did."

"Flora?"

"She seemed to think if I didn't get you back to the heart of Nelia, there'd be trouble—"

He shook his head. "There's no need for me to live amongst our people, Alanna." He kept caressing my skin. "We are no longer welcome—and besides, you are not there. Where have you been, princess? No one around me seemed to know."

"I've been on Earth."

Xerxes narrowed his eyes. "I assumed that much. No one had seen you—they weren't just keeping the truth from me with their silence. Even as I probed their minds, I saw they had not seen you. But *where* on Earth? With *him*? Don't think I haven't noticed the bond between you—"

"I only met him very recently," I said. Monroe let out a small grunt as he moved. "Until then, I'd been alone. I've always been alone."

"And now? You're not alone now, are you?" He took an uneven step, a lingering grimace forming on his lips. "Are there any others with you?" His eyes fell on Monroe and Monroe spit in his direction. Xerxes laughed, not even flinching. "I'll assume that means no. Let's go," he said to Thorn, and the Nelian sheathed his arrow, slinging his bow over his back to take hold of Monroe by the wrists. Monroe looked as if he wanted to fight, but he stumbled, his shoulders drooping forward and the color draining from his face.

He had really gotten hurt in our tumble.

"He's in pain," I said as Xerxes took hold of my restraints and tugged me after him. "Please. Let me help him."

"I don't think so." He pinched his lips tightly and spoke no more for some time.

Monroe was hurt but making his way after Thorn. Bo had gotten hurt, too, and I didn't know how Rhett and Caspian were doing. I should have never have let them come with me. I did better on my own—no one else got hurt, then. No one else was powerless.

We were quiet the rest of the way to the cabin, the sound of our feet rustling through the grass and Monroe's heavy breathing the only things I focused on.

"You've been hiding out in my cabin? No one's looked for you here?" I asked as we approached the cabin door.

"No one but you," Xerxes said, a smile twitching on his lips. "I suppose even if they thought of it, no one else knows where to find it. How many visitors did you have during your sojourns here?"

"You and Alarik." My brother knew where to find this place.

Monroe stumbled over the threshold as Thorn held the door open, kicking at the Natch's back with his foot.

"Stop!" I tore myself from Xerxes to ram my shoulder against Thorn's chest, lest he try something like that again. Thorn stumbled against the door, then pushed back. Monroe did his best to catch me despite his hands being tied, grimacing as my body slammed against his.

Thorn reached for a dagger at his belt.

"That's enough!" called Xerxes.

I hadn't known Nelians could be so quick to rely on weapons for anything besides the wild boars. Nelians didn't kill. They weren't supposed to.

We stumbled into the cabin to find flames already roaring in the fireplace, a boiling clay pot of stew above it, an array of vegetables partially chopped on the table. They must have abandoned the meal when they'd heard the boar. Xerxes shoved me toward a chair and Thorn forced Monroe to sit beside me.

"Head back into the forest and take what you can from the kill," he said to Thorn. "Remember we have *guests* and bring an extra portion."

Thorn grunted but exited without a word.

Monroe's breathing was ragged and my stomach churned as I looked at him. He was only here because of me. He hated me, yet he'd put himself in harm's way for me. "He needs treatment," I said. Monroe shook his head glumly, but the confidence he seemed to try to convey didn't reach his eyes.

"That was quite a tumble you two took," Xerxes said. "But I'm afraid I can't trust you not to attack us. You're with a *human*."

"I'm not here to hurt you!" I shouted. "I was *worried* about you—"

"*You* were worried about *me*?" He laughed hollowly. "You left me." His voice went quieter.

My mouth grew impossibly dry. "You gave me no choice."

"And now our bond has weakened." Xerxes' chest hitched. "How? How could you walk away from what we had? How could you make it so that the love between us—"

"Has faded," I finished for him.

Xerxes' lips flattened but couldn't stop the sneer that worked its way onto his face. Before he could say anything, though, Monroe let out a small grunt and fell sideways onto the bed.

"Monroe!" I shrieked.

Sighing, Xerxes withdrew his dagger and stomped across the room.

"Don't—" I started, but Xerxes simply cut the vines tying Monroe's wrists. He grabbed hold of Monroe's legs and lifted them up so Monroe lay down. I stood beside my one-time lover, gazing down at the injured leader of the R.I.A.

Xerxes put a hand to his forehead, then recoiled.

"What is it?" I said, my heart thundering.

"He feels… strange."

With his dagger, Xerxes cut the cords from my wrists. That

hadn't lasted long. I didn't stop to thank him, though, and felt Monroe's forehead. With relief, I didn't feel too much heat or anything strange.

His skin. The feel of human skin was softer than a Nelian's. I supposed few Nelians would know such a thing. "That's normal for a human," I said to Xerxes, but I didn't take my eyes off Monroe. "Where does it hurt?" I asked him.

"My back," he grunted.

Carefully, I rolled him over, pleading silently with Xerxes for help. He sighed and added his strength to mine.

The back of Monroe's shirt was ripped and dirty, red seeping through the fabric. Rolling the shirt up carefully, I kept peeling even as Monroe let out a sharp intake of air.

A short, pointed stick punctured his flesh. I gasped and covered my mouth.

"It's nothing you haven't seen after an encounter with a boar before," said Xerxes, stepping forward. "I'll rip it out."

"Wait!" I said.

"What is it—" started Monroe, but he screamed as Xerxes yanked out the stick.

A pool of blood formed on Monroe's back. Xerxes tossed the sharp object aside. "Get the bandages."

Yes. I needed to keep my composure. I ran to the cupboard where I'd kept such things and found it adequately stocked. Medicine, spices, condiments, and even my concoction of plant oils for sleeping darts was still half-full. The mixture brought on a near-instant sleep and was quite useful when taking on a raging boar, though I did not see any darts left in the cupboard. Sometimes I used it on myself to allow those around me to use their abilities, but I didn't care for the way it made me dizzy afterward.

I handed the plant silk bandages and cleaning cloths to Xerxes.

"Water," he said. "Use the cooking water."

As if I wouldn't know such a thing. Standing next to the bucket beside the fireplace, though, I realized I hadn't grabbed a ladle or anything else to hold it in. Maybe I really wasn't thinking.

The thought of Monroe's suffering removed all sense of the focus.

Then there was the fact that my other three men were out there, lost…

My men. As if Monroe were one of them. As if I could stay with the rest of the R.I.A. after this was all over. As if they'd even want me and my poison that nullified their powers.

Focus, I reminded myself, and I scooped the water with a wooden ladle from the table.

Xerxes worked quickly, his hand steady as always, his previous experience helping those injured in boar attacks clearly on display. My heart melted as he cleaned the wound and wrapped the bandages around Monroe's shoulder, keeping the wound sealed up tight, then went to work cleaning at the other scratches, his touch gentle around the forming bruises.

Despite everything, Xerxes was still… kind. His assault on Earth hadn't destroyed his true nature completely.

Monroe's breathing slowed until finally Xerxes stepped back and Monroe's eyes fluttered shut, falling into the steady rhythm of sleep.

"Thank you," I said hoarsely as Xerxes got up and tossed the cloths in the wash bin.

He stared at me. I stared at him.

The attraction between us was not gone. But it was clouded with all that had passed between us. Diminished in the face of the stronger bonds I'd felt with the R.I.A. almost instantly.

But he was the first man I'd ever loved. The first man who'd truly disappointed me.

Xerxes seemed to feel the brunt of my thoughts then, shaking his arms at his side as he moved out of his unnatural stillness. He rinsed his hands in the washing basin and then stepped to the table full of half-prepared vegetables, picking up a knife and chopping.

He'd often cooked alongside me during my long, lonely periods keeping to myself in this place.

"Why have you come?" Xerxes asked after a bit, the chop, chop, chop of his knife on an onion punctuating the silence hanging between us.

"Flora told me you'd escaped from under the guards' eye," I answered. "I barely had time to consider it before I found myself here—"

"With him," he said. The stew water bubbled over the fire, sizzling as it turned to steam once it met the flame.

"And three others," I admitted, knowing I might need help to locate them.

Xerxes slammed the knife down on the table. "And do you feel for them what you feel for this one?"

That was what bothered him. He could feel the attraction between Monroe and me. Though I could not say if it was mutual. I had not experienced enough of humans' love to know such a thing. Aurora and her non-Nelians lovers did not exude quite the same level of aura between one another, for example, that I felt from my brother to her. But I did not doubt her affection for them. Humans were strange, hard-to-understand creatures at times.

"Yes," I said, knowing I could not hide this truth if he ever saw me beside them.

"And yet *our* bond has weakened," Xerxes said, running a hand over the smooth dark green hair at his scalp. The movement ruffled the ends of the loose lock hair, which danced over his broad shoulder. A mimicry of a smile danced across his lips, the feeling not reaching his eyes.

I stumbled backward, the table working its way into the flesh at the small of my back. He was right. It was there—there was no denying it—but it was faded.

I hadn't known that was possible until I'd seen him again.

Nelians found new loves, new connections, but I hadn't heard of anyone breaking off old ones.

Not if they'd felt the bond, the *need*. It was why I'd avoided being where he was—I hadn't trusted myself to be able to stop it.

"You're the only one I've ever felt such a connection with before," said Xerxes, taking my hands in his. He examined them. They were rough and scratched, though they seemed unblemished compared to the injuries Monroe had suffered keeping me from the worst of harm. He put a scratched knuckle gently to his lips. "But I know I have done much to betray that love," he said softly. "I just want you to know... I *need* you to know... I am sorry. I never meant to pay the price of the love we had."

I didn't know what to say as he went back to chopping the vegetables, unnaturally focused on that work. He'd used me —and my powers—to try to take over the Earth his way. He'd betrayed my brother, the true ruler of our people.

But I'd loved him. I'd almost wed him once. Though now I could never picture such a thing, never picture returning here to a life without my men.

My men.

I didn't get to tell Xerxes I forgave him—I wasn't sure if I did. Forgiveness was a strange thing for a Nelian, a thing I'd learned about more in depth on Earth, a thing wholly unfamiliar to me.

"If you won't go back to the heart of Nelia no matter what," I said, "then there was no reason for me to come here."

"Stay," Xerxes said quietly. "With me. Here. Far from our community. Away from the cold, unblinking stares of those who think us *different*, who are disappointed with us."

Monroe's steady breathing filled my ears, sent a jolt of warmth from my head to my toes.

"I won't," I said. "There's somewhere I can do some good." Second Hope. Even if my men wouldn't have me, to be on the same planet as them, to be doing something *useful* with my power… I could be content.

"And where is that?" Xerxes snapped. "On a polluted, dying human planet?"

"Yes," I said, and I explained Second Hope to him—the Natch children, the suffering they were in. "They're different, too. Disappointments to those around them. If I can only convince their human guardians, stay with them—"

"You'd leave me to help a handful of human children?" Xerxes' guttural growl was louder than the clank of the knife he threw back on the table. "You think I'd be content to stay here without you? I was *waiting* for you. *Looking* for you."

"I won't stay here!"

Xerxes grabbed me by both wrists and shook me. "Don't lie to me, then! You want to go back to be with *him*! With your filthy human lover!"

"Nelians don't *lie*—"

"Don't tell me that! We both know it's not true." Xerxes dropped his grip on me and clutched the table instead. "We speak around the truth sometimes—that's how I made use of my power at all. Pulling the truth, *forcing* the truth from those around me. But you, I cannot force to speak."

"Alanna…?" Monroe said quietly. His eyes were still shut, and I couldn't tell if he was speaking in his sleep or concerned about me.

"Enough," said Xerxes. "Enough, Alanna. Enough."

Thorn returned then, the cabin unbearably quiet as we worked to make sustenance. Xerxes conferred with him quietly outside the cabin, but strain my ears as I might, I couldn't pick up what they were saying.

Then they were back, Xerxes adding some of the meat to the stone slab over the fire, Thorn heading to the cupboard to store the extra slabs of meat and pull out jars of spices that he added to the boiling stew over the fire after an inordinate amount of rummaging around.

Thorn's hard stare at me and Monroe's sleeping form as

he went to work finishing the meal said enough—he didn't like us being free, but he didn't say anything to contradict the decision of the Nelian in whom he'd put his faith and fealty.

We ate quietly together, and I roused Monroe just long enough to get him to eat just a little of my stew. There was plenty since Xerxes and Thorn saved the meat for themselves, bypassing the stew altogether, gorging themselves on the flesh of the beast until they claimed to have room for nothing more.

I'd try once more in the morning to convince Xerxes to go home. And then, if he would not be moved, I would convince him to let us go. Or I would fight my way out if need be. I had to find the others—get back to the heart of Nelia myself and find a pair to teleport us back to Earth.

But for now, I wouldn't argue the point. I would stay. Let Monroe rest. Just for tonight. I was *tired* after eating. So tired.

The three of us lay on makeshift bedding made of blankets on the floor that evening, Monroe taking up the bed.

And when I woke, the day well underway, the two other Nelians were gone, the lingering smoke from the charred wood beneath the clay cooking pot the only sign they'd ever been here.

CHAPTER TWENTY

My hand clutched the blanket I'd used to make a makeshift bed as I took in the empty space around me. My ears strained for sounds of movement, but all they picked up were the sounds of Monroe's gentle breathing.

My first duty was to him. I stood and put a hand to his forehead and let out a hitched breath—it was the right temperature, not overly warm or clammy to the touch.

I needed to examine his wound, but I didn't want to disturb his sleep. And then there was the matter of finding the rest of the R.I.A. now that we were no longer under the watchful eye of Xerxes and Thorn—and then finding where they had gone off to.

Xerxes was a truth-puller, a Nelian with a rare power like me. Thorn could produce vines from his palms and bend them to his will, as most Nelians could. Without two portal-creators to assist them, though, they wouldn't be able to travel to Earth. So where had they gone?

A hand seized mine in its sturdy grip—Monroe had awoken, had found me kneeling at his bedside.

"Where are they?" he asked, his voice stern—stronger than it had been the day before.

"I don't know," I answered truthfully. "I woke and they

were gone. If they've not gone back to the heart of Nelia, then they're wandering the endless forest. There are simply no other shelters like this to be found anywhere—everything my people could possibly need is within a short distance to the heart of Nelia."

"What about other cities?" Monroe grunted as he lifted himself up on one elbow, his grip on my hand going slack. "Other Nelians?"

"There are no other cities. No other Nelians."

He chuckled darkly. "You speak to us about preserving a planet when your own is so much easier to take care of—because the population of a single city can't possibly do the damage that seven billion people can, even if you did have all our technology."

"I don't know if we *could* have all your technology without your seven billion people," I pointed out. "Or at least a significant number of them. I've been researching your world while living in it, Monroe. The cycle of production, of cash money to lay claim to food and a roof over your heads. The extra cash money that goes into buying others' products, which sustain those workers' habitats and ability to eat."

"Capitalism in a nutshell," he said. He winced as he sat up straighter on the bed and this time I stood to slide next to him, to offer my body as full support.

"I need to check your wound."

He grunted and I rolled up his tattered shirt. "It doesn't seem a fair system," I said as I helped him remove his arm from the sleeve. He bit down on his lips, making the succulent things turn into a thin line as I slowly peeled the bandages away. "With so many of your planet's people struggling—some without homes and many more without enough food to sustain themselves—when there are an extremely small number in giant dwellings with more cash money than they know what to do with."

"Are you Nelians taking on capitalism now?" He winced as the last of the bandage peeled away, taking a small amount of dried blood with it, opening part of his wound anew. "How's it look?"

"How you would want it to at this stage." There was no sign the wound was turning to infection. Xerxes had cleaned it well. Monroe was a stranger to him, and Xerxes had known he had my heart. The reminder of Xerxes' kindness made me feel just a little more broken inside. I got up to dispose of the bandages and wrap him with a new set.

"It's easy to pass judgement on a place from a moral high ground," Monroe said as I returned to the bedside. He gazed toward the nearest window—not made of glass like it would have been on his world, just an opening left in the walls of the cabin, an opening covered in green. The gentle rustling of leaves from the forest around us penetrated the silence between us. "I get it. It's beautiful here. But Earth… Earth is so much more complicated."

"I know," I said, and it was true. Cleaning around the wound, I wrapped it up once more.

"What's that made of?"

"Vines," I answered. "We dry them and cut them for many uses."

"You're a resourceful people, I'll give you that."

"As are you," I said. "So many of you. You find an objective and you focus on it, letting the state of the world at large slip away from your sight." I tied the bandage off. "I can understand that. What I don't understand is why you won't let us help you with those things you cannot do yourself."

Monroe gripped my hand as I pulled it away. "We're not children."

"I know," I said, my core vibrating, growing steadily sleeker and damp. My eyes darted shamelessly to his crotch, at the bulge I saw there, grown harder the longer I looked.

Dropping my hand, he gripped his knees, staring down at the floor. "Our world is flawed—it always has been. But *because* it's flawed, I've learned not to trust the word of anyone who claims they're just doing what's best for me, that I don't need to think for myself." He jutted his chin toward the blankets left on the ground. "Perhaps such an instinct could have come in handy around your Nelian friends. All it took was one man speaking a little differently than a king, and he gathered people around him to his cause, right?"

"You don't hurt people," I said, as much to convince myself as him. "For your beliefs—Xerxes does not enjoy the act of violence, but he was not as careful as my brother in ensuring the humans suffered little during his excursion to your planet."

"Don't be so sure I don't hurt people." Wincing, he flexed his arm nearest the wound. His knuckles popped white against his skin as he clenched his fist on his lap. "I will if I have to."

"But to do that, you'll have to be away from me," I said. The words left a sense of melancholy behind them in the air between us. It was my turn to offer him a flittering smile. "I won't let you use your powers to hurt even a little insect. Because I know you're better than that."

"You *know*, huh? We'll have to agree to disagree," he said gruffly. He moved to stand. "Come on. We have to find the others. They could be hurt, too. If not, why haven't they located us?"

He was right. An ache in my throat overtook me, but Monroe stumbled slightly and I had to jump up to offer him support. "You're in no condition," I said. "Stay here."

Monroe took a few shaky steps and leaned on the table. "No," he said sternly. He stood straighter, his eyes watering. It wasn't just the wound that hurt him, but the bruises—who knew what kind of other damage he had. I guided him back to the bed and he offered little resistance. He breathed deeply as he sat on the edge of it, then slammed a fist against the soft cushion beneath him. "I have to go." He shook his head. "We should never have come. If the others had objected, I should have *made* them stay on Earth."

"That sounds like someone telling others you know what's best for them."

He looked at me and chuckled. Then he started laughing harder, wincing all the while. He fell backward on the bed. "Oh, princess," he said. "If only you knew how badly you've turned my world upside down."

"I stopped you from putting my loved ones, my friends, in danger," I said. "But only for one night. That was all I could do with my nullification powers."

"You've done so much more than that," he said softly.

"I have?"

"Goddammit." Growling, he gritted his teeth. He seemed frustrated, and I still didn't understand what he was talking about. "Tell the truth."

"I always speak the truth," I said, though my conversation with Xerxes tugged at the back of my mind. Did I? Did all Nelians truly speak the truth or did we speak around it sometimes?

No matter. I would speak the truth to him. I had nothing more to hide.

"Was seducing my friends part of your plan?" he asked. "To get them on your side?"

"No, I had no such *plan*," I said. "But I will not deny the attraction I felt to every one of you the moment I met you. Such a thing is plain to see—as easy to sense as the warmth of a beam of sunlight on your face—for my people. I forget that it is not so for yours."

"Every one," Monroe said gruffly. "But you did not seduce me."

I rested a tentative hand on his bare abdomen. The muscles beneath it were solid, defined. "I do not *seduce*," I said. "I love. I give in to the love I feel as naturally as I breathe air." My fingers danced in circles over his abdomen and his muscles clenched, a quick shudder taking over his body. "But I would love you if you would let me. I would love you for all my life," I said, and though I thought of

179

Xerxes then, how I'd once spoken the truth of the same feeling toward him, I realized with sudden clarity that the attraction I'd felt for him had never been *this*. Had never been this strong. This unyielding. This unbreakable.

He'd been kind to me when few others had. He'd accepted me. There had been the faint scent of a bond between us.

That wasn't the same as this, this unruly, unyielding passion that I fought only out of respect for this man, out of the realization that I could not be so greedy as to demand my fourth love when I had already secured three.

Monroe stared up at me. His eyes softened, the muscles beneath my fingertips relaxing.

I opened my mouth and then shut it, jumping to my feet. "I should go," I said. "Stay here and rest—I'll be back as soon as I can with word of them."

I grabbed my belt with the daggers' sheaths from the corner of the room where I'd put it before going to sleep. Xerxes had never taken it from me.

"Alanna, wait," Monroe said as I reached for the doorknob and opened the door. "You can't go alone. Those giant pigs might still be out there. We need a plan."

But any plans were going to have to include making our way through the giant web of vines blocking our path forward.

CHAPTER TWENTY-ONE

"They trapped us!" I shouted. "Thorn must have waited until I was asleep and then wrapped the cabin with his vines when his power returned. How did we not wake as he worked?"

I ran back to the cupboard and found the jar of sleeping concoction empty. I growled. "They added a sleeping oil to the stew." As if only knowing that I'd consumed some could trigger the feeling, I suddenly felt unbearably nauseous. "*Sediment!*"

"I thought I was just tired because of the injury." Monroe let out a seething breath through his teeth. "But I was *out* like a light last night."

I pushed through my queasiness and tossed back my shoulders. "How long were we asleep?"

"I don't know. But that's beside the point now, isn't it?" He nodded toward the knives still on the table. "But they're not exactly geniuses, are they? Let's get to work and cut them." He picked one up, then grabbed hold of the nearest vine and began sawing at it. A guttural scream passed out from his lips as his back wound strained.

"You can't!" I said. "Your injury."

He ignored me and kept sawing, kept grunting, a sheen of

sweat appearing on his brow. I tried to follow suit, but it was hard, slow work.

"*Dammit!*" Monroe threw his knife to the ground and then grabbed a vine with both hands, trying to tear it in two. Nothing happened besides a patch of red leaking through his bandages.

"Stop!" I said, letting my own dagger clatter to the ground. "We can't do this. It'll take days and you're opening your wound."

"So what do you propose?" Monroe pounded a fist against the doorframe. "We just sit here—doing *nothing*? Hoping the guys find us and can get us out?"

Monroe's stomach growled and I took a deep breath. We had to take stock of what we had—what we *could* do. I went back to the cupboard. There were a few withering vegetables and some of the meat from the boar left as well, though that wouldn't last long without proper curing. And I had no intention of being here long enough to cure it.

"What are you doing?" Monroe asked, his stomach speaking louder than him. I took the food out of the cupboard and picked up another knife.

"Eventually, my brother will check here for me," I said, chopping greens to make salads for our belated first meal of the day. "Then we can look for the others."

"*They could be hurt,*" Monroe snapped.

"There's nothing we can do right now. Alarik can bring a force stronger than just you and I—"

"I can use my powers if you're unconscious."

"Lightning?" I asked.

"Lightning causes *fire*," he said. "A good, raging fire would take care of that mess outside."

"It would also burn the cabin down—and us with it," I pointed out. "Why do you think I didn't suggest setting them aflame to begin with?" Monroe's stomach growled once more, and my own joined him. "We must have been out a long time. We need food."

Monroe slapped a radish I'd been chopping off the table. "We *need* to get out of here."

"I can't go unconscious on command," I said. "They used up all the sleeping oil." I stared up at him. "But if you won't wait for us to gain our strength first, to have some sustenance as we go out traipsing around Nelia's endless forest to search, then knock me out again. You have my permission. Then rely on your lightning power after enough time passes and see if that actually manages to fix our problem."

Monroe took a step back, picked up the radish, and sighed, slamming it back on the table. "Eat. Sleep. If you don't sleep fast enough, we'll discuss knocking you out."

He grabbed for a knife and chopped. A small, uneven piece of the radish went flying across the room as his knife came down too harshly. "Guh!" he shouted, dropping the knife and shaking his hand out.

I stopped mixing greens and went to his side, taking his hand in mine. There was no sign of a cut at least—perhaps he'd pinched the skin with the handle.

Monroe stared down at me, his lips parting. Clearing his throat, he pulled away and focused down at the radish. The red skin chipped, the slices askew—it looked like it had been stabbed by a child during his first practice with a dagger.

"Again," I said, moving to roast some of the meat. I stoked the embers of the dying fire and added some of the wood beside it. "My nullification proves nothing but a hindrance. Useless."

"I would hardly call your powers useless," said Monroe. "For one, you forced me to slow down and not set the cabin on fire." He flexed his fingers. "It feels so weird not to be able to use my Natch abilities." He gestured toward the open door and the vines built around it. "But it's certainly useful against your enemies."

"And sometimes even your allies," I said, flipping the meat over with a stone poker. "Did you know about Lacey?" I asked.

"Lacey?" Monroe asked. "How do *you* know about her?"

"Bo told me. I met her."

He let out a disgusted sigh. "Of course. My team has dicks for brains since they met you." He took a seat and tapped his heel against the floor.

"You think I would hurt her?"

Monroe took another whack at the radish. He chopped with too much force and his knife got caught halfway. "Well, if you were our enemy, you might." He struggled to get the knife out. "Why would he—oh. You can take her powers away. Bo must have been really happy about that." He froze.

"Yes," I said. "Here." He yanked the knife free of the vegetable. I placed my hand over his and guided the knife into the vegetable in a smooth, measured motion. "Like this," I said, and he let me guide him. When we finished, he dropped the knife and traced smooth circles on my palm.

"Your skin *is* like rubber," he said.

I laughed. "You all keep saying that. That word sounds like it's not something nice."

He took hold of my wrist and yanked me closer. He wasn't wearing his shirt and my hip rubbed up against his other arm, the hardened bicep digging against me. "On you, it's beautiful," he whispered.

My jaw dropped open, my words lost on my tongue. Our breathing grew in sync in the relative quiet of the cabin, the crackling of the meat over the fire the only distraction.

"The meat," I said quickly, extracting myself from his grip to head toward the smoky meal over the fire. Using the poker, I flipped and watched until both sides of each piece were cooked, then I removed the meat from the rack that hung over the flames and put a slice on both of the wooden plates I'd set out for us on the table.

Monroe appeared behind me as I wrapped my hands in bandages to move the pot that had caught the meat's drippings to the hearth, then dig it into the dirt so the hot grease wouldn't catch fire.

"You know, humans put the Stone Age behind us tens of thousands of years ago. Metal has a lot of uses, like cooking, for one."

"I know," I said, unraveling the bandages from my hands. "Don't think I haven't noticed how much easier some things are there." I nodded, staring down at the bowl full of grease as the sizzling died down. "But our way works. And besides, we do not have this metal your people found on Earth." My nose wrinkled. "And though I can stand *that*, I'm not really a fan of the *plastic* you get from the oils in the Earth."

"You don't want plastic anywhere near an open flame anyway." He stood next to the fire. The flames flickered, casting dancing shadows over his face that saturated the crevice between my thighs.

His shirt was soaking in the basin, but I was in no hurry to give it back to him. It was in pieces anyway.

"Let's eat," I said, as much to distract myself as to satiate my growing *need*—for food, for him, for everything. I sprinkled his chopped radishes on our greens and placed those plates beside our portions of meat. "Then, once my hunger is satisfied, perhaps I can fall asleep and you will gain your powers after a time. If my brother doesn't appear by then, you can try to take the vines down. But be careful."

"It was a bad idea," he admitted. "But I can try to narrowly focus the bolt, see what happens." He dragged his chair beside mine so that instead of sitting across from me, he sat just around the corner of the table. He reached over the table to bring his plate to his new seat, flaunting his well-shaped muscles. My wooden fork dropped from my weak grip.

Monroe smiled just slightly. I so rarely saw smiles on his face like this one—genuine, radiant, confident, and not tinged with a sense of despair about his surroundings. It suited him.

"I thought you had to be unconscious for your abilities to wear off," he said, digging in to his first bite of greens. "Like knocked unconscious with force or drug. Sleep counts?"

"Sleep counts," I said, my voice trembling. He knew too much about me. Why was it I trusted him so—trusted them all so—when I knew they were still my friends' enemies? That was a foolish thought. I knew why. "But I don't fall asleep easily."

"Hmm."

We ate in silence. My stock of seasonings was still in the cupboard, and I'd used some to make the meat more palatable.

"This is delicious," Monroe said, and there was that bright smile again. "I wish you'd been in charge of the cooking last night."

The heat that flushed to my cheeks and then to somewhere far, far below wasn't from the fire.

"I wouldn't have put the sleeping concoction in the stew as a spice, for starters." Putting my fork down, I folded my hands together as I examined him. "You look better," I said.

"You look amazing," he said quietly.

That could not be true. I grasped at my hair, felt its wild, uncombed nature. My Earth clothes were dirty, torn in places and tattered. It was a far cry from playing dress-up when I'd dined with Rhett.

"You hate me," I said, and even then, some small part of me knew that wasn't the entire truth.

"I don't," Monroe said softly. He pushed his empty plate aside, and his lips pinched tightly together, but they were trembling as he gazed at me. "Not anymore. Not ever, not really. But I can't—we can't—"

"Don't." I moved a hand to rest atop his thigh. "Don't fight it. Please."

He chuckled, but it wasn't a happy laugh. "You're my enemy."

"I'm not," I said, though I'd just reminded myself he was mine. "If you don't hurt my friends, I'm not."

"You're a Nelian," he added. "And a *princess*."

I swallowed. "I am."

"And you've fucked my three best friends." His words were sharp, tinged with anger. He took a deep breath then. "I shouldn't care except—"

"You think I did it only to make them turn on you," I said.

"No." He ran his thumb over the back of my hand. Shivers wracked my body from such a small touch. "I'm sorry I ever accused you of such a thing." He rubbed his closely-cropped hair, the follicles practically nothing more than fuzz. It looked so soft. No Nelian had ever worn their hair like that before. I wanted to rub my fingers over it.

My fingers were already there before I realized it, and Monroe laughed, lighter this time, as I massaged his scalp. It tickled my skin and I freed my other hand from his so I could run fingers over his jaw, which was dotted similarly with the hair that grew on his head.

He let me massage his skin for a bit and then captured my wrists in his large hands. "I was jealous," he said. "Plain and simple. I never would have imagined you'd work your way through all of them and still I'd—"

I moved forward and kissed him quickly, firmly. His startled grin curled into a mischievous smile as he seized me back, pressing his lips against mine—more aggressive, hungrier.

We were both breathing harder when he broke the kiss.

"I love differently than many of you humans are used to," I said, my heartbeat thundering so wildly in my ears, I could hardly hear myself speak. "When I feel a *bond* with others, there grows room in my heart for all of them."

"The guys have been talking like some hippie commune thing is going on with you," he said. "That they'll *share* you—"

"I love all four of you," I said, watching the words take him aback. "If you love me—if you *want* me too… I will be your *hippie myun*."

"*Commune*." He snickered and then grew serious, his eyes piercing mine. "I want you," he whispered, then he crushed his lips to mine, taking my face in his hands gruffly—firmly but without hurting me. "So I *will* have you."

A fever raged from my core out to the very tips of my pointed ears.

"You know there's something we haven't tried to get you to fall asleep faster," he said, leaning forward to place his forehead against mine. He took a series of deep breaths that I echoed as the tingling consumed me at his proximity.

"What's that?" I asked, my heart beating so loud, I could almost hear it.

"Making sure you get plenty of exercise."

CHAPTER TWENTY-TWO

Part of me felt ashamed that when so much was unknown —where Xerxes was, the danger my brother and Earth friends were in, the condition the rest of the R.I.A. was in—my mind was so fully focused on the man in front of me.

But I *ached* for him, from my nub to the very tips of my fingers and toes.

And there was nothing we could even try until I fell asleep. There was only now. Only this moment.

Pushing his chair farther from the table, Monroe pulled me to straddle his lap. "I thought you hated me," I whispered into his ear.

"Never," he said, gnawing at my earlobe. His fingers caressed the pointed tip at the top, one of the sole visible differences between us. That and the green hair and his soft, soft fuzz. My own hands massaged his scalp again.

He moaned. "Why?" he said quietly. "Why, after all this time, when I've been so good at not being distracted, do I have to fall for someone who threatens to derail everything I believe in?"

My pulse thumped wildly. I had not set out to change their minds through my love, but if that was a consequence of it, I could hardly complain.

"Tell me what you would have us do so you would no longer view us as the enemy," I said between gentle kisses along his forehead. His hands roved down my back, cupping my butt cheeks.

"Not now," he said before his lips moved to my neck. "Right now, there's only this moment."

And then there truly was.

Monroe took hold of my shirt and rolled it up. "Lift your arms."

I obliged, and he removed my shirt, grunting at the pain in his back.

We sat there, flesh against flesh, Monroe's hands cupping my breasts as his thumbs moved in circles around each nipple.

"Do they taste like rubber?" he asked.

I giggled, resting my arms gently over his shoulders, avoiding the bandage at the shoulder blade. "I wouldn't know."

Launching forward, he took my left nipple into his mouth and bit down—hard, but just enough to make me cry out without causing true duress. His bite loosened and his tongue moved in circles, pebbling the nipple stiffer than I'd thought possible.

Instinctively, I squeezed my thighs tighter, trying to rein in the juices pooling between my legs. But with Monroe's legs on either side of mine, it was his thighs, his groin I squeezed.

He gasped, pulling back, craning his head backward as he shoved against his chair. The hardness in his pants punched up against the simmering wetness in my own.

"Get on the bed," he said, craning his neck back to face me, his breaths heavy and warm, as frequent as mine. "Now."

I stood on shaking limbs, then he followed suit and yanked me toward him, pressing my naked chest hard and overpoweringly against his own. He stared into my eyes for a moment, his brown irises as vibrant as soil itself.

Without another word, he smashed his lips to mine.

Fierce, commanding, each kiss was like wildfire, and it caused me actual pain to have to rip away and come up for air. He pushed his tongue greedily inside my mouth, his hands squeezing harder, moving down beneath the fabric of my leggings into the soft flesh of my rear. In sync, we moved to the bed.

He pulled his tongue from mine and pushed me to the cotton mattress. "You've been a bad girl. You've taken too long to get around to me," he said, his words punctuated by a guttural groan. "Haven't you?"

I gripped both of his strong, sturdy biceps. "I've been bad," I said, breathless.

He leaned forward, his hands on either side of me, his head tracing the curve of my arm up around my shoulder to my neck. "Bad girls get punished," he whispered. "But… *gently*. With great care." He pulled back, the temperature between us growing warmer with each of our heavy breaths. "And only bad girls who've been punished get rewarded."

The curl of his lips sparked a light within his eyes. "Tell me you're sorry, princess."

"I'm sorry," I said. My groin pulsated at the way he called me "princess." It wasn't how others said my title. The way he said it was more endearing, like a pet name.

He reached for the waist of my leggings. "You don't seem sorry."

His fingers danced around the hem of my leggings, dipping inside to the plush of green hair over my vulva. It was blazing and drenched in there, his two fingers coming out glistening after a quick plunge between my outer folds. The tease of the movement across my pleasure point left me frustrated. I arched my back. "I'm *sorry*!" I shouted.

"Sorry… What?" he asked.

I cocked my head quizzically, my mouth hanging open, ready to say anything, *do* anything to get this going, but not knowing what.

"When we're alone, princess," he said, "you'll address me as 'Daddy.'"

I choked, remembering this was a word some people on Earth called their fathers—usually very young children. And I had certainly never been close enough to my father—king of Nelia, the ruler who lost his powers in proximity to his own flesh and blood—to call him such a term of endearment.

"Not like your real daddy, princess," he snapped. "I'm your motherfucking boudoir *daddy*, and you will address me as such." He pushed one of my legs up and spanked my butt cheek. The crease between my legs was positively creamy now.

"I don't know what a *budoa* is," I said, breathless. "But I'm so sorry, Daddy, that I took so long." I squirmed under his gaze.

The slow smile that built on his face didn't warn me of how quickly he'd move, yanking at my pants until they came off both legs.

His fingers danced up the length of my legs, then stopped, hovering frustratingly on my thigh, so close but too far from my moist, eager entrance.

Still, his extremities came back sleek, coated with my wetness. He stuck them in his mouth and sucked—*hard*. "Beautiful. *Delicious*. Who knew a bad little princess could taste so good?" Straightening, he removed his own pants, grimacing slightly with the effort.

I leaned up on my elbows. "Do you need my help?"

His eyebrow arched. "Did I tell the princess she could lean up like that?"

"No," I said, plopping back down. I lifted my hands above my head, running them through my long, green hair as I squirmed. "I'm sorry, Daddy."

"Now you're getting the hang of it." He pulled down his *boxer pants*, and there was his phallus, erect and flaunting, calling out for my thighs to squeeze themselves around it. "Bone me, please, Daddy!" I called out.

192

"*Bone* you?" he chortled. I opened my mouth to speak, but he shook his head and leaned over, laying a gentle finger over my lips. "No, it's cute. It's just what my bad little princess would say." His finger trailed down my chin, down my neck, between my breasts. "Now tell me you're sorry you took my power away without telling me you were the one doing it," he said. Those fingers moved frustratingly closer to the mound at my apex.

I grinned. "I'm not sorry, Daddy."

He pulled his hand away. His lips were in a tight, tight line, but there was a sparkle in his eyes as he gazed down at me. "What did you just say to me, naughty girl?"

"I'm *not* sorry, Daddy."

"Oh, that's what I thought." He took hold of my waist and flipped me over fast, tugging on me until my rear was anchored up in the air. He shuffled onto the bed behind me, resting on his knees and making the mattress rock beneath us. "Bad little princesses get their asses spanked," he said. "Are you sure you want to be so naughty?"

"I am, Daddy," I said, clenching my fists together as I arched some more, the stretching making my muscles sore, but my body afire.

He slapped my butt cheek—hard. It stung, but it drove me wild all the same. I bit down on my lip as he did it again.

"Bad little princess, what do you say?" His finger traced down around the flesh of my rear, to the slit between them, massaging my clitoris and making my toes curl. He spanked again. "I didn't hear you."

"I didn't say anything."

He spanked me again. And again. The sounds coming out of my mouth were guttural, deeper than I thought possible, the area between my legs sleeker, shimmering with each moment his skin made unyielding contact with mine.

I said nothing for a long while as his slaps grew faster, *harder*.

I screamed. It hurt, but it *felt so good*. "I'm sorry, Daddy," I said at last, my core about to burst.

"Good girl." Monroe seized my hips in both hands. "Here's your reward."

His head dipped, his tongue slithering through my folds, dancing over my entrance, slicking up to my clitoris and sending a wicked shudder throughout my body. I gasped and almost lost the strength in my thighs and arms to keep me up, but Monroe squeezed harder, pushing up on my hips as his tongue worked as if he were born with such a Natch ability. I let out a quick little peal of laughter between moans as I thought that—knowing if there were ever such a Natch ability, I would never be awake to experience it.

He pulled back. "Is this funny, princess?" He leaned forward and stuck his tongue into my tunnel, pushing through greedily, sending a new coat of slickness out to meet him.

"Yes!" I gasped, not even meaning that to be the answer to his question.

He pulled out and chuckled. "Oh, we'll see what a naughty little princess finds funny, won't we?" He pushed down on my arched back so my rear was lower and guided it firmly to line up with his *boner*. It danced teasingly at my entrance, sliding in between the folds and rubbing vigorously across my apex. "Is this funny, princess?" he purred from behind me, his voice deep and exacting.

"No," I said, then I gasped again. "But please keep doing it!"

"Please, *what*, you naughty little princess?"

"Please, Daddy," I breathed. I ground against him, shoving my rear tightly against his chest. Even as he winced at the pressure, he pushed back, slipping his *boner* in and out along my folds. Moisture was dripping down my thighs now.

"Good girl," he said, and he shifted back just slightly to plow his stalk through my entrance. I yelled, a jolt of wildness settling into my bones as I kept screaming out in joy, not caring even if it drew wild boars to our door.

"Yes!" I screamed. "Yes, yes, *budoa* Daddy!"

He obliged, impaling harder, going deeper, and then pulling back, smacking my butt cheeks as he did. Harder, deeper, back, and a smack. We settled into a rhythm, my limbs positively shaking from the movement, the only thing keeping me from collapsing his strong and steady grip on my breast from below.

At last he shuddered inside me, and I exploded as well, my throat going sore with the sounds ripping past my tongue. I collapsed, utterly spent, but he held me up. "Hang in there, bad little princess," he said between labored breaths. Kissing my shoulder, down my back, he finally pulled out and let me fall flat against the bed.

Without another word, my *budoa* Daddy pulled me against his chest, his arms encircling me from behind. Our labored breathing slowed and the dull light of the dying fire grew weaker until at last I fell asleep, the warm touch of his hands on my skin the last sensation to go.

CHAPTER TWENTY-THREE

I woke to the sound of thunder roaring in my ears—and cut short the moment my eyes opened.

The sole pillow from the bed was over my head. Rubbing my eyes, I sat up slowly, taking in the sight of Monroe—clothed once more, though his shirt was torn and wrinkled—standing in the open doorway.

A sizzling, pungent smoke poured in between the vines covering the door to the outside.

He shook his arms out in front of him again and then turned to look over his shoulder. "Oh. You're awake. I tried to muffle the noise—"

"I should have had you render me unconscious again," I said.

He grimaced. "I don't think it's a good idea for you to get knocked unconscious so often." He put one hand on his hip. "I'm sorry I did that to you before. I didn't know sleeping was an option."

"An unreliable one," I said, gesturing around me. I caught Monroe staring at my bare chest and a smile fluttered across my lips despite everything. "It's okay. I asked you to last time." I got up to find my clothes. They'd been scattered throughout the cabin, but Monroe must have gathered them up and folded them on one of the chairs at the table.

"It was never going to work anyway," he said, staring at the sizzling vines in front of him. "My powers are too dangerous in confined spaces like this. You're right. I could have set the whole cabin on fire." He walked over to the fireplace and stoked it. He must have started it up again after I'd fallen asleep. "Same thing if we try burning the vines down with fire. Too unruly. More likely to hurt us than help."

Fully clothed, I marched over to the doorway to peer through. The smoke was dying now. I grabbed hold of the nearest vine and tugged at it. "I can see a tear in the vine on the outer layer," I said.

Monroe came up behind me, sending a shiver down my spine. His chest pressed against my back as he peered beside me. "Yeah, I was aiming to call the lightning at the very outermost layer," he said. "Figured it was safest that way."

"It was only a moment," I said, turning and finding myself embraced in his arms, "but I got to witness your Natch abilities. *Feel* the power you called to you." My fingers danced around his collarbone as I leaned in. "It was incredibly attractive."

Monroe squeezed me and laid his lips on my forehead. "I didn't think I needed my Natch abilities to be *that*."

"No, you don't, Daddy," I whispered, though he was nothing, nothing like my father.

"Good girl," said Monroe quietly as he took hold of my chin. His lips pressed against mine softly, but hungrily, stirring an ache inside me all over again.

We kissed for a few moments until the sounds of voices rung out through the forest at a distance. "This way! Yes! I can't use my vines. She's here."

"Alarik!" I called, pushing back. "It's my brother," I added, patting Monroe's chest.

His pectoral muscles clenched as he spoke in a carefully controlled manner. "Great. Just great."

It was indeed a great thing to have been found. "Alarik! Brother!" I called, pressing myself against the vines.

I peered through the hole as Alarik approached, Zander the Renegade leader and Torynt, Kouta, and Lila behind him, as well as several Nelian warriors and… Flora caught between two of them. She looked terrified. What had happened?

"Flora!" I shouted. "Three of the others who came with me —we got separated! Have you seen them?"

"They're well, princess," she said, but Alarik cut her off with a wave of his hand.

Alarik rushed to the growth and reached a hand toward mine. Our fingers grazed. "Thank the mother you are okay." But the sense of relief clear in his expression vanished as his lips grew pinched, his eyes narrowed. I looked over my shoulder to find a similar expression on Monroe's face.

I turned back to Alarik. "Why is Flora being held captive like that?"

"Your R.I.A. friends are back on Earth and tracked us down to explain everything they could," my brother said. Relief flooded through my entire body and Monroe slackened beside me. "They remembered her name and when we located her, she told us everything. Including the fact that she, Tianah, and Renaya helped Xerxes flee to Earth after they sent your *lovers* home. Though she doesn't know where on Earth Xerxes may have gone."

Monroe's growl behind me made me tense.

"What?" I asked. "*Why* would they send him there?"

"We just wanted him gone," said Flora, who straightened her back between the two guards who had her held tight. "He does not belong here." Her eyes sharpened as they narrowed on me. "Some Nelians simply don't." I hadn't known she'd harbored quite this level of distaste for me and my own abilities.

I'd thought she'd wanted to *help* Xerxes. She'd made it seem as if *others* wanted Xerxes gone, not her.

She'd… lied. Or hidden the truth. It was the same thing, really, now that I realized that.

"Quiet," Alarik snapped. "You do not speak for my kingdom." He turned back to me. "I'm not worried about him. Or Thorn. I tasked Normak with finding out where they've gone. He will alert me if either causes an issue on Earth."

He seemed so *prepared* for this.

"You knew Xerxes would leave Nelia?" I asked.

"I thought it a possibility," he said. "I just didn't know which of my people he would tempt to help him." He glared at Flora. "Thorn was little surprise, but the others…"

Monroe appeared beside me at the hole, his arm pressing against mine. "Are my people injured?"

"The R.I.A.?" asked Zander, speaking up for the first time since their arrival. Torynt waved at me, then he turned his hand so that his thumb stuck up. He pointed to Monroe and wriggled his eyebrows. Lila elbowed him. "I don't know. I didn't exactly ask them if they needed a mint and a pillow," Zander continued.

"They're fine," Lila added. "Waiting for you downtown."

"I want to go back," I said. "To Earth."

"And to your array of traitor lovers, I presume." Alarik sighed. "Can you get them to call off their efforts to take us down once and for all? It's like swatting an insect, I assure you, but it is a truly aggravating insect."

Monroe slammed a fist against the nest of vines. "We tried to negotiate with you without letting anyone get hurt, but you wouldn't listen. So listen to me now. If you think what you're doing on *my* planet is something I'm going to just sit back and let happen—"

I grabbed hold of his face and turned it toward mine, planting a long, steady kiss on his lips.

When I pulled away, Monroe's gaze darted to the ground. "Princess," he said quietly, this time submitting to *my* command.

"We're going to have to wait until you fall asleep," Alarik

said, ignoring Monroe's outburst. My lover's hands clenched into fists at his side at the sleight. "It'll be quicker work if we can knock these vines aside with new ones."

"Render me unconscious," I said to Monroe. "Then take me back to Earth." I spoke the second part louder so Alarik could hear me.

He nodded. "Very well. We'll rest here until the effects wear off."

"No." Monroe's eyebrows scrunched together. "I won't do that to you again."

He hadn't even hesitated the first time. "It's all right," I said to him, cradling his cheek. The short, short hair there felt so much like the soft hair on his scalp. "You did it painlessly last time. Please."

Monroe looked through the hole to Alarik, who gestured to either side of him. "We can do nothing until she's been unconscious for a time," he said. "The sooner we work, the sooner you are both on Earth."

Monroe sighed and planted another kiss on my forehead. "All right," he said, guiding me to the bed.

"I'm sorry," he added, his shoulders tensing as he raised his arm, his hand a stiff straight line.

There was a thunk on my neck. The last thing I knew before everything went dark was not the feel of the bed beneath me, but the sturdy, loving grip of Monroe's arms.

"I love you," he said—unless I was just dreaming it.

FOR THE SECOND TIME IN WHAT FELT LIKE A VERY SHORT WHILE, I woke up disoriented, the sense of something crackling in the air and then cutting out abruptly.

"Hello, princess." The words should have sent shivers of arousal down my spine, but I knew the voice wasn't the one I ached for—though it was familiar nonetheless. "Torynt...?" I sat up. I was on a bed in what looked like a human abode.

He cracked his knuckles. "The one and only. I was playing around with a little tornado on my palm when whoosh, it just vanished. I guessed that meant Sleeping Beauty was waking from her slumber."

I rubbed my forehead. "How long have I been asleep?"

He counted items off the fingers on his hands. "Long enough for us to twiddle our thumbs out in that mighty Nelian forest waiting for our powers to come back, then for us to use said powers to push those vines away, then for those hot Nelian chicks to create a portal again, then for us all to come back to Earth, then for us to split up and drive you back here, then for a change in shift watching over you—"

I clamped a hand over his endless counting fingers. "Where's Monroe?"

"Hotshot R.I.A. guy?" His eyebrow darted up and down. "Sorry, I don't know my enemies on a first-name basis."

I stared pointedly at him until he actually shirked back somewhat. "Yeah, him," he continued. "Veras was insistent they escort him to meet up with his friends downtown. Without you."

My stomach hardened and spots seemed to flash in my vision as I thought about how they were gone. Away from me. How my friends would keep insisting on keeping us apart.

"Where's my brother?" I asked. "Xerxes?"

Torynt scratched his cheek. "Big brother elf king is conferring with his soldiers to find out where the other big bad elf might have gone. Don't worry about it. I *think* they have it under control."

Torynt didn't seem so certain. I supposed I could expect as much, considering what Xerxes had done the last time he'd been on Earth.

A hard knock on the door startled both Torynt and me. Without even waiting for either of us to speak, the door whapped open. Lila's lips pinched as she took me in. "You were supposed to tell Zander as soon as she awoke."

"Give me a break," said Torynt. "She woke up like two seconds ago. I thought you'd all notice it anyway. Losing powers and all?"

"Not all of us whittle time away playing with ourselves," Lila snapped. "Do you think I just teleport around the house for fun?"

"Right," Torynt said coolly. "But I thought if you and Kouta were left alone, maybe he was using his water streams like little massaging kisses all over your naked body—"

"Shut it," said Lila, stomping into the room. I realized my clothes had been changed—I now wore a new set of soft, blue pants—*yogi* pants, I think Lila had called them once—and a soft blue long-sleeved top that matched it in feel and look. "Your brother needs you *now*," she said.

My breath caught in my throat.

"Who died?" Torynt asked, chuckling. Then the smile fell off his face. "No, seriously, what happened?"

"Got a call from Zander." Lila tugged me to my feet. Kouta appeared in the doorway, a set of keys jingling in his hand. "Aurora is missing. She was last seen *with the R.I.A.*"

My ribs squeezed tightly in my chest as a wave of nausea soared through me.

CHAPTER TWENTY-FOUR

Lila continued to explain as we descended the stairs. "Aurora and Chastity saw the R.I.A. leader off to his friends and then went their separate ways downtown. Aurora was supposed to meet up with Roulette, but the former never showed. Jayden is pissed at Chastity for ever leaving her alone, but apparently, Aurora had been insistent she *didn't need a guard dog*." She scoffed.

"So why do you think that means the R.I.A. has her?" I slipped on some shoes—they fit well enough, so they would do. I headed for the door.

"They could have easily followed her after they parted ways," said Lila. "And hostage-taking is just about the only thing they have in their playbook."

"You're wrong!" I said, not bothering to look behind me as I raced outside.

"Alanna," said Kouta, trailing after me. "Wait up!"

I looked both ways. I didn't recognize where I was. The Renegades moved too often and I had explored this city too infrequently for me to figure out where we were.

Kouta reached my side and jangled the keys. "We're taking the car."

Of course. I'd run out without thinking, my quivering muscles making each step harder than it ought to have been.

I wouldn't believe my men had become my enemies once more. Not after everything we'd been through together. I had to find them, to find Aurora—to figure out what had happened.

Torynt took hold of my arm and dragged me toward the car. I realized with a start that I had still just been standing there and Kouta and Lila had climbed into the *beeacal*.

"Should we even be taking her with?" Lila asked, though not unkindly. I was quite used to comrades debating whether or not my presence's benefits outweighed the drawbacks.

"None of us can use our powers for an hour now anyway," said Kouta, making the car shake with a roar as he brought it to life.

"I need to be there," I said, clearing my throat so they would hear me. Any other mission and I would defer to their judgement, but these were *my* men. *My* brother-consort sister.

My breath hitched. Was it possible that they had tried to take a hostage again? Would I ever be free of the guilt, the shame of loving those who stood in the way of my loved ones' happiness?

That was why I'd preferred solitude to begin with. I couldn't trust my own heart to keep me steady.

But no. No, they wouldn't. They might not have agreed with my brother, but they'd seen the folly of their methods by now.

A small crackle sounded from the backseat and Lila drew the *tech* bracelet Veras had given each of the Renegades—though Torynt was only putting his own on now, drawn out from a pocket—to her lips. "Zander?"

Zander could only telepathically communicate with people other than those he'd truly bonded with when he had the gift of Aurora's boost. And when the people he was communicating with weren't suffering the ill effects of my nullification. He could also project an image of himself to speak with people far from him, so I'd heard, but he couldn't do that so long as I was around them.

"I figure Alanna is up since I can't project into HQ," came Zander's voice from the communicator. "Is she with you?"

"I am," I said, leaning forward to be heard.

"We're on our way," said Lila.

"*No,*" Zander snapped quickly. "Keep her away from Veras HQ. We might need to send her in wherever those assholes have holed up, but it's best the rest of us retain our abilities."

"The R.I.A. didn't do this!" I shouted, ready to speak up in their defense, but my speech was lost as Kouta quickly moved the car in front of another, causing it to let out a shrill, loud sound, almost like a wild boar of Nelia.

"Take it easy," Torynt said. "Wherever we go, we want to get there in one piece."

"*Dammit,*" came Zander's quiet voice over the comm.

I reached for my phone in my back pocket, only I realized I wasn't wearing what I had been before. I must have left it back at the Renegades' temporary HQ.

"Any activity?" Zander asked again, but his voice was fainter, like he was speaking to someone with him, not to us.

Lila and Kouta exchanged a look and nodded. "We're heading to the park by the beach," she said. "Close enough that I can warp us to just about anywhere in town when needed."

"Only *after* you drop Alanna off somewhere else entirely," Zander said bitterly. "Alanna!" he called out louder, though I had no communicator of my own. "What do you know about these punks? What do we have on them?"

"*Have* on them?" I repeated. I sort of understood what he meant and I wasn't sure I liked it.

"Who can we use as a hostage to make them give back the love of my life—and the mother of your own future ruler?"

Hostage.

Bella. Drake.

Lacey…

Bo's worst fear, his enemies knowing about the one he loved the most.

The fear he'd trusted me with.

Torynt knew about the bar, though. I'd told him. And he'd told Lila, who had been nearby to pick me up. There was no hiding it.

Torynt looked to me, observing me, his mouth slightly hung open.

"There's a bar kind of out in the middle of nowhere outside of town," he spoke into his own communicator when I didn't. "They were hiding there. I suppose that means they got along with the people who worked there?"

"We don't need hostages!" I shouted. "We need to find the R.I.A. They didn't do this!"

Zander ignored me. "Head to that bar, then. Let me know when you're there." The communicator crackled and then went silent.

With another loud squeal and a few more angry boar-like cries, Kouta directed the car in the opposite direction, flinging us back and forth tightly against our *chair belts*. Then we were off again.

———

It was quite a while later that we arrived at Drake's. There weren't any cars parked outside. True, Bella had told me that when the sun was up, there were fewer customers, but the place seemed unnaturally quiet, unnaturally still.

I dragged my feet outside the car as Torynt and Kouta charged ahead. "It's locked!" Torynt shouted as he tried to open the door. Kouta tried and also failed. "Shouldn't they be open?" Torynt continued.

"Not if the R.I.A. thought ahead and got their allies into hiding." Lila growled from where she leaned against the front of the car. "Bastards!" she cried, kicking at the thin metal exterior.

"Hey, hey," said Torynt, jogging up beside her. "Don't take it out on the Charger."

No. If they weren't here, I couldn't prove their innocence.

And I *would* prove it. I had to.

The communicators crackled to life. "Update?" came Zander's curt voice.

"The place is closed," Lila said into her communicator.

"Yeah, well, that doesn't mean we can't bust a few windows and climb in and find out," Torynt muttered. He searched near his feet and picked up a rock. I laid a hand on his wrist. I didn't want those kind humans—the kind of Typicals who clearly accepted Natches without issue at that, meaning they weren't the Renegades' enemies—to be involved at all if I could help it.

I leaned forward toward Torynt's wrist and he had to drop his rock and push a button on his device so I could speak into it. "Where's my brother?" I asked.

"Gone back to Nelia," Zander said. "Coming back with warriors to show the R.I.A. the full might of the enemies they just insisted on making of us." He growled. "Before they were insects. Now they're a motherfucking swarm and we need to get the exterminators in."

Air got stuck in my narrowing throat.

"Easy," said Kouta, catching me. I hadn't realized I'd started to wobble.

"Whoa, whoa, princess," said Torynt, and again the title stabbed me in the heart as I thought of Monroe calling me the same back at the cabin. He turned to his communicator. "Zander, you know she's, like, in love with half of them?"

"All of them!" I said, leaning on Kouta to stand up.

Torynt's eyebrows shot up, but he grinned. "Look at you, princess. Making friends on Earth."

Lila rolled her eyes. "Not helping, Wind-Brain."

But Zander hadn't heard everything we'd said to each

other—I was just realizing that unlike a phone, the things at their wrists required someone to push a button to be heard.

"Alarik is quite aware," said Zander. "And he's said they've crossed a line. I agree with him—and so do Jayden and Nash."

All of Aurora's lovers would be angry, I knew that, especially since Aurora was carrying their children.

"We should have never have let those assholes live," Zander said. "How many times have they been within our grasp? How many times could we have ended them?"

"No!" I shrieked, grabbing Kouta's wrist and pushing hard on the button. He stumbled but let me speak into it. "Don't even say that!"

It was probably the loudest I'd ever spoken to any of them. To anyone.

Everyone stared at me. There was only crackling coming from the devices for a moment.

"Oh, shit," Zander said again. "We have another problem."

"Really?" Kouta took his arm out of the tight grip I had on it. "How much more fucked-up can this day get?"

"The rogue Nelians who got away? Well, we know where they are now," Zander explained.

Lila's jaw dropped. "They can't be attacking now…"

Xerxes…

"It's a targeted attack?" said Zander, and it was a question. There was a voice I recognized as Veras member Wade's in the distance, but I couldn't be sure what he was saying. "They're… kidnapping? Natch children?"

A sudden iciness struck my core. Roots and sediment, there was no way in both worlds…

"An orphanage-slash-institution for Natch kids whose powers are out of control," said Zander quickly. "Second Hope."

Second Hope. I'd told Xerxes about that place. How had he found it so quickly? *Why* had he gone there?

What did he want with them? With innocent children?

Who had powers they couldn't control…

"Vines are surrounding the property," said Zander. "It wasn't Alarik, so it has to be him."

"We've wanted to do something about that place for ages," Lila said quietly. "Though we didn't know how—how to help the kids whose own powers hurt them and others without them even trying." She kicked the car again and Torynt let out a little shriek as if she'd kicked him. "We've been so damn focused on the Nelian goal of turning us all into environmental hippies, we've been pushing aside our own goal of making sure Natches get a fair shake for too long."

"That's not entirely true," said Kouta. "We're working together with the Nelians—"

"Yeah, and we all freaking forgot about those kids." Lila's mouth pinched into a straight line. "It's run by a bunch of freak Typicals, Kouta. We should have brought it down ages ago."

"I've been there," I said quietly. "The humans there didn't understand what I was able to do, but…"

"Holy mother of pearl fucking hush puppies." Torynt stared at me. "You! *You're* the answer to helping those kids."

Lila grabbed hold of me. "Let's go," she said, dragging me back into the car.

"Police blocking off traffic," said Zander. "You'll have to bust through. Hurry so we can get back to finding Aurora."

Torynt sat behind the wheel. If I'd thought Kouta could make the *beeacal* do some erratic, heart-pounding moves, I took that back. He had nothing on how fast we moved now.

CHAPTER TWENTY-FIVE

"What are they doing to those kids?" Lila asked.

I wasn't sure myself. I knew what *I* could offer those kids, but Xerxes...

"Nothing good." Kouta gripped the armrest on the door beside him.

That much we all seemed to agree on.

The roads became busier and busier as we approached town and the Second Hope home, only there were few cars headed toward the place. Cars came at us from both sides of the road, causing Torynt to shout out a choice collection of Earth's curse words as he honked and swerved our car between obstacles, eventually bypassing a bunch of black and white cars with red and blue lights flashing above them. Down the street, a giant vine twisted up and down through the concrete. There was a car caught between two tendrils of the green lifeform. Torynt slammed his foot down, causing the car to lurch and the belt against my chest to dig into my flesh.

My heart was thundering as he made the car go quiet.

A couple of screaming humans rushed past as we all climbed out and stared up at the enormous plant.

"Well, that's going to cause some political setbacks,"

Torynt muttered as he stared up at it. "Zander and the pointy-eared elf king promised no more if everyone complied."

"And no police or military force is likely to come this close to the action," said Kouta quietly. "Not when we made it clear that they're not to interfere with Natches or Nelians if they don't want to face worse consequences."

"So we cover it up later and say someone didn't *comply*," Lila snapped. "Politicians and policymakers lying. Shocker. Can we worry about cleanup after we stop the elf invaders from kidnapping the orphans?" She looked at each of us in turn. "So what's the plan? Get the princess close enough to shut down their powers and then punch the living daylights out of them?"

"Let's go." I raced toward Second Hope and started climbing the maze of vines in front of me.

"Alanna!" The sound of my name came not from behind me and the Renegades, but from in front of me. "I know you're here!"

It was Xerxes' voice. I was near enough to get rid of Thorn's ability to produce vines, so he must have noticed.

I gripped another offshoot of the vine and went soaring, launching my feet over to the other side. When I landed, I reached for the daggers at my hips, only to realize with a start I wasn't wearing them.

Xerxes stood before the Second Hope building, a line of human Natch children of various ages streaming from the building to a large, long, yellow *beeacal* I remembered was called a *boos*.

And in the back of that *boos*, visible through the back window… was Aurora, a piece of vine wrapped around her mouth.

"Aurora!" I gasped. I'd been right. It hadn't been the R.I.A., but Xerxes had somehow found her and taken her before she could meet up with her friend. She seemed to notice me and she twisted in her seat, lifting her elbow at an awkward angle, revealing that her hands were tied behind her.

The children all froze as I'd called out, but Xerxes quickly motioned for the nearest child to keep moving and some did, but some walked toward me instead.

"It's the princess!" said a little boy I recognized. "I *knew* she was the one who sent these elves to rescue us!" The smile on his face melted my heart.

My eyes darted around the place. Thorn was helping some of the children up into the *boos* with a snarl on his face. The adult Typical humans who'd been charged with caring for these children in their cold, unloving way were all tied up outside the door to Second Hope, smaller vines coiled around them, some unconscious and others squirming and screaming obscenities that I ignored.

"What are you doing here?" I asked Xerxes even as the gaggle of children who'd charged at me all came to embrace my legs. "What have you done with Aurora?"

"She is unharmed." Xerxes crossed his arms tightly over his chest. "And as for my objective *here*, did you not tell me about these poor, mistreated children?"

"I didn't mean for *you* to save them!" My muscles went rigid. "What can you do for these kids that—"

He interrupted me. "I'm recruiting them."

There were dulled shouts now from behind the vine that I'd leaped over as the Renegades tried to join me but seemed to lack the Nelian grace and training necessary to make the climb in a single leap.

"Recruit...ing?" I asked. We had that word, but it was so underused, it felt odd on my tongue. But Xerxes had used it before. Recruiting Nelians to be warriors, to take on the glorious goal of saving humanity's planet from its ungrateful inhabitants...

Xerxes was taking Natch *children* to be his warriors?

The shock must have been apparent on my face.

"Do you know what those *humans* think of the children in

212

their own care?" Xerxes said, pointing to the tied-up adults across the way. "I pulled the truth from them. They consider the Natches *inferior*. Inferior! When Natches have the powers to *kill* them in an instant if they so choose."

One of the children at my legs gasped as she looked up at Xerxes, her arms hugging me tighter.

I did feel sorry for the children being left in the care of such humans.

"How did you find where this place was exactly?" I asked. "How did you find Aurora? Why did you take her?"

"I made it my first objective when I came to this planet to find... insurance. We noticed right away as we wandered through this poisoned planet that Normak was on our trail. We caught him unawares and Thorn made sure he couldn't follow us for *quite* some time." He smirked. A shot of pain went through me at anything he might have done to Normak. Would Xerxes and Thorn go so far as to *kill* him? How could that be? Killing wasn't the Nelian way.

Xerxes didn't seem to notice the effect his words had had on me. "But how fortunate that we caught sight of the *royal* consort shortly thereafter and waited until she was alone to take her with us. From there, it was a simple matter of pulling the truth from her to ascertain the location of this place." His lip curled. "From her mind, I discovered this place is common knowledge here, and yet no one did *a thing* to help these poor, suffering children."

I faltered just a little in the face of that truth. Aurora, the Renegades... People here had known about Second Hope and no one but Bo had thought to show me, to give me purpose in aiding these children.

But this wasn't the way to help them.

"Let her go," I said. "And leave this place. You don't need to *recruit* anyone. We don't *do that* anymore, Xerxes. Alarik promised the humans here. If they cooperate—"

"*Please*." Xerxes gestured again toward the human caretakers. "As if they deserve the courtesy of a promise such as that."

"You have no idea what my brother has been up to. His new methods have been doing more to secure this planet's safety —"

"Alanna!" a high-pitched and sweet voice called.

Lacey climbed out of the back of the *boos* and right into the arms of Thorn, who impeded her ability to run toward me as she so desperately wanted to.

No. "Let her go!" I bent down and whispered for the ones nearest to run behind me. Torynt was shimmying down the vine now, with Lila on top just as Kouta poked his head up from the other side.

The kids did as I asked and I bolted for Lacey, easily dodging Xerxes, who only snapped into action after he'd realized I was on the move. I skidded around some more children as I approached Thorn, then leaned down to sweep his leg out from under him, snapping back up to catch Lacey in my arms as he tumbled.

She squealed in delight. "I felt your presence," she said, her overall demeanor simply glowing with joy. "The pain… gone. I *knew* you sent these elves," she said. "We all did." She grew thoughtful. "But who's the lady in the bus?"

"I didn't send them, Lacey," I said. "And I don't want you to follow them. They took that woman against her will."

But two of the other children were already helping Thorn to his feet. His mouth was in a thin line as he stared at me, and I shuffled to put the *boos* at my back as Xerxes joined him.

Across the way, the Renegades had finished climbing down and were attending to the children I'd sent over to them.

We were all powerless here in my presence regardless.

I chuckled. Actually, I was the only one whose power was still working, now that I thought about it. I just had rarely recognized it as such. Monroe had been right.

"You're amused?" Xerxes asked, his head slightly tilted.

"It's nothing," I said.

Thorn kept directing the children to climb the *boos*.

"You're not taking these children," I said. "Or Aurora."

"I am." Xerxes opened his mouth and then closed it before taking a step toward us. "With the royal consort as our *guest*, Alarik will have no choice but to let me do as I please. And you can come with us. We'll figure out how and when to keep you away from the rest of us so we can successfully go about our plans."

"You're not *taking* children to destroy Earth cities. And I'm certainly not going with you—"

"Where's your new lover?" Xerxes glanced toward the Renegades. He wouldn't find my lover there. "Or your brother for that matter?"

My jaw clenched. I had no idea. Though at least now I had my proof the R.I.A. was innocent. "I don't know."

Lacey looked up at me, unasked questions in her eyes.

"Well, I imagine it won't be long before Alarik is called here." He gestured toward the giant vine and frowned. "Leave the others," he said quickly to Thorn. "Retreat with the ones we have."

"No!" I shouted, carefully sliding around Lacey to launch myself at Xerxes. My hand went as stiff as a log and chopped at his neck, but he was ready for my quick movements this time and he caught my hand as if it were nothing, twisting it until I cried out.

"Go join our friend, little lady," Torynt said as he came to a halt behind me, guiding Lacey away from the *boos* toward Kouta far behind us. One less Natch child to worry about.

Xerxes grabbed me by the hair and yanked as hard as he could.

"Hurry!" he called to Thorn, who nodded and jumped up into the back of the *boos*, shutting the door behind him.

"Stop him!" I cried out to Lila, who didn't need to be told twice. She ran for the front of the *boos*, where I realized there was another smaller door, and she launched up to grab a hole in the door that must have served as a handle just as the *boos* roared to life and started moving away. Aurora stood inside the *boos* but tumbled, her head slamming against the window in front of her, her form falling out of view.

Xerxes guffawed and I elbowed him in the gut, cutting the sound off. He scrambled to get a better grip on my hair, but I twisted despite the pain the movement caused me—a chunk of my hair ripped out at the roots—and aimed the toe of my foot right at the back of his knee. He cried out as Torynt swung a punch at Xerxes, clipping him in the jaw. Xerxes crumbled at my feet, running a hand over his face, where Torynt's punch had left a swelling mark.

I turned to look back at the *boos*. It was swerving wildly, worse than Torynt's control of his car, Lila flailing off the side. Thorn had thought to leave a gap between his vine growth for the *beeacal* to fit through, but the *boos* wasn't heading properly toward it.

"They're going to crash!" I shouted, and I ran, leaving both Xerxes and Torynt behind me.

The discharge from the back of the *boos*—dark and foul-smelling—made me cough as I trailed after it, but I kept going, my eyes watering in the face of another of the humans' foolish ways of injuring their homeland. I could hear the screams of the children through the walls of the *boos*, but the *beeacal* went faster, kept turning, and finally, Lila went flying off, tumbling, screaming all the while.

I hesitated.

"I'm all right!" she said through clenched teeth. Her arm hung off her side at an awkward angle and I knew she wasn't *truly* all right. But she wanted me to keep going. I moved faster.

Suddenly, a *beeacal* swerved through the hole between vines, careening sideways with a disturbingly loud screech.

I knew that *beeacal*. It was a pickup—the R.I.A.'s truck. *They came!*

But I couldn't be distracted. I latched on to the handle at the back of the *boos* just as it went screeching sideways.

"Lacey!" shouted an ardent, deep voice. Bo. He'd climbed out of the truck and was standing in front of the charging *boos* with as much foolishness as my men had possessed in front of the charging boar. They must have heard about the attack on Second Hope.

The movement of the *boos* wrenched my shoulder, but I gritted through the pain and climbed up. Children flocked toward the door and before I realized what they were doing, they opened it, sending me backward with a shout, but I held on to the door for dear life.

"He can't drive!" shouted one boy, leaning over to reach toward me.

I took his extended hand and another boy grabbed him. Together, they yanked me inside the *boos* just as it went swerving again, this time away from the R.I.A.'s parked truck.

I found Aurora on the seat beside me, her eyes closed, a trickle of blood leaking from her forehead. But there was no time to help her just yet.

"Stop!" shouted another familiar voice. Caspian popped out of the truck. "Alanna's here—our powers aren't working! You're not strong—the bus will kill you!"

But Monroe had already appeared from around the other side of the truck and he tackled Bo away, both of them weary and exhausted as they rolled to the ground. Rhett stepped out of the truck just as the *boos* swerved and started heading the other direction entirely, making it so I could no longer hear the R.I.A. from the open door of the *boos* as we went faster and trailed away.

Children screamed from everywhere around me as the *boos* swerved wildly. "Hold on to the seats!" I cried, stumbling up to the front and wresting the wheel from Thorn.

He pushed back and I realized with a start that we were still moving—that the feet were part of this driving thing, too.

Kicking his ankle hard, I sat on top of him and put my own foot down on a big foot-sized button on the ground. We went way, way faster and everyone screamed once more.

Screaming along with them, I let my foot off. We were headed right toward the Second Hope building, right toward the tied-up Typical human adults.

I slammed my foot hard on the other foot-button and the *boos* screeched, but it slowed. With a series of jumps, the *boos'* front wheels went up the stairs leading to the building, but I pushed harder, clutched the wheel tighter. Finally, *finally*, it came to a rest, the human adults mere moments from becoming crushed beneath the giant *beeacal's* weight.

With a grunt, Thorn squirmed from below me and shifted some stick beside us. I almost smacked his wrist, but he cried out, "You need to do that to keep it from moving! I figured that much out."

I let him shift his stick and then stood, glowering at him. Sure enough, taking my foot off the floor-button didn't cause the *boos* to move once more. I twisted the dangling metal keys like I'd seen so many others do in cars before and then ripped them out from beneath the wheel, throwing them at the wind-shield so Thorn didn't start up this monstrosity again.

"Is anyone hurt?" Kouta called from the open back of the *boos*.

Aurora.

CHAPTER TWENTY-SIX

STUMBLING THROUGH THE PATH BETWEEN THE ROWS OF SEATS, I helped the nearest child to her feet. She seemed dizzy, unsteady, but she didn't appear to be bleeding.

"We'll need to get in touch with Veras," said Kouta. "Get their healer over here—Lila is hurt the most." He reached up and helped a boy back to the ground.

Of course, for the healer's powers to work, I'd have to leave the area.

But I couldn't. Not just yet. "Aurora," I said. "She's here. Xerxes had her." I wove through the evacuating children, stumbling toward her. Lifting her in my arms, I felt for the thrum of her pulse and thanked all the forces of nature. Yanking away the vines from around her mouth and those keeping her hands tied, I called to her, lightly tapping her face.

"Leave her there," Kouta said. "You don't want to move her too much until Roulette has been to see her."

With a squeak, the door behind me opened and Thorn stumbled outside out of the *boos'* other door.

"Go," said Kouta, helping another child down. "You're a better fighter than me. I got this."

Turning around, I ran down the steep steps after the rogue

elf. He was headed for the break in the vines—the one he hadn't been able to drive to. My eyes scanned the clearing. Bo was on his feet again, though he held his forehead with one hand. Caspian stood behind him. Rhett and Monroe were fighting hand-to-hand with Xerxes—and my former lover was holding his own against two.

My heart nearly stuck in my throat, but there was no one else going after Thorn. I had to leave those three to their battle. Glancing over my shoulder, I saw Lila on the ground in front of the growing group of children and Torynt was directing kids toward the others we'd already gathered. With a start, Torynt noticed one little girl with yellow, flowing hair running toward the R.I.A.'s pickup, and he started after her a moment too late to catch up.

Only Thorn was edging toward the truck, too, since that was his escape route. The palace guard never did have the flexibility required to make a jump over the height of the vines. That was why he'd never been selected for a venture to Earth before Xerxes had taken over and had valued faith in ideals more than actual skill.

Bo noticed Lacey right away and stumbled toward her, though Caspian had to stop him from falling flat on his face once more. Rhett moved to help and then seemed to catch sight of the two speeding Nelians headed his way and darted my way to head Thorn off, Caspian taking up his spot fighting Xerxes.

Thorn saw Rhett coming and managed to dodge Rhett's flying fist, but that stopped the fleeing Nelian in time for me to catch up at last and give him another sweep of the legs. He stumbled, but this time he collapsed purposefully behind Rhett, drawing a dagger from his sheath before I even noticed and pointing it at my lover's throat.

"Do you care about this one?" Thorn asked, a sneer coloring his face. "Because if you don't let me go, I'm going to kill him like a boar."

"Since when do Nelians kill?" I demanded to know,

standing taller on shaking limbs. "Thorn, what's wrong with you?"

"As if a pampered princess would understand," said Thorn, gripping Rhett's hair and tugging on his scalp. "Even when your abilities turned into such an inconvenience for other Nelians, they *still* asked you to go on journeys to rescue Earth."

That was it? He was wounded that only Xerxes would allow him to come to Earth with him? "Xerxes only ever chose you because you were foolish enough to betray my brother for him."

Thorn's eyes narrowed and Rhett's gaze met mine. "Lana," he said quietly. He went still, his expression grave before he closed his eyes, almost surrendering to the moment.

Like roots and sediment this would be goodbye.

"I did all this!" Thorn gestured with his head toward the nearest growth of vine.

"Something most Nelians could," I pointed out. "Face it. You're nothing special. My abilities may *inconvenience* others, but they're one of a kind."

With a roar, Bo leapt up from behind Thorn and Rhett. I used the distraction of Thorn turning to see the source of the sound to seize Thorn's wrist and twist it until he dropped the dagger and cried out. Rhett took hold of Thorn by the arm and rolled away, pinning him on the ground, just as Bo's fist went down within a leaf's distance of the side of Thorn's head, stopping just short of the ground.

Thorn cried out in terror, his face paling as his jaw hung open, and then his eyes rolled back and he just lost consciousness.

Bo laughed and pulled back. "I've never scared anyone to the point of fainting without my abilities before."

Rhett smiled tightly. "To be fair, Lana did most of the work." He glanced at me, his eyes hooded as he took me in silently from head to toe.

Both he *and* Bo were looking at me—hungrily, but with a

clench of a jaw, a darted glance; it was clear they were working hard to restrain their raging desires.

I knew because I was, too. I embraced first Rhett and then Bo, the three of us grunting just a little as bruise brushed against bruise. Bo pressed his lips to mine as Rhett wove his fingers through my hair. But that was all we had time for just now.

"My friends think you took Aurora," I said.

"Who?" Bo asked.

"The elf king's girlfriend," Rhett explained.

"It was Xerxes," I said. "She's hurt—inside the *boos*. But we have to stop Xerxes. Then we explain everything."

"You don't have to tell us that twice," said Bo. He turned and I followed his gaze. Monroe and Caspian and Xerxes were still going at it, and I let out a little gasp when Xerxes succeeded in landing a blow against Caspian's temple.

"Fuck," muttered Bo.

Before we could move to help, there was another insufferable squeal of a fast-moving car and around the stationary pickup came the van I recognized as belonging to Veras, as well as a second *beeacal* I was less familiar with.

Out of the car spilled *all* of Veras, and I winced, knowing my presence kept Roulette from being able to heal any of the injured just yet. Beside my brother was Normak—astoundingly alive, though he was limping—and two other Nelian guards, along with Zander. My brother's brow pinched when he looked my way. "Alanna!" he said, charging toward me, his arms in sync with the movements of his legs. "What are you doing here? Now I can't teleport the rest of my warriors."

"Good," I said, standing between him and Bo and Rhett. "Because you misunderstood the situation. The R.I.A. didn't take Aurora—"

"Then where is she?!"

"She's here." I gestured to the *boos*. "Xerxes took her. And she's wounded."

The enlarged vein at his temple grew even more defined

as he flew past me without a word, Aurora's other lovers all pushing aside their comrades to follow suit, as if when one felt worried about their beloved, they all knew.

With all of them distracted, I tore off down the lawn after Monroe and Xerxes, stopping first at Caspian, who was on the ground, retching bile on the soil beneath him.

Placing my arms around his shaky core, I gave him the strength he needed to sit up. "You're hurt."

His dark eyes met mine and he smiled, despite the sweat cascading down his skin. "Hello, *hermosa*. It's been too long."

Rhett appeared beside me, and I looked up to find Bo exchanging words with Torynt, Lacey between them. There was a tightness to Bo's expression as he cracked his knuckles. Torynt looked from Bo to Lacey and he smirked. He was figuring out the connection, that much was clear.

"Your pupils are dilated," Rhett said, taking hold of Caspian's face to get a good look in his eyes.

He was right. I was no expert at healing, but that didn't seem to be a good sign.

"Roulette," I said. "From Veras." I nodded toward her. "Only she can't heal for a while yet—and I have to get away from her."

Caspian chuckled, but the movement hurt him. "I don't think Veras is going to help us, *hermosa*. Not after what we did."

I kissed his temple. "I don't care that you took me hostage," I said. "I *let* you."

"That doesn't change our intentions." Caspian murmured something in his other language and caressed my face, shifting aside a tendril of hair, his touch lingering on my ear.

"Lana said they thought we kidnapped the elf king's girlfriend," added Rhett.

Caspian let out a deep breath. "Then we're fucked. They'll never work with us."

"It wasn't you," I said. "They know that now—or they will."

The last-minute arrivals were spreading out around the open area, some heading toward Kouta and Lila and the rest of the children, others toward Bo and Torynt.

"Believe in me," I said to my lovers. "Have faith that I can make this work—can make your complaints heard."

Rhett and Caspian had a silent discussion between them. "We're yours," said Caspian.

Rhett nodded. "From now on and always."

My clenched fists relaxed somewhat and I nodded, placing a kiss on both of their temples, being especially careful with Caspian's wound. "Watch over him," I said to Rhett, indicating Caspian. I bolted toward Xerxes and Monroe.

Remembering how Aurora had defeated him during his last visit to Earth, I leapt on top of Xerxes' back, as creeping and as quiet as the passage of day into night, not letting him know to expect me.

And just as his hands reached up to take hold of me, I squeezed his throat, harder and harder until his muscles went weak beneath me and we fell in a pile to the ground.

Monroe, panting, stared down at us both.

"Alanna!" he cried, trying to get me to unfurl my limbs from around Xerxes. It took some effort, as I was still crushing hard, my heartbeat roaring wildly. "You'll kill him, princess." He spoke softly, gently, without his usual force. "'Killing isn't the Nelian way.'"

That snapped me out of it and I let go, collapsing back against my lover. I stared down at Xerxes. He'd been bleeding profusely after Aurora's attack a few months back.

I'd thought I'd lost him then. Thought I couldn't live anymore if I had.

But now... I'd wanted him dead. When he'd lain there, still and lifeless at my own hand, all I could think about was how he'd hurt my brother, Aurora, these children, Caspian, Monroe... The bond between my first lover and I was now snapped clean.

What was I becoming?

Monroe took me in his arms. "It's over, princess." He soothed me with gentle rocking. "I mean it. The R.I.A.—it's over. We won't fight against you. You've turned my world upside down." He shuddered, but still he focused on me, on keeping me safe in his arms. He was covered in bruises and cuts all over—and he was still wounded from our battle with the boar.

There were voices, and in the distance, the shrill cry of alarms. But I didn't care about any of it. I just breathed in his musky scent, his warmth, and all felt right with the world.

CHAPTER TWENTY-SEVEN

ALARIK APPEARED BESIDE US, BENDING DOWN TO FEEL THE PULSE of life on Xerxes' neck. "He breathes."

"Where's Aurora?" I asked, my cheek still against Monroe's chest.

"Conscious now. Roulette and Wade are with her," Alarik said. "But you need to leave. *Now.* So Roulette can get her powers back and heal her."

"I'm going with her," said Monroe.

Alarik glared. "I don't trust you."

"*I* do," I said. "You were wrong about Aurora—the R.I.A. didn't have her."

"The R.I.A. is disbanded," Monroe said as Bo and Rhett walked toward us, Caspian supported by them and limping between them, and Lacey on Bo's heels.

"Boss?" said Bo.

"Enough," he said, clutching me harder and placing his lips atop my forehead. "Enough fighting."

"We'll discuss this later," Alarik snapped. "Alanna, please. *Aurora.*" He shut his eyes tightly, and I knew Aurora's injuries were eating at him. The babies being in danger would devastate him.

"Let's go," Monroe said, helping me to my feet.

Before Monroe could even take the keys out of the back door of Drake's Bar, Lacey pushed past him to run inside.

"Whoa, hello there!" Bella called from inside. She was lingering in the hallway between the back entrance and the kitchen. Lacey didn't even pay her any mind; she kept running past her into the bar proper.

"Lacey! Don't just run off!" Bo sent me an apologetic smile and trailed after her.

"I take it whatever business you were so secretive about is over now?" Bella sniffled. Her face was painted with powder, but there was still some puffiness under her eyes and around her nose from her illness. "Though you lot look like something the cat dragged in."

"I thought we told you and Drake to get out of town," Monroe snapped. When?

"And hunker down where? Our personal yachts?" Bella scoffed. "Some of us have to make a living. We got out of town for a couple of nights and figured whatever danger you wouldn't explain was over."

"Danger?" I asked.

"Monroe asked them to leave town before we left for Nelia," Rhett explained. "In case that elf escaped to Earth."

"*Nelia*?" Bella's head jerked back.

"Long story, *amiga*," Caspian added. He was standing straighter now, whatever dizziness had caused his unsteadiness before thankfully on the mend.

"I take it you haven't seen the news," Monroe said curtly. "Or been in town today."

Bella tugged on the hem of her tight shirt. "It's been quiet out here. Just trying to get the bar ready for the night. Did those elf freaks—" She stopped herself and looked at me. "Sorry, sweetheart."

"It was a rogue elf," Monroe explained. "But yes, there

was an attack in town. Stay away from uptown during the clean-up."

"A *rogue* elf?" she asked.

"They're not all bad," said Caspian, sliding an arm around my back and pinching my side playfully.

"We'll explain everything," Monroe said. "But later." He grimaced.

Bella jumped, as if truly noticing the dried blood and bruises on our skin for the first time. "Get on upstairs and I'll bring you something to treat those wounds with."

As Bella brushed past them, Bo and Lacey shuffled back in to the back room, Drake on their heels. Lacey was unwrapping a *peppermint* and Drake handed her a few more. "Never thought I'd see you lot so soon," he said. His face fell. "You all look like death."

"Thanks." Monroe's jaw clenched through his stiff smile. "We've seen better days, sure."

With much shuffling and assistance from Drake and Bella, we all managed to get upstairs, directing Caspian to a mattress, though Monroe refused to take a seat until he was sure everyone else got their injuries tended to.

"You might be hurt the most," I said, taking in the red stain leaking through his shirt from the wound during the boar attack.

Monroe wouldn't be moved. "Princess, sit your ass down and let Bella get a look at your wounds."

I did as commanded. By the time everyone was done helping everyone else—Lacey running around and rifling through what little there was the whole time—we all looked like a collection of fluffy white wrappings and shredded clothing. Only then, when Monroe couldn't argue that it wasn't his turn for treatment, he shook his head. "Drake? Bella? Do you mind giving us some time to discuss a few things?"

Drake let out a heaving sigh and required Bo's help to stand after crouching beside Caspian on the mattress. "You boys need to invest in some actual beds." He scratched his chin. "And we need to get the plumbing running. That stove needs fixing—"

Monroe shook his head. "We won't impose on you much longer."

My blood ran cold.

Were they leaving me?

"That so, huh?" Drake shuffled to the door. "Well, we can talk about that later when you're rested."

"Here, hun." Bella handed me her box full of bandages and salves. "Don't let him call *all* the shots. He needs treatment."

I didn't let her know that the idea of letting him call all the shots thrilled me.

"C'mon, sweetheart," she said, reaching her hand out toward Lacey. She looked to Bo for confirmation and he gave her a nod. "Why don't we make you something to eat before the regulars start flooding in?"

"Cake!" Lacey hollered. "No, wait—pizza! *And* cake. And burgers. I haven't been able to *eat* when feeling this wonderful in all my life!" She scurried forward and gave Bo and then me each a hug so fast, I barely had time to hug her back before she was running toward the door.

"Screw the regulars," Drake said as he waited for Bella and Lacey in the doorway. "We'll close down for another night. Use the time to catch up on inventory. Give you all some time to *talk* about whatever it is you need to discuss." His head dipped toward Lacey as she skipped ahead of him. "We'll be sure to keep her busy. Got some booths she can nap on if she gets tired." He winked.

Monroe mumbled his thanks and then Drake, Lacey, and Bella were gone, closing the door behind them. Rhett locked it after they left.

The dim light from the windows threw shadows over each of my lovers' faces, and all avoided my gaze as I looked from one to the other. Undeterred, I approached Monroe with Bella's healing implements in hand.

"Sit," I said.

He stared down at me, then waved me off.

"Help me get his shirt off," I said to Rhett, who stood nearby.

Rhett gave me a nod, and he and Bo both began directing Monroe to one of the mattresses.

"All right, all right. I'm not a child." Monroe avoided their grasp and sat down on the mattress himself.

"That's better," I said.

Monroe let me rip what remained of his shirt off rather than have him lift his arms above his head, and Bo and Rhett sat down on either side of Monroe and me as I went to work cleaning and wrapping the wounds with the soft cotton.

"Feeling kind of lonely over here." Caspian got up off his mattress and dragged it across the room until it lined up against the other three, forming one giant bed. "That's better." He grinned broadly at me.

"Be careful," I said to Caspian as I patted Monroe's skin. "You need your rest. And you"—I caught Monroe's eyes—"ripped open your wound again."

"Happens when you take on a maniacal elf in the process of kidnapping children," he said grimly.

The room went quiet again, and I finished tying up Monroe's bandages, letting my hand linger on the solid bulge of his bicep. The longer I stayed unmoving, the bigger the bulge between his legs grew.

He ripped his arm away. "We have to discuss this."

"*This*?" I asked softly. "How you plan to leave me?"

"What? No." Monroe wrapped his less-injured arm around my waist and yanked me toward him. His lips hovered over my face, his steamy breath sending a tingle straight down to my groin. "Never. Never again."

Rhett slipped an arm around me from the other side and the tingling grew stronger. "Not if you don't want us to go."

Bo crawled behind Monroe to lay a kiss atop the back of my head, his fingers brushing aside my hair to caress my cheek, my ear. It was ticklish and invigorating at the same time. "I'm yours for life, sweetheart."

"Me, too," added Caspian. He crawled forward on hands and knees, his bright, white teeth gleaming. He placed insistent, feathery kisses on my lips, my cheek, my throat.

Groaning, I fell backward against Bo, who caught me firmly, sliding his arms through Monroe's and Rhett's.

"We'll work with Veras and the Renegades," said Monroe. "If you're sure they'll listen."

"They will," I promised. "They'll listen to me. I'll explain everything."

"We'll need their help to find a place for the Second Hope kids." Bo massaged my thigh in probing, teasing touches. "Not just Lacey. If we can build a better shelter for Natch kids who can't control their abilities…"

"If we can assure the people have more say in how we save the planet…" Caspian added, his lips trailing down my neck and wandering atop my chest.

"If your friends are willing to work with their former enemies…" said Rhett, tasting my shoulder, curling the bottom of my shirt up to slip his hands underneath.

"They will," I said. "We've done it before," I added, thinking of how Veras and the Renegades had accepted Alarik and me and the other Nelians. Even after Alarik had taken hostages of his own, had done so many things they hadn't agreed with.

We'd work together for a better world.

But right now what I wanted most was just a little piece of it to myself and my men. "I want to share a home with you."

"Wherever you are is home," said Monroe. The other men made murmurs of agreement, their mouths too busy landing kisses wherever they could find space.

"But we'll find a place," he added. He seized my chin and whipped it toward him. "A permanent place. No more being on the run. No more skulking in the shadows." He kissed me gluttonously, his tongue slipping inside, caressing mine.

"Yes," I breathed the moment he pulled back. "Yes," I added, quieter. "Take me there now. All of you. Take me *home*."

They all pulled back long enough to have a silent conversation and each pulled away from me in turn, standing and peeling off their clothes. Shivering, I settled back onto the mattress, feeling the loss of their nearness as an actual chill in the air.

"Patience, princess." Monroe traced a thumb over his lips and then removed his pants. The twitch of his jaw belied the strain the movement caused him, but he didn't hesitate. He stood over me, his phallus stiffening as it came to attention, his thighs slightly parted.

Caspian moved much faster, letting out a thrilling cry as he stood naked before me, as eager as if he were about to dive off a cliff to crash into a lake. He spoke in his second language, though I could feel the meaning of "*mi corazón.*"

As he slipped back beside me and began rolling up my shirt, his *boner* taut and temptingly within reach, Bo undressed and shook out his golden hair, scratching his beard before landing on his knees on my other side. As he tugged off my pants, being careful around the bandages, his stalk was alert as well, and my other hand could have reached right for it. I did.

"Uh-uh-uh." Monroe wagged a finger at me. "No touching. Not today. We touch you."

I didn't want to argue with *Daddy*. His admonishment had sent my vulva into a frenzy. Vibrating, unyielding, damp, my clitoris buzzed as my back arched and Bo finished removing the pants. Animalistic gasps escaped from my throat.

Rhett approached me from above, his naked form sleek and trim and glorious, his *boner* at the ready as well. He sat above me on our giant array of mattresses, sitting on his calves and pulling my head to rest on his lap, his bulge pushing against my scalp.

I moaned, and he began caressing my face, my ears, his hands moving down to grip my breasts. His hands mixed with Caspian's and Bo's as they trailed across my torso to my legs, down between the crevasses of my folds, all in constant motion, the hands crossing over and under each other's.

My muscles buckled, my back arching more as my head ground into Rhett's lap above me, the guttural sounds escaping my mouth unlike any I'd produced before.

"Good," said *Daddy* Monroe, pacing back and forth at my feet above me. "More."

The hands of my three other lovers moved quicker, Bo's and Caspian's lips alternating with their hands, Caspian taking a nipple between his teeth and pinching it, Bo's tongue sliding between my folds.

I cried out, my hands reaching for their hair, and *Daddy* Monroe barked, "No! Naughty girl."

I settled for clutching the mattress instead, writhing from all of their touches.

Monroe gripped his plump, jutting phallus and slipped his fist up and down, first in beat with his pacing steps, then rapider, his feet coming to a stop as he stared down at me, his gaze snatching mine to his, *demanding* my attention, even as I writhed and *burned* inside with *need*. "Please," I said between panting breaths, punctuated by another cry. "Oh, *please!*" Every part of me was getting tighter, *tighter*, the building tension too much to bear.

"Beg all you want," said Monroe, his arm pumping, his expression tightening even in the face of the discomfort the rapid movement must have been causing him. "I'll come when I'm good and ready."

I screamed, but Caspian planted his mouth over mine, muffling my cry, threading his tongue around mine. Squirming, twisting, I leaned into the kiss, shifted my apex to press harder against Bo's lips down there.

"Now," Monroe said, and both Caspian and Bo pulled back, letting Monroe kneel before me, grabbing hold of my thighs and splaying them, ramming hard against them. His eyes locked on mine, my other men's hands roving over my breasts, my ears, my rear, Monroe thrust inside.

My back arched, my whole body buckling. I couldn't speak—could just make moaning sounds. Monroe slipped partway out again and then buried back in, clutching my thighs oh-so-tightly.

We moved together in a steady beat as he slipped in and out, my groin so sleek and wet, he met little resistance. It kept building and building, the buzz within me, no quarter given to a single cell of my body—the love, the burning, the *need* coming from everywhere all at once. Too soon, Monroe released, my insides clamping around him as the blood rushed to my head, and I called out.

Monroe bent to kiss my knee. "Good girl," he said, his grin wider than I'd ever seen. He slipped out, and I buckled at the loss of him. "Now it's Rhett's turn."

My ecstasy went on and on as each of my men took a turn sliding inside me, as all of their hands roved around me, touching every speck of my flesh, pressing their lips to every part of me until I collapsed, spent, in the arms of those I loved most in every single world.

EPILOGUE

"You look *amazing*," said Aurora as Roulette reached under her bathroom sink for what seemed like an all-too-familiar can.

"No," I said, putting a gentle hand on her arm. "No more hairspray."

Roulette chuckled. "Oh, yeah. Forgot we've been here before, haven't we?" She reached for a little metal pin instead. "We'll just go with the coiled curls, then. Who cares if it stays put all day? Four eager sets of hands are going to rip it all down come this evening anyway."

"*Roulette*," Aurora said, trying to sound harsh, but she was smiling. The grin fell quickly off her face, though, as she clutched her giant belly, protruding through the Regency-period dress she was wearing to match my own Jane Austen-style wedding dress. I had learned a lot about history from Rhett in particular over the past few months, and we'd ordered a pale cream dress with puffy, short sleeves, and a long skirt cinched under the breasts. There was a lovely lace trim up and down the material and at the edges, topped with a silk shawl. Aurora had pointed out that severely pregnant women hadn't been fit to be seen in "society" in those days, but I also pointed out that no Jane Austen heroine had ever had a wedding ceremony to wed four men at once.

She'd laughed pretty hard, then, to the point of "leaking," she'd told me.

"Sit down. Sit down," Roulette said hurriedly, guiding her best friend to the edge of the nearest bed in their formerly shared room. Roulette subconsciously rubbed her own belly —not yet showing, but filled with a child as well—as she stared down at Aurora with tight lips. Aurora took deep breaths.

"Is it time?" I asked, sitting beside her and wrapping an arm around her back. "I should have never held my wedding around your due date—"

Aurora cut me off. "Nope. None of that. This is your day. When else would Alarik and Zander and Monroe all be able to agree to slow the hell down and take some time off from all the politics? They had to *schedule* time off to be sure they were ready for the babies' arrival." She patted her stomach gently. "And there's nothing my babies would love more than knowing they were coming into the world just as their most beloved aunt is celebrating her bonds." She ran a finger under my chin and smiled.

It had been a hectic few turns of the moon. Xerxes had been turned over to the Typical human *authorities*, they'd called them. He would be a *prisoner* here on Earth for quite some time. I should have felt worse about that. I knew there was some shred of kindness in him, had seen it for myself in my cabin on Nelia. He'd had more comfortable accommodations on Nelia, laxer guards. But he had gone too far, attempted to ignore my brother's decrees too often. He wouldn't be able to escape the Typicals without the ability to conjure vines.

Thorn had been sent home to Nelia. He'd have been able to get out of a Typical *prison*, and so he would be exiled to the cabin I no longer needed in the forests of Nelia, a rotating set of guards to watch over him. For aiding Xerxes in his escape to Earth, Flora, Tianah, and Renaya had been sentenced to some more careful monitoring as well, though they'd stay in the heart of Nelia. It was just as well. That was no longer my home.

Most importantly, my men and my brother and my friends had agreed to work *together*.

It had all led to today.

Aurora hadn't held a ceremony like this with her lovers—had said she knew she loved them and that was enough. Roulette *had* married her husband, Ice-Blast, also known as Darien, some months back and that had given me an idea. That and finishing the rest of Austen's works and talking them over with Rhett. He'd always wanted his own happily ever after and a wedding. Caspian, Bo, and Monroe hadn't been hard to convince to join us.

Though they hadn't understood why I'd insisted on costumes from Earth's England in the nineteenth century.

What could I say? Rhett had taught me that this world had so much to say about love—and Austen was how he'd first shown me.

A squeal echoed out from the hallway and Lacey and one of her little friends formerly from Second Hope came charging in. She was dressed like a Regency English girl, too, complete with a basket of flowers. "It's almost time!" she cried. "Are you ready?"

Standing, I held out a hand for Aurora to take. With Roulette on her other side, we lifted her to her waddling feet, my shawl getting caught between us and Aurora having to straighten it before we exited the room.

We were at Veras HQ, where some of Second Hope's children lived, and I made frequent visits to offer them some relief from their painful and often uncontrollable abilities, just as I did to the large house the Renegades had purchased to make their own permanent residence of sorts, complete with a "guest house" out back for some privacy for the adults on a rotational basis. However, I didn't dwell full-time with either group, knowing that I could never stay with each child for the rest of their lives—that they'd have to learn to cope with and control their abilities as best as they could, even if it was unpleasant.

It was just... Who they were. And they were special, every one of them.

Lacey had her own room in the cozy country cottage just outside of town that my friends had secured for me and my men. But she, too, spent much of her time here with her friends, learning to cope with a condition that caused her pain whenever I wasn't near. She was making better progress with Natch teachers instead of Typical, cold-hearted guardians.

We were holding the ceremony in the backyard. As I approached the door, Lacey and her friend leading the way, Aurora and Roulette behind me, I gasped at the sight of the yard. There were vines grown like a forest, cloaking the entire seating area in a lattice design. Flowers grew from the entire canopy, and I knew Aurora had given my brother a *very strong* boost to make this happen before I'd arrived. On either side sat my friends. Children from Second Hope. A few Nelians. Veras members. The Renegades. Torynt gave me a wink and a thumbs-up as I passed by. And at the end of the path ahead, covered in beautiful sprouts from the grass beneath my bare feet, were my four men—standing in front of my brother, who would bless our union.

Caspian adjusted his *cravat*, as I'd learned it was called, looking a little stiff, but his muscles visibly relaxed as my eyes caught his, his breath hitching noticeably as he took me in.

Bo's beard was trimmed neatly, his hair perfectly styled beneath his large *top hat*. He shared a quick smile with his sister and then looked toward me, his jaw dropping and staying that way as I approached.

Rhett held his head high, looking so handsome in his Regency suit, facing me straight on, a wild fire in his eyes as he looked at nothing but me.

Monroe ran a shaking hand over his fuzzy scalp, so at

odds with an old-fashioned suit, licking his lips and staring at the ground. When he looked up, his skin flushed and a slow smile built on his lips that felt like he was welcoming me home.

And he was.

Taking both Rhett's and Monroe's hands, I stood at the middle of my lovers and waited for my brother to speak.

"Welcome, everyone. Friends, former foes… Thank you for being here." Alarik tossed his head back. "It is my pleasure as king of the Nelians to give away my sister, our only princess, to the men with whom she has most adamantly bonded."

I grinned at each of my men in turn, felt a shiver go down my spine when Caspian and Bo moved to stand behind me and place a hand on each shoulder.

"Alanna, do you take these men—Monroe, Rhett, Bo, Caspian—as your mates?" asked Alarik once the group quieted. "As your husbands for life?"

"I do," I said.

"And you?" Alarik asked of each man in turn. "Do you take Alanna, my precious sister, jewel of the Nelian people, to be your mate and your wife?" His expression sparkled mischievously as he added each ridiculous descriptor. As if I were ever Nelia's *jewel*. But I knew I had been my brother's. And that was truly enough.

But my men were not cowed. "I do," said Monroe, followed by Rhett and Bo.

"Oh, motherfucking god, believe me, I do!" shouted Caspian, bouncing on his heels.

Everyone laughed.

"There are kids here." Bo nudged him.

"My bad, *hermano*." Caspian grinned.

"Then as king of Nelia, and brother of the bride, I pronounce you husbands and wife!"

Monroe kissed me first and it was like a chilly evening in a cabin warmed by a fire, all passion bursting through me as my *daddy* dominated me, his tongue entangled with mine.

He wiped his mouth as he pulled away and Rhett stepped in, kissing me sweetly, hesitatingly at first, but then digging his hands into my shoulders as his tongue found mine, his *boner* digging into my hips as he pressed harder against me, seeming all proper on the surface but so naughty beneath.

He stepped back graciously to allow Bo a turn, my golden-haired lover's soft, fuzzy beard tickling my cheek, his fingers tracing a line from my temple to my chin as he stole small kisses over and over, trailing a few down my neck.

Caspian put a hand on Bo's shoulder and finally got his turn, seizing hold of me and dipping me downward so my head was halfway to the ground as he leaned over and seared a ravenous kiss onto my lips.

When he leaned me back up, he let out a wild cry and pumped a hand above his head.

I laughed. My face was burning, my breaths were hitched, but I couldn't stop laughing—couldn't stop the sensation of pure joy.

"And now we have food and song—" began Alarik, but with a loud, piercing cry, Aurora stumbled, Roulette catching her, Zander, Jayden, and Flayme jumping up from the front row to assist.

Aurora stared down at her dress, which grew wetter between her legs.

I didn't think it was a matter of "leaking" this time.

"It's time," she said, and my brother pushed past me to join the other men at her side.

And so it was that on the same day I gained myself four husbands that I danced, I dined, I laughed as we all waited for the news from down the hall, where Veras' doctor, Wade, attended to my sister-in-spirit. And a few hours later, still clothed in my Regency bridal gown, I walked into the lab and was handed my nephew and niece, a dark-haired, wide-eyed, rosy boy who gripped at the lacey fabric of my dress and a pale brown-skinned beauty with pointed ears and a tuft of green fuzz atop her head. Her eyes were shut, her little mouth opening a few times as she lulled herself to sleep.

With the babies in my arms, I felt warm and strange… Cushioned. Cuddled. *Protected* somehow. Despite the fact that I should have nullified all sense of gifts, of powers, from anyone around me.

There was something formidable washing over me, generating from the infants in my embrace.

That was how I first met Bryony and Sage.

Succubus Soul, a standalone sequel to *Succubus Lips* and
Succubus Heart

Blessed with the power to protect. A princess born to two

worlds. But despite being the star pupil at Veras Academy for superpowered young adults, all she wants is to be "normal."

Bryony Haddix is the heir to the Nelian throne, but the world of elves from which one of her fathers hails is a strange, mystical place, and Bryony is much more comfortable at Veras Academy on Earth, home to the rest of her family. Born a Natch with superhuman abilities, she's called on to protect and defend Earth's Natches from prejudice so that they may flourish on a once-doomed Planet Earth.

Now that she's come of age, Bryony vows to live as ordinary a life as possible, despite the weight placed on her shoulders. That also means that unlike her mother and her elven princess aunt, she's certainly never going to fall in love with more than one man. If only her parents didn't expect her to pick a husband from among the three fetching exchange student Natch princes who just transferred. If only she could stop herself from succumbing to the magnetic allure of her rival for valedictorian/best friend. If only she didn't start to think that maybe loving more than one man did run in the family, after all...

ABOUT THE AUTHOR

Lina Jubilee loves reading, writing, drinking tea, and rooting for her favorite fictional romances. When not lost in a book, she cooks dinner at lunchtime, plans errands in fewer trips, and does everything she can to get back to romping through fictional worlds ASAP.

Ravenous readers, if you liked this book, please consider joining my Facebook street team! Connect with me:

https://authorlinajubilee.wixsite.com/books/

    a amazon.com/author/linajubilee
    BB bookbub.com/profile/lina-jubilee
    O instagram.com/linajubilee
    f facebook.com/authorlinajubilee

MY RACY REVERSE HAREM BOOK CLUB
STANDALONE CONTEMPORARY REVERSE HAREM

Nothing can keep Rose away from Romance Book Club at the library—not even the snowstorm of the century. Catching a ride home through the storm with Lance, the stunningly attractive librarian who happens to be her neighbor, and Vaughn, his chiseled, alluring housemate, Rose takes them up on their invitation to drop by sometime and join them for their own book club. Rose gets more than she bargained for when she's introduced to Rafael, their magnetically charming third roommate, and the surprising genre of books they love to read and discuss. As the blizzard rages, Rose joins the Racy Reverse Harem Book Club, whose members are open to trying just about everything together to get warm.

A standalone novelette by Lina Jubilee, author of the reverse harem urban fantasy series Succubus Sirens.

REVERE ME: FLEEING FROM THE FAE KING
STANDALONE FANTASY ROMANCE

Brecc

I've waited an eon to find you. You, my bride, the other half to my soul. But I noticed you too late, the annual fete that was supposed to bring us together not your time to shine. My need for you threatens us all... Nonetheless, I will have you.

The world is meaningless without you. Love me. Bow to me. Revere me.

Edony

I was supposed to be safe. My years as an eligible maiden were behind me, so no fae should have sought my hand at the Fae King's Fete. Yet you caught me breaking the rules, and my fate rested in your hands. Instead of banishing me to the labyrinth of madness surrounding your castle, you vowed to let the world crumble to have me at your side. But I won't let you sacrifice everyone I care for—everyone in your kingdom —for me. To escape you, I'll go willingly into the maze. I'll keep running so you never find me. You will never break me. I will never yield to your desires.

Even though I crave you. Even though when I close my eyes, all I see is your face.

Revere Me is a steamy fantasy romance recommended for ages 17+ for mature themes and scorching romantic tension. First serialized on Kindle Vella, this episodic novel reads as a dark fairy tale in the vein of *Beauty and the Beast*.

Wallflower bookworm Quinn curates her neighborhood's Mini Donation Libraries, paying special attention to the Ooh-La-La Box filled with romance reads. When a series of steamy donated books wrecks her life for a few days, she's left wondering if the author is local. Before she can get her sleuth on for long, a friend introduces her to Allen, a man with deep pockets who wants Quinn to set up a Mini Library on his street—and can take her wildest fantasies from the page to under his sheets.

First serialized on Kindle Vella, *My Mini Library Romance* is a contemporary romance with plenty of sizzle and a dash of humor. Perfect for every booklover who's ever dreamed of becoming a romance novel heroine.

READ MORE HOT ROMANCES
FROM CRIMSON FOX
PUBLISHING

Crimson Fox
PUBLISHING

THE MADRID MISTAKE

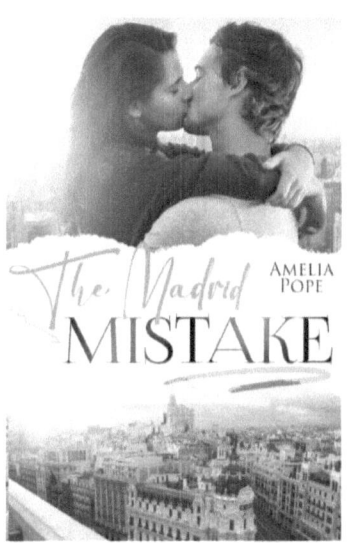

When Layla arrives in Madrid for her sister's wedding, she's brokenhearted and ready for a rebound. What she finds is more than a rebound: She finds Mateo, the first man to truly see her for who she is and make her feel worthy of love. And he just happens to be an international superstar.

As the wedding approaches and family drama escalates, it becomes clear that secrets will come out. Secrets that just might ruin the wedding—and cost Layla the love of her life.

A DAGGER IN THE IVY

In a world plagued by darkness and deceit, half-fae Celeste Westergaard is torn between her duty as the Commander of the Royal Regiment and her station as the next in line for the throne. Attacks from supernatural creatures are on the rise, the carnivorous beasts sent by the Shadow Tsar to claim the lives of third-born fae throughout the realm of Terre Ferique.

But as Celeste's homeland of Delasurvia faces turmoil and unrest, she is thrust into an arranged marriage to the prince of Hedera, the Land of Ivy.

While the destiny of her kingdom rests on Celeste's shoulders, she must also face the threat of madness, a fate which could befall her if her fae powers do not manifest. And to make things worse, the prince's brooding half-brother carries a hatred for her she can't understand.

As Celeste unravels the mysteries hidden within Hedera, she must navigate a treacherous path to protect her kingdom and uncover the truth hidden within her own bloodline.